THE INN AT NETHERFIELD GREEN

What Reviewers Say About Aurora Rey's Work

Recipe for Love

"So here's a few things that always get me excited when Aurora Rey publishes a new book. ...Firstly, I am guaranteed a hot butch with a sensitive side, this alone is a massive tick. Secondly, I am guaranteed to throw any diet out the window because the books always have the most delectable descriptions of food that I immediately go on the hunt for—this time it was a BLT with a difference. And lastly, hot sex scenes that personally have added to my fantasy list throughout the years! This book did not disappoint in any of those areas."
—*Les Rêveur*

Autumn's Light—Lambda Literary Award Finalist

"Aurora Rey has a knack for writing characters you care about and she never gives us the same pairing twice. Each character is always unique and fully fleshed out. Most of her pairings are butch/femme and her diversity in butch rep is so appreciated. This goes to prove the butch characters do not need to be one dimensional, nor do they all need to be rugged. Rey writes romances in which you can happily immerse yourself. They are gentle romances which are character driven."—*The Lesbian Review*

"Aurora Rey is by far one of my favourite authors. She writes books that just get me. ...Her winning formula is Butch women who fall for strong femmes. I just love it. Another triumph from the pen of Aurora Rey. 5 stars."—*Les Rêveur*

"This is a beautiful romance. I loved the flow of the story, loved the characters including the secondary ones, and especially loved the setting of Provincetown, Massachusetts."—*Rainbow Reflections*

"[*Autumn's Light*] was another fun addition to a great series."
—Danielle Kimerer, Librarian (Nevins Memorial Library, Massachusetts)

"Aurora Rey has shown a mastery of evoking setting and this is especially evident in her Cape End romances set in Provincetown. I have loved this entire series..."—*Kitty Kat's Book Review Blog*

Spring's Wake

"The third standalone in Aurora Rey's Cape End series, *Spring's Wake*, features a feel-good romance that would make a perfect beach read. The Provincetown B&B setting is richly painted, feeling both indulgent and cozy."—*RT Book Reviews*

"*Spring's Wake* has shot to number one in my age-gap romance favorites shelf."—*Les Rêveur*

"The Ptown setting was idyllic and the supporting cast of characters from the previous books made it feel welcoming and homey. The love story was slow and perfectly timed, with a fair amount of heat. I loved it and hope that this isn't the last from this particular series."—*Kitty Kat's Book Review Blog*

"*Spring's Wake* by Aurora Rey is charming. This is the third story in Aurora Rey's Cape End romance series and every book gets better. Her stories are never the same twice and yet each one has a uniquely *her* flavour. The character work is strong and I find it exciting to see what she comes up with next."—*The Lesbian Review*

Summer's Cove

"As expected in a small-town romance, *Summer's Cove* evokes a sunny, light-hearted atmosphere that matches its beach setting. ...Emerson's shy pursuit of Darcy is sure to endear readers to her,

though some may be put off during the moments Darcy winds tightly to the point of rigidity. Darcy desires romance yet is unwilling to disrupt her son's life to have it, and you feel for Emerson when she endeavors to show how there's room in her heart for a family."
—*RT Book Reviews*

"From the moment the characters met I was gripped and couldn't wait for the moment that it all made sense to them both and they would finally go for it. Once again, Aurora Rey writes some of the steamiest sex scenes I have read whilst being able to keep the romance going. I really think this could be one of my favorite series and can't wait to see what comes next. Keep 'em coming, Aurora."—*Les Rêveur*

Crescent City Confidential—Lambda Literary Award Finalist

"This book blew my socks off. …[*Crescent City Confidential*] ticks all the boxes I've started to expect from Aurora Rey. It is written very well and the characters are extremely well developed; I felt like I was getting to know new friends and my excitement grew with every finished chapter."—*Les Rêveur*

"This book will make you want to visit New Orleans if you have never been. I enjoy descriptive writing and Rey does a really wonderful job of creating the setting. You actually feel like you know the place."—*Amanda's Reviews*

"*Crescent City Confidential* pulled me into the wonderful sights, sounds and smells of New Orleans. I was totally captivated by the city and the story of mystery writer Sam and her growing love for the place and for a certain lady. …It was slow burning but romantic and sexy too. A mystery thrown into the mix really piqued my interest."—*Kitty Kat's Book Review Blog*

"*Crescent City Confidential* is a sweet romance with a hint of thriller thrown in for good measure."—*The Lesbian Review*

Visit us at www.boldstrokesbooks.com

By the Author

Cape End Romances:

Winter's Harbor

Summer's Cove

Spring's Wake

Autumn's Light

Built to Last

Crescent City Confidential

Lead Counsel (Novella in The Boss of Her collection)

Recipe for Love: A Farm-to-Table Romance

The Inn at Netherfield Green

THE INN AT NETHERFIELD GREEN

by
Aurora Rey

2019

THE INN AT NETHERFIELD GREEN

ISBN 13: 978-1-63555-445-8

THIS TRADE PAPERBACK ORIGINAL IS PUBLISHED BY
BOLD STROKES BOOKS, INC.
P.O. BOX 249
VALLEY FALLS, NY 12185

FIRST EDITION: OCTOBER 2019

CREDITS
EDITORS: ASHLEY TILLMAN AND CINDY CRESAP
PRODUCTION DESIGN: SUSAN RAMUNDO
COVER DESIGN BY TAMMY SEIDICK

Acknowledgments

I've been an Anglophile since I discovered Jane Austen and the Brontë sisters in high school. Loving all things British only grew when I became an English major in college. London is special, but there's something about the English countryside that calls to me. It's like where I live now, only the cottages are older and there are a lot more sheep. Writing this book is my homage to a special place, fueled in part by a magical ten days in England with some of my favorite folks (I'm looking at you, WEGs!). I'm grateful for those friendships and the others I've been lucky enough to build with the amazing writers and editors at Bold Strokes Books.

Special thanks to my expert on all things British, the delightful Eden Darry, and my beta reader extraordinaire, Leigh Hayes. To my word count and writing process buddies—Maggie Cummings, Erin Zak, Carsen Taite, and Georgia Beers—thank you for all the processing, motivation, and occasional flashes of inspiration. Thanks to the whole team at Bold Strokes Books, most especially Ashley Bartlett. Your feedback makes me slightly cooler, way smarter, and an all-around better human.

Finally, thank you to everyone who has given me the gift of buying and reading my books, and for the kind words and encouragement along the way. You've given me more joy than you know.

Dedication

For Mitch
My favorite Anglophile

CHAPTER ONE

L auren's head spun, making her queasy. This could not be happening. Her eyes darted around the room as she searched for cameras or some other sign she was the butt of a cosmically terrible practical joke. There were no cameras, no Ashton Kutcher lurking behind the furniture. But there were two security guards, each holding a box. "I—"

"Ms. Montgomery, I would encourage you not to make a scene." Eric, her boss, looked at her with something that resembled regret. Like he knew this was bullshit but didn't have the balls to do something about it.

It was not only bullshit, it was probably a setup. On the heels of that revelation came the realization of exactly who stood to gain by setting her up. Betrayal twisted her stomach as anger pulsed through her veins. Lauren closed her eyes for a second and took a deep breath. She wouldn't vindicate herself by yelling or throwing things or having herself forcibly removed from the building. Although every fiber of her being told her to fight back, this wasn't the way to do it. No, causing a scene now would make her look desperate. Desperation was a sign of weakness. She was not weak.

She moved to take the boxes, but Eric lifted a hand. "They will escort you down."

Lauren turned and walked straight to the elevators, past the conference room where she'd nailed a pitch just two days before, past the reception desk with the KesslerAldridge logo hanging behind it. She held her shoulders back and her chin high, but refused to make eye contact with anyone she passed. Part of her wanted to know if her colleagues' stares were curiosity or condemnation, but looking wasn't worth the threat to her composure. She was holding on to that by the thinnest of threads and couldn't risk losing it.

The ride to the lobby passed in a blur. The next thing she knew, she was sitting in the back of a cab, a box on her lap and another one next to her. The butterfly orchid that had been a gift from her father for landing the Starbridge account poked out of the box in her lap, its blossom broken off in all the jostling. Something about the sad, flowerless stem broke something in her. Tears welled up. She blinked furiously, reining herself in with the pathetic image of smeared mascara and a runny nose.

She just needed to get home, to the quiet and privacy of her apartment. She could fall apart there, and then figure out what the hell she was going to do.

Two blocks shy of her building, her phone buzzed. She fished it from her purse, almost too afraid to look. It wasn't a call though, or even a text. It was a calendar alert. She had the meeting with the attorney about her great-uncle's estate in fifteen minutes. Fuck.

The cab pulled up to her address and the driver turned to look at her. "You need a hand unloading?"

"Yes. And actually, we're just dropping them off. I need to go back downtown."

He gave her a funny look but didn't argue. Why would he? He wasn't likely to pick up a return fare in her neighborhood at ten in the morning. "You got it."

She hefted the box in her lap and got out, not waiting to ensure the cabbie followed. Seeing her approach, Nevin opened the door and held it. If he was surprised to find her returning from work an hour after leaving, he didn't show it. He offered her a nod and his usual smile. "Good morning, Ms. Montgomery."

"Good morning, Nevin. Would you see these two boxes make it to my apartment? Right inside the door is fine. I'm running to a meeting."

"Of course, Ms. Montgomery."

She handed him one box and gestured for the cabbie to set the other on the counter of Nevin's desk. "Thank you."

Back in the cab, she gave the address of the law firm and then closed her eyes for a moment. She had no desire to keep this meeting, but hopefully it would be quick. And maybe Uncle Albert had left her a giant pile of money that would make her care less about her entire career going up in a conflagration of false accusations. Yes, it was far-fetched, but she'd have said the same thing about getting fired a couple of hours ago.

Twenty minutes later, she found herself shaking the hand of a nervous-looking lawyer and apologizing for running late. Mr. Brightwater pushed up his glasses and shook his head. "It's no trouble, ma'am."

If she wasn't having the shittiest day of her life, she might find him entertaining. But since she was, she wanted to get this over with and get on with it already. "So, how does this work? I must confess I've never inherited anything before."

"If you'll take a seat, I'll walk you through the provisions of the will and answer any questions you may have."

"Sounds good."

Mr. Brightwater started talking. It took more effort than she cared to admit to remain focused. She caught no surviving children and something about his favorite niece, then realized she was the niece. Even though she'd met him maybe half a dozen times in her life. All his worldly possessions. The Inn at Netherfield Green. Rose & Crown pub. Derbyshire.

For the second time that day, her head spun.

Eventually, he stopped talking and Lauren just stared. Surely, she'd misheard him. "A pub? As in public house, as in bar."

"Yes, ma'am." He pushed his glasses up for at least the tenth time. Did she intimidate him or did he always have that nervous energy? "It's also an inn with twelve rooms."

She shook her head. Officially the strangest meeting she'd ever had, which given her morning, was saying a lot. "What am I supposed to do with an inn?"

"Well, Ms. Montgomery, you own it, so you may do whatever you'd like with it."

She owned an inn. And a pub. In England. From a great-uncle she'd met a handful of times. Insane. "Including sell it?"

He frowned. "There's nothing in the will that would prohibit it, once you've taken possession."

Maybe this wouldn't be all bad. Sure, inheriting money would have been a lot easier, but if she could sell it quick for even three or four hundred grand, her nest egg would almost double in size. That would give her time to hire a lawyer and strategize her next move. Like suing KesslerAldridge for an obscene amount of money and vindicating herself and her reputation. And making Philip suffer, because did she ever want him to suffer.

Mr. Brightwater cleared his throat. Clearly, she'd gotten ahead of herself. She refocused her attention on the task at hand. "And when can I take possession?"

"As early as next week. You do need to be physically present, however. That is one of the stipulations."

She could handle a few days in the UK. A couple of nights in London, some shopping, a quick jaunt to Derbyshire. Wherever the hell that was. "Perfect. I'll arrange travel and let you know the details. Will you be handling that side of things as well?"

For the first time since the meeting started, Mr. Brightwater seemed to relax. "No, Ms. Montgomery. I'm based here in the US. There will be a local solicitor to manage that end. I'll be happy to give you her contact information. I believe she helped your uncle create his will."

She imagined a female version of Mr. Brightwater, complete with little glasses and hair in a bun. "Excellent."

"Very good. I think we're done here." He stood and extended a hand. "I'm sorry again for your loss."

She stood and shook his hand, offered him a subdued smile. No point in telling him she hardly knew her uncle, or that at ninety-four she'd hardly consider his passing tragic. "Thank you. And thank you for everything."

"Of course, Ms. Montgomery. You take care." He walked her to the door, offered her a final nervous nod.

Outside, Lauren turned right and walked with purpose to Sixth Avenue. Once there, safely out of view of Mr. Brightwater's office, she paused. She needed to make a game plan. One that didn't involve asking her admin to make travel arrangements for her. Which sucked, really, because Chrissy was amazing at travel plans.

The events of the morning came crashing back, threatening to suffocate her. She needed a game plan for that, too. But the idea of dealing with it a couple thousand miles away suddenly had far more appeal than holing up in her apartment. Even if she loved her apartment.

She stepped to the curb and hailed a cab. It was fine. Everything would be okay. She had no idea how, but it would. She would make it so. She refused to consider the alternative.

❖

Cam Crawley set down her glass and leaned forward on the bar. "What do you think will happen to the place?"

Charlotte, the bartender at the Rose & Crown and Cam's ex-girlfriend-slash-best-friend, shook her head. "No one knows. Rumor has it Albert left it to some distant relative living in New York. Of course, the other rumor is that he left it to Tilly."

Tilly was Albert's springer spaniel. Cam wasn't sure which of the two would be worse. "Such a sad state of affairs."

She'd been coming to the Rose & Crown all her life—with her grandpa when he was alive, with her parents and sisters for an occasional dinner out of the house. She'd brought dates there, celebrated weddings of friends, and toasted the lives of people who'd passed. In a lot of ways, the pub felt more like home than home. And now its future hung in some mystery bequeathal.

Charlotte shrugged. "Sad for us, at least. I hope I can be so lucky as to go the way Albert did."

He'd passed on right there in the pub, during a short afternoon nap in one of the booths and with a pint of his favorite ale in front of him. "I'll drink to that."

"To Albert." Pat, a pub regular and the local electrician, raised his glass.

There were fewer than ten other patrons in the place, but they all joined in. The already subdued atmosphere mellowed even further. Charlotte resumed wiping glasses. "Are you sure you can't get anything out of Jane?"

"I've tried." She had, too. She'd played the family loyalty card, the sentimental attachment one, and even the business necessity. Jane's lips remained firmly sealed. Even poking fun at her unwavering commitment to the confidentiality of a dead man hadn't swayed her.

"What good is having a solicitor for a sister if you can't call in a favor every now and then?"

"Well, she did sort out my trademark business. And she reviews all contracts before I sign them."

Charlotte waved a hand, her towel swinging precariously close to Cam's glass. "A fat lot of good that does me."

Cam chuckled. "Fair enough. Perhaps you should try to sway her yourself."

"Who are we swaying? I'm very good at swaying." Jane perched herself on the stool next to Cam's.

Cam hadn't heard her come in. "One, stop sneaking up on people. You're liable to get yourself a bloody nose. Two, you. We were talking about you."

"Oh." She frowned. "Why do I need swaying?"

Cam glanced over at Charlotte, who sighed heavily and placed her hand on her chest. "Cam was merely trying to console me on the precarious nature of my future. She thought you might be able to give me the tiniest nugget of information to ease my poor nerves."

"Oh, poor Charlotte. I can only imagine what you must be going through." Jane patted her hand. "Hopefully you won't be stuck in limbo much longer. The new owner arrives this week."

"Seriously?" Cam set her glass on the bar with more force than she intended.

"What?" Jane seemed genuinely confused, with a little bit of hurt thrown in for good measure.

"I've been after you for weeks about what's going to happen. And you give it up for Charlotte at the drop of a hat."

Jane had the good graces to look offended. "I only spoke with her today. She's very excited to see the place, hoping to spruce it up a bit. I think it's a good sign."

Charlotte visibly perked up. "Is that so?"

"But who is she?" Learning it was a she only piqued Cam's interest further.

"Albert's niece."

Charlotte frowned. "I didn't know Albert had a niece."

"She's American," Jane said, as though that explained everything. Well, it sort of did, or at least none of them having any idea who she was.

"Is she moving here?" Cam asked.

"She didn't say. She just asked me to recommend places for her to stay."

Cam folded her arms. This was getting more interesting by the minute. "And what did you tell her?"

"I told her this was the only hotel in town."

Charlotte snickered. "What did she say to that?"

Jane shrugged. "I think her exact words were, 'Right, thanks.' And then I gave her the telephone number."

As if on cue, Mrs. Lucas burst through the door that led to the office, waving a piece of paper excitedly. "You'll never guess who just rang."

Charlotte turned and made a show of pointing at her. "Albert's niece, who now owns the pub and is coming to town?"

Mrs. Lucas stopped in her tracks, appearing equal parts confused and deflated. "How did you know?"

Cam tipped her head toward Jane. "The loose-lipped solicitor here spilled the secret."

"I am not loose-lipped." The comment clearly horrified Jane, even if made in jest.

"I'm joking." Cam patted her arm to show her sincerity. "Jane's been the pillar of confidentiality. She only let us know just this minute that the new owner does, in fact, exist."

"And that she's coming," Charlotte said. "What else do you know?"

Mrs. Lucas's chest puffed up. Clearly, she had more details to share. "She's from New York."

The words were spoken in a hushed tone, like it was some exotic place she'd only seen in movies. Cam chuckled at the idea. New York was an exotic place they'd all only seen in the movies. "That could spell trouble."

"What do you mean?" Mrs. Lucas asked.

"I mean if she's not from here, she might not understand how things are, how they work. She might want to come in and change everything." Cam hated being the killjoy, but she didn't put a lot of stock in people from the big city. And New York was about as big city as it got.

"Like the staff?" Mrs. Lucas once again looked deflated. This time, her frown was laced with worry.

"She has no reason to do that." Charlotte glared at Cam. "We're the ones who know how to run the place. She doesn't know anything at all."

"That's true." Mrs. Lucas nodded hopefully.

"I just don't like that, for as far as we know, she's never been here. And, like you said, we didn't even know he had a niece. Why would Albert leave the place to someone he hardly knew?"

The question had a sobering effect on the room. Whether it had to do with the woman coming to town or realizing maybe they didn't know Albert as well as they'd thought, she didn't know. After a long minute, Charlotte squared her shoulders and broke the silence. "Well, there's no use in worrying on it until we know what we're dealing with."

As usual, her practical way of looking at things put the situation in perspective. Paired with her sharp wit, it was one of Cam's favorite things about her and one of the main reasons they were able to stay mates when their romantic connection fizzled. Cam nodded. "And it sounds like we'll know that soon enough."

That effectively closed the conversation. Jane, who'd stopped in for lunch and not simply to gossip, ordered a sandwich. Charlotte scribbled her order on a ticket and fixed her a glass of club soda. Mrs. Lucas bustled off to start preparations for the new owner's arrival. Cam bid them all a good day and headed back to work. She was glad the pub hadn't been left to waste away, but she was equally glad she wouldn't need to be intimately involved in the process, whatever that turned out to be.

CHAPTER TWO

L auren never slept on planes. Well, that wasn't fair. If she booked first class and took a Benadryl with a vodka tonic, she slept. But this wasn't one of those times.

She spent the six hours between JFK and Heathrow researching everything from her legal options regarding wrongful termination to commercial real estate prices in the English countryside. The result: a complete one-eighty in her plans.

No matter how in the right she was, suing KesslerAldridge had, at best, a fifty percent chance of success. It didn't help that she didn't document the incident or tell anyone, which Philip had probably anticipated. A lot of good hindsight did her now.

And the hotel and pub were only worth three or four hundred grand if she could find a buyer. In its current state—tired, dated, and in the middle of nowhere—she'd be lucky to find someone willing to pay half that.

Fueled by coffee and a refusal to give in to despondence, she cooked up a new plan. She'd take everything she knew about the hospitality industry and put it to work for herself. She'd turn the inn into a destination, a whimsical escape from the crush of city life and a charming adventure for tourists looking for an authentic English experience. With the pub downstairs, she could market it as a bed and bar. Much hipper than a bed and breakfast. And then she'd sell it for a killing.

With the money and the attention she'd garner from that, she'd be poised to start her own agency. Sure, that had been her ten-year plan, but the universe had just given a giant middle finger to her plans. This would be so much more satisfying anyway.

By the time she claimed her luggage and found the driver she'd hired to take her to Netherfield, Lauren bordered on manic. She told herself it was the lack of sleep, not a hyper-emotional state that might be spurring her to make rash decisions she'd regret in the light of another day. She took a steadying breath and settled herself into the back seat of the black sedan. This would be the ride many of her future guests would take. She should pay attention to it.

The bustling streets of London gave way to the suburbs, with row after row of brick houses tucked close together. Suburbs yielded to houses more spread apart, interspersed with rolling hills bursting with lush green and small yellow flowers.

"What's that growing?" she asked her driver.

"Rapeseed. They harvest it for oil."

"Ah. Thank you." She settled back into her seat, not wanting to encourage more conversation than necessary.

It didn't take long for sheep sightings to begin. Sheep, cows, those shaggy things she'd learned were highland cows. It was quite picturesque, really. She'd be able to tell potential guests it would be like stepping into the quaint British village in *The Holiday*. Which was exactly the kind of escape up-and-coming urbanites craved— Instagram fodder as far as the eye could see. She'd definitely have to work that angle when putting together her listing for potential buyers and developers.

The driver exited the highway and Lauren glanced at her watch. Odd. She thought they still had a good hour to go. Perhaps Google had miscalculated. Not that she was complaining.

Forty-five minutes later, she sat with her eyes closed and one hand gripped on the handle of the car door. She'd given up after the third narrow escape from a head-on crash on the impossibly narrow road. If this was going to be how she met her end, she'd just as soon not see it coming.

When the car came to a stop, she opened her right eye, then her left. The massive hedge that made the road even tinier had disappeared. In its place, a rather quaint looking building. The sign over the door announced that she'd arrived, alive, at the Rose & Crown. She couldn't decide whether to be relieved or to ask the driver to turn around and shuttle her immediately back to London.

The place wasn't a total disaster, at least from the outside. She climbed out of the car and studied the building while the driver unloaded her luggage. The row of twelve-pane windows that lined the front of the pub looked original, or at least really old. She glanced at the year carved into a large brick to the left of the door: 1794. That meant the building was almost the same age as the US. Holy crap.

"All right, miss?" The driver had a worried look on his face.

Lauren schooled her expression into an upbeat smile. It might have felt like a near-death experience, but he got her there in one piece. "Yes, thank you."

"I just need you to sign this and I'll be off." He handed her a small electronic signature pad. "Unless you'll be wanting help getting your things inside."

She added a generous tip to the total and penned her signature on screen. "That won't be necessary. It's a working inn. Surely, there are some staff around somewhere."

That earned her a chuckle. The driver wished her well and climbed back into his car. With him gone, she was left standing alone on the street. Like, completely alone. Not another person in sight. She glanced at her watch. It was eleven in the morning on a Tuesday. Hopefully, everyone was at work. Whatever people did for work in a place like this.

Since no one was there to steal them, she left her bags on the street to go in search of a bellhop.

The inside of the Rose & Crown was dim, at least compared to the relative brightness outside. It wasn't large, but not really small either. A beautiful wooden bar dominated the wall opposite the windows. Stools lined about half the length. Sofas and tables and chairs added seating for close to thirty. It could have been a movie set—charming, if a bit drab. And nearly empty.

A woman stood behind the bar. She had strawberry blond hair and looked to be in her early thirties—younger and more beautiful than Lauren would have expected for a place like this. She appeared deep in conversation with the sole patron, but must have caught movement out of the corner of her eye because she stopped talking and looked Lauren's way.

She said, "Hello. I'm guessing you're Miss Montgomery."

Lauren barely caught the greeting through the haze that had settled over her brain. She'd made the mistake of glancing at the person sitting at the bar and the result was a short-circuiting of her entire system. The woman there looked nothing like the bartender. Her short hair was so dark it was almost black, paired with fair skin and absolutely ridiculous blue eyes. The bartender was beautiful. This woman was stunning.

Lauren licked her lips, mostly to make sure her mouth wasn't hanging open. She tore her gaze away and focused on the bartender. "Hi. Yes, I am. Lauren, please."

The bartender came around and offered her hand. "I'm Charlotte."

Lauren took it, feeling better somehow that the place had someone like Charlotte working for it. "It's a pleasure to meet you."

"This is Cam. She runs Barrister's Distillery. It's based here in town." Charlotte angled her head toward the drop-dead gorgeous woman.

Oh, that could be convenient. Or really fucking dangerous. She braved looking at the woman—Cam—again. "It's nice to meet you, too."

Cam offered a nod that seemed mildly interested, at best. "You as well." She got up from her stool. "I'm sure you two have plenty to talk about, so I'll be on my way."

Cam walked toward her. Lauren's heart rate spiked and the temperature in the room seemed to jump ten degrees. And that was before Cam smiled at her. Lauren reminded herself to breathe. This could prove very dangerous.

"Is something wrong?" Charlotte asked.

Lauren had turned to watch Cam go, and she realized she was shaking her head. She focused her attention on Charlotte. "Not at all. A little jet lag maybe, but I'm good."

"You're staying here, right?"

"I am." She needed to get a grip. She was about to become this woman's boss.

"I'll just go get Mrs. Lucas to help you get checked in and settled."

"That would be great."

Charlotte disappeared through a door behind the bar. Lauren used the minute alone to study her surroundings. She could imagine fresher furniture, a combination of high-top tables and cozy seating areas. And people. In her mind, a good two or three dozen people laughed and talked, drinking craft ales and interesting cocktails. The first she knew she could manage. The second, given the ride she'd just endured, felt much less certain. She shook her head. It would all be part of the charm, and that's exactly how she'd sell it.

Cam drummed her fingers on her desk and scowled at the spreadsheet open on her monitor. She'd promised Sophie she'd look at the distribution numbers before their meeting tomorrow. Well, look at them and have something meaningful to say. She'd stared at them for the last twenty minutes and not managed to do more than think about Lauren Montgomery.

The way she'd walked in like she owned the place, which, technically, she did. The way her hair fell over her shoulder and her dangly earrings swayed as she spoke. That no-nonsense American accent and the way she looked all fresh and glamorous even though she'd probably been traveling for the last eight or ten or however many hours. The way her shirt dipped into a low vee that showed just the right amount of skin.

"Earth to Cam."

"Huh?" She looked up to find Sophie standing in the doorway, a look of amusement on her face.

"Really absorbed in those numbers, eh? Or are you watching porn?" Sophie folded her arms.

"Hey!" Cam whipped the screen around to prove her innocence. "I'm looking at your numbers."

"I know that's not true because you've got a real puss on your face and the numbers are great."

"Oh."

Sophie tipped her head to the side and her face softened. "What're you so pissed off about? You can tell me."

"I'm not pissed off." She wasn't. Distracted, maybe. Wondering what the hell Charlotte and Lauren might be talking about. Wondering what Lauren had in store for the Rose & Crown. Wondering when she might have an excuse to see Lauren again.

"Well, I'm not going to argue with you about it. Do you want me to walk you through the numbers so you don't have to fight with the spreadsheet?"

Sophie had gone to business school so she could oversee the business side of Barrister's, but she'd discovered a love and aptitude for all things financial. They were lucky she wanted to stay in the family business because she could have likely taken her talents elsewhere for far more than her company salary. "Will you tease me mercilessly if I say yes?"

"No, it's probably a more efficient use of time overall."

She opened her mouth to protest, but Sophie was right. And having Sophie explain things would save her having to pore over the numbers one at a time. "I am at your disposal."

Sophie came the rest of the way into Cam's tiny office. She sat in the chair opposite Cam and pointed to the monitor. "May I?"

"Please."

Sophie angled it so they could both see the screen. She grabbed the mouse and positioned it so she could use it. "So, like I said, the numbers are good. Barrister's had a one percent growth in sales compared to the same quarter last year."

"And Carriage House?" She cared about Barrister's, but that was the number she truly wanted to know.

Sophie tipped her head back and forth. "Up four percent over the same period. It's in almost ten percent of the stores that carry Barrister's."

By some standards, that level of penetration in under two years on the market was excellent progress. Cam had used the company's existing relationships to get meetings at many of those stores. Meetings that led to samples and samples that led to orders.

Carriage House was her baby, the product of five years' worth of blending and sampling and perfecting a gin both delicious and distinct from the company's signature spirit. It stood on its own when people tried it, but she knew it was Barrister's reputation that got its foot in the door. "There's a but, isn't there? I can see it on your face."

"But it's still less than two percent of net sales. That's not terrible, but not where I'd like it to be. Especially since Carriage House makes up eight percent of our production costs."

Cam groaned inwardly. Smaller batch production would always make Carriage House more expensive to produce, but the premium price was supposed to balance that out, at least over time.

"It's just not flying off the shelves. I think we need to boost brand awareness, beyond tastings. You need to look at bars."

"Are you the marketing department now?"

Sophie shuddered. "God, no. I have no idea how you should do it, and I have no interest in figuring it out."

Cam laughed. "Oh, good. I was worried there for a minute."

"You can bring it to Rohit. I'm sure he'll come up with something."

"Maybe." Rohit oversaw the marketing for Barrister's. He did his job well, but he was pretty set in his ways. Selling a new craft line was an entirely different animal than maintaining the reputation of a hundred-plus-year-old brand.

"Or you could go door-to-door with that gimlet you made the other day. That drink would sell herself."

She imagined traveling the Midlands with a case of Carriage House and a cocktail shaker. It might not be a bad idea. Even if the thought of doing it sent a shiver of dread down her spine. Not the making cocktails. She could do that until she was blue in the face. It was the door-to-door salesman bit. She could think of little she'd want to do less. "I'll take that under consideration. Does this mean we don't need to meet tomorrow?"

"That depends. Were you planning to serve cocktails?"

"Always."

"Then we need to meet." Sophie stood and offered her a wink. "I'll think of something we absolutely, positively need to discuss."

"And I'll come up with something good."

"You always do."

Sophie left and Cam readjusted her screen. Sophie's advice played through her mind. As much as she didn't want Carriage House to follow in the footsteps of Barrister's, she also didn't want it to become some trendy darling of overpriced cocktail menus. The rise of gastropubs, complete with those cocktail menus, threatened the existence of traditional English pubs, the kind that kept their prices reasonable and catered to locals more than tourists. Places that were the heart of the community. Places like the Rose & Crown.

Cam shook her head. If she decided to take Carriage House on the road, she'd avoid the tourist traps and pretentious bars whose patrons were more interested in taking pictures of their drinks than talking to their companions. She'd hunt out the funky restaurants and the pubs who threw a few quirky cocktails up for folks looking for a break from ales and lagers and stouts. And she'd make them a damn fine cocktail.

Still far from being on board with becoming a traveling salesman, she returned her attention to the monitor. Which lasted all of two minutes. Then her mind wandered back to her beloved pub and its distractingly beautiful new owner.

CHAPTER THREE

Lauren lugged her suitcase into the room and set it down with a grunt. So much for bellhops. She planted her hands on her hips and looked around. It wasn't a total disaster. The carpet would have to go, obviously. Hopefully, there was hardwood underneath. She didn't even want to think about how much installing new floors would cost. Plus new mattresses. The rest of the furniture looked old but sturdy. It had that kitschy, dated vibe she'd have to work with, not against.

She turned to face Mrs. Lucas, who stood in the doorway clutching Lauren's carry-on bag. "How many rooms are there again?"

"Twelve, ma'am. This is the largest, with the sitting area. There's one more like it and ten regular rooms."

She nodded. Bigger than a B&B, but manageable. Kind of like the place in the Catskills Anja had dragged her to. It had been done up to look like it had in its 1960s heyday and they'd converted one of the rooms to a bar. Not her taste, necessarily, but it worked. People flocked to it from the city, looking for something with authentic charm and personality. Here, she wouldn't even have to give up one of her rooms to get the bar.

"Is there anything else, ma'am? I do afternoon tea when there are guests. I could fix you up something if you're hungry."

When there are guests. The way she said it told Lauren it was a relatively common occurrence for there to be no guests at all. That would have to change. She couldn't just fix it up and hope someone would see potential. She'd need a track record of good bookings for proof of concept. Three months at least, maybe six.

"Ma'am?"

Lauren hurried over and took the bag from Mrs. Lucas. "I'm so sorry. My mind is wandering. It must be jet lag."

Mrs. Lucas offered her a warm smile. "You must be exhausted, flying all the way from the States. Perhaps a lie-down before you eat."

She didn't need sleep, but she could definitely use a few minutes alone. "I might do that. Thank you for helping me get settled."

"Of course, ma'am. I'm here until six. Jack will be in then if you need anything."

Lauren pulled her mind away from her plans and studied the woman in front of her. "You've been getting paid, right, since my uncle died?"

Mrs. Lucas looked down at her hands. "We have, ma'am. Since it wasn't clear in the will, Miss Crawley said things would continue as usual until you took over and decided what to do next."

The poor woman probably feared for her job. She might have reason to in the long run, but not for the moment. Lauren needed a few people who knew how the hell to run the place. "Good. You certainly shouldn't be working for nothing."

"Thank you."

"That'll be all for now, I think." Mrs. Lucas turned to go, but Lauren called after her, wanting to put her mind at ease. "I'm looking forward to working with you, to learning all there is to know."

The smile Mrs. Lucas offered told Lauren her instincts had been correct. "Me, too, ma'am. If there's anything you need, you don't hesitate to call down. The numbers are all there by the phone."

An honest to God rotary phone. "I will. Thank you."

Mrs. Lucas left, pulling the door closed behind her. Finally alone, Lauren surveyed her surroundings. She could see why guests weren't lining up at the door, but it wasn't an entirely lost cause. The work to whip things into shape didn't seem insurmountable.

Of course, she rarely considered anything insurmountable. Her train wreck of a professional life notwithstanding.

She shook off thoughts of that train wreck before they could take over too much of her brain. Being angry was a complete waste of time, as was feeling sorry for herself. Neither was her style and she wasn't about to start now.

She turned her attention to her suitcase and unpacked before heading for the shower. Afterward, she stood at the mirror wrapped in a towel. Her meeting with the lawyer—solicitor—was at ten tomorrow and would give her some information about what she was taking on, in addition to official ownership. She could stay in, get some rest, and tackle everything then. But she wasn't one to stay in or sit still.

She went to the closet and considered her options. The pub seemed pretty casual and she didn't want to stand out. She settled on a pair of jeans and a lightweight black sweater with elbow-length sleeves and a boat neck. She added her black Louboutin heels more because she liked the way they made her feel than anything else. Earrings, a spritz of perfume and she was good to go.

On her way downstairs, her mind wandered to the woman from earlier. Not Charlotte, the other one. Cam. A tall drink of gorgeous, that's what she was. And not her usual type, either. Kind of country, with a quiet confidence. And she ran a distillery.

She probably knew a thing or two about cocktails, not to mention the local bar scene. If they were working together, Lauren would be much less inclined to tumble into bed with her. Not that a tumble wouldn't be nice. She just had other priorities at the moment and needed to keep her focus on the project at hand. The more she thought on that, the more she liked the idea of enlisting Cam's help.

She walked back into the bar. More patrons had appeared in her absence, although the place remained more than half empty. She glanced at her watch. Just after four. Perhaps things would pick up after five.

She scanned the crowd. The average age had to be pushing sixty. She really hoped that had to do with the time of day more than the demographics of the town. She shook her head. Village. This place didn't even make the cutoff to be called a town.

"Something wrong, Miss Montgomery?"

Lauren looked in the direction of the voice and found Charlotte looking at her. Lauren tossed her hair over her shoulder and offered a confident smile. "Not at all. And please, call me Lauren. I thought I'd come down for a drink, get a feel for the place."

"Right, then. What can I get you?"

She crossed the room, felt a dozen pairs of eyes on her. Knowing it had nothing to do with her appearance being out of order, she resisted the urge to check her hair or clothes. She took the seat Cam had vacated earlier and tried not to wish she was still there. "What do you recommend?"

"We've got a great new cream ale if you're a beer drinker. Otherwise, you can't go wrong with a gin and tonic."

She was not a beer drinker and happy to be offered something else. "A G&T would be great."

"Preference of gin?"

The fact that they had more than one seemed like a good sign. Even if she wasn't enough of a gin drinker to know the difference. "Whatever you suggest."

Charlotte smiled. "Barrister's is local, a traditional London dry. Personally, I'm partial to Carriage House, a new line from Barrister's. A little peppery, great with tonic."

"Sold."

Charlotte made her drink and set it in front of her. "Travels okay? You're from New York, right?"

"That's right. And yes, thank you." She took a sip. It had a slice of lemon instead of lime, which actually seemed to work better. "Oh, this is very good."

"It's Cam's brainchild. She spent years perfecting the recipe."

Despite the briefness of their meeting, she had no trouble conjuring Cam's face. "Really?"

"She does all kinds of funky things in small batches. This one finally made the cut to get its own label."

Lauren had heard of Barrister's. It was one of the middle-shelf standards at a lot of bars back home. This was the first she'd heard of Carriage House though. Strange considering how good it was. "Is it new?"

"It's been in commercial production for a year or so. Everyone who tries it loves it, but I think Cam is still figuring out how to get people to try it."

"Interesting."

"Yeah. She's brilliant at making it. Marketing it is a different story."

"It always is." Lauren nodded. She was inclined to like Charlotte, if for no other reason than she was young and had the kind of energy Lauren could relate to. But she also seemed to have her finger on the pulse of things—something Lauren desperately needed if she was going to make her plan work. "So, how long have you worked here?"

"Since I was old enough to have a job. Close to fifteen years now. Albert was good friends with my pa, so I've been coming here since I was a little thing. Albert used to let me come behind the bar and fix my own fizzy orange in a fancy glass. I was hooked."

Lauren imagined she was referring to the British equivalent of a Shirley Temple. Although she'd had her share of those as a child, they'd been served to her at the club where her mother played tennis and had lunch with her friends. It was funny to have such a thing in common, yet have the fundamental experience of it be so different. "It sounds like you were very close with Albert. I'm sorry for your loss."

A look of embarrassment swept over Charlotte's face. "Oh, bollocks. You're the one related to him. I should be saying that to you."

Lauren waved a hand and offered a sympathetic smile. "That's very kind, but not necessary. I'm sorry to say I hardly knew him."

"We were wondering about that. No offense, but none of us even knew he had a niece."

She appreciated Charlotte's frankness, and not just because she'd be able to use it to her advantage. "I'm technically his great-niece. He visited us in New York a few times when I was young. I think he was my mother's only uncle. They weren't terribly close, but she always spoke fondly of him."

"Ah."

"That side of the family is very small. I don't have any cousins through my mother, at least that I know of." As she explained, the why of how she came to own the Rose & Crown took shape. It made her sad to think she was perhaps the closest relative Albert had. Or, perhaps more accurately, the youngest and most likely to take on his beloved pub.

"Well, we're glad you're here. None of us who works here is keen on hunting for a new job."

Lauren hoped that had more to do with loyalty than there being no other places to work in town. "Speaking of, I have a lot to learn. I'm hoping you'll be willing to help bring me up to speed."

Before Charlotte could reply, the door opened and a group of five men came in. They all wore variations of the same outfit: work pants and boots, T-shirts or button-downs with the sleeves rolled up. Lauren glanced at her watch. Not quite five. Charlotte excused herself and greeted them by name, filling pint glasses without needing to know their preferences. Lauren chuckled to herself. Like *Cheers.*

The evening continued like that. Lauren asked questions and Charlotte answered in between pouring drinks, mostly beer. A handful of people ordered food and Lauren snagged a menu to peruse the offerings. Fish and chips, pies filled with chicken or lamb or vegetables. Realizing she'd not eaten all day, she ordered a lamb pie. A bit heavy for her, but probably a local specialty. And assessing the quality would be step one in revamping the menu.

When her food came, she switched to wine. There were exactly two reds to choose from, a situation she'd need to rectify sooner rather than later. She went with the Cab Sav and was relieved to find it not a total disaster. The pie was good, too, even if it seemed more suited to a chilly winter evening than a day in the middle of June.

By eight, her lids felt heavy and her eyes grainy. The travel and the time change had caught up with her. She bid Charlotte a good night and excused herself. Back in her room, she didn't bother with another shower, choosing instead to swap her clothes for a tank top and a pair of boy shorts before crawling into bed. She shut off the light, expecting to spend a good hour or two mulling everything over and starting to formulate a game plan. Instead, she drifted off almost immediately, falling into the kind of deep sleep that eluded her most of the time back home.

CHAPTER FOUR

C am rarely had a poor night's sleep, but when her alarm went off at six, she rolled over and groaned. Strange dreams and a seemingly never ending cycle of being too hot and then too cold had kept her awake more often than not. Irritated, she threw off the covers and headed to the bathroom. She cranked the shower to cold and stepped in.

The temperature of the water shocked her system, leaving her alert if no less wound up. She brushed her teeth and worked her fingers through her hair, then padded to the kitchen in her robe. She put on the kettle and added an extra spoon of tea to the pot, leaving it to steep while she got dressed.

Two cups and two pieces of toast later, she pulled the door closed behind her and started the walk to work. She passed her parents' house and contemplated stopping in for a real breakfast. It didn't matter the day, her mother prepared the works: eggs, sausages, beans, and at this time of year, tomatoes. She'd gotten out of the habit of eating that much after moving to the cottage on the far side of the property, but she liked knowing it remained an option when the mood struck.

In the end, she kept walking, deciding she'd rather be first into the office.

She let herself in via the side entrance, the one used by the production crew and delivery people. She flipped on lights, enjoying the way it made the space come to life. She went to her office and booted her computer but didn't linger, heading instead for the main still room. She fired up the two main stills, getting them ready for the alcohol and botanicals that had been left to macerate overnight. She'd mostly stepped back from the larger-scale production side of things, but it felt good to keep her fingers in it, keep herself fresh.

"Am I late and don't know it?" George's voice boomed across the room.

Cam turned and offered her production manager a smile. "No, I'm early and thought I'd start things in here instead of in my office."

He let out a dismissive sniff. "Can't blame you there."

They'd had countless conversations through the years about the production and sale of gin. She'd learned as much from George as Harry, the old head distiller whose job she'd earned when he finally—finally—retired. Unlike Harry, who she'd butted heads with incessantly, she and George always got along. He was smart, had great instinct and an even better palate, but he had no interest at all in the business side of things. Or the people. He was gruff and prone to surliness, even with the people he liked. Considering she had a less extreme version of the same tendencies, she could relate. "I'm going to do some blending later. Care to join me?"

The space between his bushy eyebrows closed. "It depends. You aiming to put something else in production?"

Cam chuckled. When she'd made the decision to put Carriage House into commercial production a couple of years prior, George hadn't been pleased. Mostly it had to do with how much he disliked change. But she'd won him over with another part-time assistant and by including him in the final round of refining the flavor profile. By the end, he'd become a friend as much as a company employee and one of Carriage House's biggest champions. "Just some things for the tasting room."

He nodded, seemingly satisfied with her answer. "You know where to find me."

Before Cam could answer, Dev and Tom walked in. They rounded out the morning crew and would get the gin to the point of being ready to bottle. If she wasn't careful, she could while away her entire morning on the production floor. It would be a nice way to spend her time, but would mean she spent her afternoon in her office instead of the blending room. She bid the three men a good morning and headed to the work waiting for her.

An hour later, she'd sorted through the production schedule for the next month, making sure it matched up to the standing orders and inventory needs. Thanks to her impromptu meeting with Sophie the day before, she had a handle on Carriage House's place in all that, and spent a few minutes thinking about how she could make its sales match her vision.

After twenty minutes of staring at the wall, she had nothing.

Cam sighed. Her brain just didn't work that way. Not that she wasn't creative at all. She could create flavor profiles and craft cocktails every which way. She simply wasn't a marketer. In her mind, an outstanding product sold itself. It seemed to work for Barrister's. The problem was that people didn't buy something they didn't know about, no matter how good it was. Obviously, Barrister's had that sorted out before she was born. She shook her head.

Maybe she should talk to Rohit after all. Or consider bringing in someone from the outside. She hated the idea—from the expense to the thought of some slick-talking Londoner strolling in and telling her what to do.

"You're looking glum again."

Cam looked up to find Sophie hovering in the doorway. "You've got me thinking about marketing and it makes me sour."

Sophie smiled. "I'm not sure if I should apologize."

"No. You're right, I just don't like it." Cam rolled her head from side to side, trying to loosen the tension that had settled at the base of her neck. "I'm going to go walk it off."

"Always a good idea."

Sophie headed to her own office and Cam stood. Taking a walk in the middle of the day made her feel like her father, but she didn't mind. It worked for him during his years at the distillery and his father before him. Her mother had encouraged it, saying it was good for the body and the soul.

She left the way she came, heading into town rather than toward home. As she often did on her walkabouts, she decided to pop by the pub. It was too early for a pint, but Charlotte would be opening up and there'd be few if any customers. They'd share a pot of tea and Charlotte would tell her of her latest girlfriend or, now that she'd expanded her pool to include trans guys, boyfriend. It was like a queer soap—entertaining, but made her glad she was watching and not a participant.

She was halfway there when Lauren's face popped into her mind. They'd barely met and somehow this woman had gotten under her skin, although it was hard to tell if it was the woman or what she represented—modern, trendy, and urban. Either way, Cam had no desire to bump into her. She'd pop by Kitty's office instead, pet some animals, and catch up with Charlotte later.

Satisfied with her plan, Cam turned up Baker Lane and continued walking. She realized her mind had drifted away from her marketing problem and landed squarely on the beautiful new owner of the Rose & Crown. What she couldn't decide was whether that situation made her mood better, or worse.

After getting directions from Mrs. Lucas, Lauren set off in the direction of the solicitor's office. It was all of a three-minute walk. A small brass plate on the door announced the office of Jane Crawley, Solicitor. Inside, she found a tiny waiting area with a pair of chairs, but no reception desk. The door to the inner office stood open. Before she could call out a greeting, a woman appeared. She had golden hair pulled back from her face and blue eyes that seemed vaguely familiar.

She offered Lauren a smile and said, "Good morning. You must be Miss Montgomery."

Lauren shook her hand. "I am. And please, call me Lauren."

"Of course. And you must call me Jane. It's so nice to meet you, although I'm sorry it's under these circumstances."

"Thank you. Although, by all accounts, my uncle seemed to have lived a full and happy life."

Jane's smile softened and kindness seemed to radiate from her. "He certainly did. Please, come in and take a seat."

Jane's office seemed a perfect mirror of her demeanor. Unlike Mr. Brightwater's office, the room was light and airy, the shelves and walls painted a pale green. There were a few rows of books, but the other shelves and surfaces held photos and knickknacks. The result made the space feel feminine but not cluttered.

"How much did Mr. Brightwater convey to you?" Jane laced her fingers together and set them on her desk. The calmness of her demeanor, especially compared to the fidgety Mr. Brightwater, was striking.

"Not much. Only that I inherited the pub and inn and everything that came with it." Even after spending the night there, it was kind of surreal.

"That's correct. The building, its contents, and all of Mr. Collins's personal effects, including Tilly."

"Tilly?" Please let that be a cash till full of money.

"Mr. Collins's springer spaniel."

A dog? Seriously? What was she supposed to do with a dog?

"Of course."

"The local veterinarian has a small kennel. Tilly's been staying there since Mr. Collins's passing."

It wasn't that she disliked dogs. No wait, it was. Smelly and full of energy and always wanting to go outside and chase things. She shook her head.

"She's a very sweet dog, no trouble at all." Jane looked at her with concern.

Lauren pinched the bridge of her nose. Shunning the companion of the uncle who just left her everything would make her look like a total bitch. As much as she didn't mind that reputation in New York, it would work against her here. Here, she needed to win people over. Fortunately, she was really good at that. Even if it meant doting on some dog. She smiled. "I'm sure she's a doll. I don't have much experience with animals, but we'll work something out."

Jane's features softened and she smiled. She was quite pretty, in a sweet, wholesome sort of way. "The veterinarian is my sister, so I can say with confidence she would be more than happy to help."

Lauren bit back a laugh. "Small world."

"Small town, at least. Four of us still live here, one is off in Scotland."

Wow. She couldn't decide what was stranger—having three siblings close by or having so many siblings in the first place. "What do the others do?"

"Cam and Sophie both work at Barrister's. It's the family business."

Wait. This woman was Cam's sister? Cam, the gorgeous woman who barely spared her a second glance the day before? Fascinating. "I think I met Cam briefly yesterday, at the pub."

"Oh, you may have. Charlotte, who manages the bar, is her best mate. She has lunch there more days than not."

Lauren's brain kicked into overdrive, filing away all the points of connection and overlap. Although the advertising industry had a fair amount of cross-pollination, it had nothing on this. Good thing she was used to keeping track of massive amounts of detail. "Is everyone in town connected?"

"In one way or another." Jane shrugged like it was the most natural thing in the world.

"Good to know." Lauren waited a beat, trying to settle on the most tactful way of asking if Albert had left any money that she might be able to use to overhaul the place.

"Mr. Collins also left his car, the apartment attached to the inn, and a small stake in the Winslow sheep farm."

A sheep farm. Of course. "I hope this won't come across as tactless on my part, but—"

"There are no liquid assets, I'm afraid. Mr. Collins did not keep any personal bank accounts. The register at the inn shows a balance of six hundred and eighty-three pounds."

Her shoulders slumped. She should have known better than to think this whole thing would amount to a windfall.

"From what I've been able to surmise, the pub is solvent, if for no other reason than it was owned outright. The monthly income typically covers wages and inventory," Jane said.

Typically. That meant there were months when the place didn't even break even. If she was going to do this, it would mean dipping into her savings. The payoff might be totally worth it. Or she could wind up broke on top of jobless. Not a decision to make lightly. Even if she'd sort of already made it. "Do you have the books?"

Jane offered a sympathetic smile, as though she could read Lauren's thoughts. "They're in the office over at the Rose. I believe Mrs. Lucas has been handling the day-to-day of the financials for the last couple of years."

That was a relief. Even if things weren't in great shape, she was glad to have someone who understood them. Although it did raise concern that the woman who oversaw reservations and the kitchen also had time for the books. "I'll set up a time to go over everything with her."

"Excellent. When you're ready to get Tilly, let me know. It's just a short walk and I'd be happy to show you the way."

Of course it was. Well, no time like the present. "Would you have a few minutes now?"

"Absolutely."

She hadn't really expected Jane to say yes. What kind of lawyer had random free time during the day? Lauren sighed. One in a tiny village where nothing ever happened. "As long as you're sure I'm not interrupting anything."

Jane beamed. "Not at all. I like to take a walk late morning anyway. And this way I'll get to say hello to Kitty."

A veterinarian named Kitty. She couldn't make this shit up if she tried. "Lead the way."

CHAPTER FIVE

C am made a face and sighed. "Shit."

"What? What's wrong?" Kitty looked at her with alarm.

"Nothing." Did she really have to run into her again? Already?

"Clearly, you're lying." Kitty came over to peer out the door. "Who's that with Jane?"

"It's the woman who inherited the Rose & Crown. Lauren Montgomery." Cam realized Kitty was giving her a funny look, so she added, "Or something."

The funny look turned suspicious, but Kitty didn't work in a jab the way Sophie would. "Oh, Jane must be bringing her here to meet Tilly. I do hope she's a dog person. Poor Tilly's been so lonely."

Without having anything to base it on, Cam assumed Lauren was not a dog person. She came across as a little too neat, a little too polished, to enjoy the fur and slobber of canine affection. Or maybe she had one of those little dogs, the kind women carried around in purses.

"Why are you sneering?"

"I'm not." She needed to get a grip. She'd spent all of two minutes in the same room as this woman and she was letting her get under her skin. It was not her style, and she didn't like it.

Fortunately, Kitty didn't get the chance to argue with her. The door opened and in came Jane and Lauren. Cam couldn't resist looking at her. Their gazes caught for a second, but Lauren quickly looked away. Clearly, Cam didn't even register as a blip on her radar.

"I didn't expect to see you here," Jane said.

Cam lifted the pill bottle she'd thought to procure for their mother's dog. For some reason, it made her feel better to have a justification for being there. "Just picking up Seamus's meds."

"That's good of you." Jane smiled and gestured to Lauren. "I understand you two have already met?"

Lauren offered a smile that, honest to God, kicked Cam's heart rate up a few notches. "Briefly."

"Are you settling in all right?" Cam asked.

"So far, so good. Although, ask me again after I've met my new dog."

Cam chuckled and tried to think of a clever reply, but Kitty jumped in. "She's just in the back. I'll go get her for you."

There was no reason for Cam to linger, but she was curious. Kitty disappeared and returned a few seconds later, Tilly loping happily behind her. She came up to Cam and leaned against her legs. "Hi, pretty girl. I missed you, too."

Cam bent down to scratch her ears, but Tilly immediately rolled onto her back and flashed her belly. Unable to resist, Cam got down on one knee and rubbed her with both hands. Lauren joined her and, after a moment of hesitation, extended her hand. "Hi, Tilly."

Tilly rolled onto her side and sniffed Lauren's hand. Once she'd given it the once-over, she nudged it with her snout. Lauren froze. Cam smiled. "That's the universal signal for 'you passed the test, please pet me.'"

Lauren laughed and stroked the dog a few times. Kitty said, "I think she likes you."

Lauren continued to pet her. She looked uncomfortable, but like she was trying. Like what might happen if someone tried to hand Cam a baby. She wouldn't hate it, but she wouldn't quite know what to do with it, either. For some reason, Cam respected that. "I could pick up some food for you, if you'd like. I pass the feed store on my way to work in the morning."

Both Kitty and Lauren looked at her with surprise. Not as surprised as she was, though. Where the hell did that come from?

"Um, that would be great." Lauren seemed uncomfortable accepting help, but also like she was smart enough to know she needed it. "Let me give you some money."

Cam waved her off. "You can repay me in beer."

Lauren smiled in a way that, if Cam were inclined to be susceptible, could be damn dangerous. "Deal."

Kitty handed Lauren a folder. "I made a copy of her records so you'd have them. She's very healthy for a dog her age."

Lauren stood. "And how old is that?"

"Eight."

Since that number didn't seem to mean anything to Lauren, Cam added, "It's middle age in dog years. She'd old enough to be mellow, but has a few good years in her still."

She nodded slowly. "Right."

Jane, who'd been quiet thus far, chimed in. "Tilly is the epitome of mellow. She spent most of her days in the pub, sleeping on a bed in the corner."

Lauren furrowed her brow. "Is that legal here?"

She sounded so scandalized, Cam laughed. "Let's call it a gray area."

Lauren resumed nodding. She seemed so much out of her element, Cam had a flash of sympathy for her.

Kitty said, "That will give her plenty of socialization, but she'll need exercise, too. A good walk more days than not."

Finally, Lauren smiled. "That I can do. Do you think she could handle running?"

"If it's nothing too crazy or strenuous, I don't see why not. You'll likely have to ease her into it, though."

Jane lifted a finger. "Unless there are rabbits. Then she'll tear off like nobody's business."

"So I can let her off leash?"

Cam might have felt bad for laughing, but both her sisters laughed, too. "I'm pretty sure Tilly has never seen a leash in her life," Cam said.

"Oh. Okay, then."

This poor woman. If her adjustments to life here thus far were anything to go on, she was in for a bumpy ride. Of course, she might not bother sticking around. Not that it was any of Cam's business what her interests or immigration status were. "I'm heading back that way. I can walk with you if it would make you feel more comfortable."

Lauren frowned but nodded. "That would be nice. Thanks."

Cam stood. "Come on, Tilly. Let's go home."

The dog stood and wagged her tail. Poor thing. Hopefully, she'd take to Lauren. And vice versa.

Lauren studied Cam out of the corner of her eye, trying not to be obvious about it. Even after learning Cam was related to Jane and Kitty, seeing her at the vet's office caught her by surprise. The flash of attraction hadn't been a surprise, but it threw her nonetheless. Everything about this experience seemed to be throwing her off. Being off balance was a foreign feeling for her and not in a good way.

She just needed to shake it off and take charge. Once she had her bearings, she could start making decisions and making things happen. Whether that involved Cam or not shouldn't be at the forefront of her mind. She'd worked through distractions before. This time would be no different.

Since Cam hadn't uttered a word since they'd started walking, she decided to venture conversation. "So, did you grow up here?"

Cam glanced at her, then down at Tilly, who loped happily between them. "I did."

"What is your favorite thing about living here now, as an adult?"

The look on Cam's face told Lauren it was the last question in the world she expected. "The people, I'd say. It's a small community, close-knit. People take care of each other."

"I've never lived anywhere like that." The words were out of Lauren's mouth before she realized it. She was supposed to be getting personal details, not giving them.

"Have you always been in New York City, then?"

Lauren figured she already knew the answer, but decided to ask anyway. "How do you know I'm from New York?"

Cam gave her a knowing smile. "Surely you're not surprised to be the topic of conversation."

Lauren chuckled, not as bothered by the idea as she might have expected. "I suppose not. And yes, I have always lived in the city."

"You're in for quite the culture shock, I'd say."

"I venture out to the country now and then." She thought about the place in the Catskills that had given her ideas about revamping the inn. It was in the middle of nowhere. Not her speed for any length of time, but it had been rather charming.

"Right." She nodded and looked unimpressed. Why did Cam seem to have such indifference for her already?

They walked in silence for a bit. Lauren weighed her options. She could steer clear of Cam moving forward, focus her attention on people who seemed likely to be her allies. People like Charlotte and Mrs. Lucas. Or she could try to win Cam over. Having Cam and her distillery in her corner could be quite advantageous. And she did love a challenge. She smiled, her mind made up. "So, what about the Rose & Crown? Are you a regular patron?"

Cam looked at her sideways, like it might be a test. "Three or four times a week I'd say, for lunch or a pint."

Interesting. "Would you say it's busy a lot of the time?"

"There are regulars, the odd person passing through town. I'm not sure I'd use the word busy."

That's what she was afraid of. "Is it that there are better places in town or that no one comes to town?"

"Some people visit." Cam scowled.

Lauren wondered if she'd hit a nerve. Before she had a chance to ask about it, they rounded the corner near the pub. Tilly, as if sensing how close she was to home, took off. Well, took off might be a bit of an overstatement. She trotted ahead, tail wagging. Maybe having a dog wouldn't be such a bad thing after all.

Arriving back at the Rose & Crown saved her from having to continue the conversation with Cam. Apparently, winning her over and pumping her for information were going to be mutually exclusive. Lauren opened the door, and Tilly walked in like she owned the place. Kind of endearing, really.

One couple sat at a table, having what appeared to be breakfast. Charlotte stood behind the bar, arranging glasses. Not the most inspiring scene to walk into, even if it was only eleven in the morning. Charlotte looked her way and smiled, then her gaze landed on the dog.

"Tilly."

The reunion that followed warmed Lauren's heart, even if she didn't consider herself a dog person. Tilly's tail went into overdrive. Charlotte came from behind the bar and leaned over, rubbing Tilly's face and ears with both hands. Tilly flopped onto her back and Charlotte got down on her knees to rub her exposed belly.

"I think she missed home," Cam said.

Lauren chuckled. "It looks like it."

"You're going to keep her, right? She belongs here."

Lauren thought about her long-term plans, the plans that included selling the pub and going back to New York. Other than her initial conversation with Mr. Brightwater, she'd not disclosed the idea of selling to anyone. Now that she was here, she realized she should keep it that way. It would be enough of an undertaking to overhaul things. If people thought she was in it for nothing more than a quick buck, she'd only make things harder. She looked over at Cam and smiled, keeping her answer specific to the dog. "Yes, she definitely belongs here."

Cam left and Tilly settled into her bed near the fireplace. Even without a fire, she seemed perfectly at home, which technically, she was. Lauren contemplated going to the office to do some planning, or tracking down Mrs. Lucas to go over the books, but neither task appealed to her. She wasn't opposed to the unpleasant or the mundane, but there were plenty of ways to be productive.

Charlotte offered to make coffee for her and she gladly accepted. She set herself up at the bar with the paperwork Jane had given her related to the estate and started reading through everything. The stake in the sheep farm was interesting. She'd have to investigate that further. And find the keys to the car.

"Can I get you some breakfast? Toast?" Charlotte set down a cup of coffee and looked at her expectantly.

"No, thank you. This is great."

"Cream? Sugar?"

"No, thanks. I take it black." Lauren smiled and took a sip. It was all she could do not to spit it out.

"Is it bad?"

Well, it wasn't good. Not terrible, necessarily, but definitely instant. She couldn't remember the last time she'd had instant coffee. "It's fine."

"A rotten liar, you are."

Despite the judgment behind the statement, Lauren couldn't help but smile. "Not what I'm used to. I'll get some to brew when I go out. There's a market, right?"

Charlotte nodded. "A Tesco. Small, but it has the essentials."

"Perfect." Lauren took another sip. Now that she knew what to expect, it wasn't quite as jarring. She turned her attention back to Charlotte. "You seem like a smart woman."

Charlotte narrowed her eyes. "Should I say thank you or is there a however coming?"

Lauren smiled. "Neither. I'm merely making an observation. One I hope will serve us both well."

"How's that?" She didn't seem suspicious, but reserved. Lauren respected that.

"From what I can tell, people aren't beating down the door to drink here. Or eat. Or spend the night."

Charlotte tipped her head back and forth. "You're spot-on there."

"I've done an initial review of the books, and it looks like the place is barely staying afloat. The inn is in even worse shape than the pub."

"It's through no fault of Mrs. Lucas. The guests that do come are happy."

Lauren appreciated the loyalty, in principle but also because it matched her initial impressions of the inn and Mrs. Lucas. "That's good to know. Do you know if Albert did any advertising or other promotion of the place? I did find the website."

Charlotte let out a snort of laughter. Then she covered her mouth with her hand and looked horrified. "Sorry."

Lauren lifted both her hands. "Don't be. It's terrible. It actually makes me feel better that we agree. We can work with that."

"What do you mean?"

No need to elaborate on the exact whys, or why she wasn't in a huge hurry to get back to her life in New York. "I happen to work in marketing. And I'm invested in making this place work. For that to happen, I think we're going to have to make a few changes. I think you're the perfect person to help me implement them."

"You do?" Charlotte blinked a few times and then something passed through her eyes. "I mean, you're right. About the changes. And me being the one to help you."

Charlotte didn't strike her as an insecure person, but maybe she'd been wrong. Or maybe she'd not been entrusted with any of the business side of running things. Either way, Lauren intended that to be one of the things that changed. "So, you're on board?"

Charlotte beamed. "Completely on board. I think we could update the look of things, and maybe the food. I don't have much to do with the inn, but I could help there, too. I don't mind hard work."

The level of enthusiasm made Lauren smile. "Excellent."

"You know who you should get to help?"

Please let there be a sexy butch contractor in town she could hire. "Who's that?"

"Cam."

At the mention of Cam's name, Lauren's stomach did a flip. She hoped it didn't show on her face. "Cam?"

Charlotte nodded. "She's a bloody genius when it comes to making drinks. She could probably do the whole cocktail menu."

"Really?" Oh, this was very interesting. Assuming, of course, Cam would agree to help her.

"Oh, my God." Charlotte's face lit up.

"What?"

"You could help Cam with Carriage House."

"What's Carriage House?"

"It's her new line of gin. She's been hemming and hawing about how to increase sales. You mentioned you're in marketing, right? You could totally help each other."

Right, right. She'd had Carriage House in her G&T last night. The idea of having something to barter made Lauren's mind hum. The fact that it was something she was really good at? Icing on the cake. Since she and Charlotte didn't know each other well enough for her to do a happy dance, she tapped her finger on the bar and nodded. "Interesting. You think that's something she'd be interested in?"

"She ought to be. This would be perfect."

A thought crossed Lauren's mind. "You and Cam. Are you?" She hesitated. Knowing was more important than not coming across as nosy, but she wasn't sure how explicit or direct she should be.

Understanding flashed in Charlotte's eyes. She shook her head. "We used to be. Ages ago."

"Ah." The relief was maybe more pronounced than professional curiosity warranted. "So you're…" She trailed off again, feeling like it was none of her business but like she still wanted to know.

"Mates. Very close, but no funny business."

Lauren laughed out loud at the description. "Okay. For what it's worth, your private life is none of my business. Unless, of course, it overlaps with business."

"Oh, no, no. I understand completely. Work and play do not mix. It's one of my rules."

Lauren had a flash of Philip. Not that she'd have wanted to play with him under any circumstances. But his inability to follow that basic principle had seriously fucked her over. She shook her head. Asshole.

"Did I overstep?" Charlotte made a face. "Cam always tells me I don't have a filter."

Lauren schooled her expression. She'd need to be careful how much she let her mind wander. "Not at all. I was thinking about something else. I think that's an excellent rule, one I share."

"Oh, good. If you want, I could talk to Cam for you."

Hmm. She was accustomed to handling her own negotiations. But if Cam and Charlotte were as close as Charlotte implied, she might have better luck swaying her. She also didn't want to lead with the idea that Cam needed help. "Maybe you could break the ice, see if she'd be interested."

Charlotte grinned. "I'll convince her she'd be crazy not to be."

Whether it was the prospect of working with Cam or being included more generally, Lauren couldn't be sure, but Charlotte's enthusiasm radiated from her. Either way, she was glad to have Charlotte in her corner. "I think you and I are going to work well together."

CHAPTER SIX

If she hadn't promised to meet Jane for lunch, Cam might have skipped the Rose & Crown altogether. Not that she planned to let the new owner drive her away. But something about her put Cam on edge. She couldn't put her finger on the why, but it made her restless and she didn't like it.

Besides, she was curious about what the new owner had in mind. Would she be looking to make changes or leave things as they were? Did she plan to run it herself or put someone in charge and be gone in a week? For Charlotte's sake, Cam hoped it was the latter. She'd been taking on more and more responsibility as Albert slowed down, with the ultimate goal of buying the place from him. Cam knew she didn't have the capital yet to make that happen, but she might in the next few years. At least enough for a down payment.

If this Lauren woman was looking to shake things up, or worse, shutter the place, Charlotte would never get that chance. Imagining the pub empty and abandoned put a knot in Cam's stomach. So many pubs had suffered that fate, unable to compete with chain restaurants or adjust to the ever-shrinking, not to mention aging, populations in the villages. She was pretty sure Albert kept things going out of sheer will, combined perhaps with a relaxed outlook on profit margins.

But as sad as it was when any pub closed, or was taken over by developers catering to anyone but the locals, the idea of it happening to the Rose broke her heart. She'd practically grown up in the pub, not to mention the fact that her parents had courted there and her grandparents before them. Hopefully, that wouldn't be the case. She shook her head, shaking off the malaise that came with the direction of her thoughts, and left her office.

When she arrived at the Rose & Crown, she found Charlotte, Jane, and Lauren huddled around a laptop, seemingly all talking at once. The unease returned, although it was hard to know whether it had to do with the fate of the pub or how much the scene reminded her of school, when groups of girls traveled in packs, leaving her invariably on the outside. There was also the problematic way her body seemed to react to Lauren. She'd managed to convince herself the attraction was a fluke, some combination of novelty and beauty that would only sucker punch her that one time.

She almost backed out the way she'd come in, thinking to send Jane a text of apology and hightail it back to work. But Tilly, who'd lifted her head at the sound of the door, hefted herself from her bed to come over and say hello. Charlotte chose that exact moment to look up and her fate was sealed. "Good afternoon, Cam," she said, her voice annoyingly cheerful.

Both Lauren and Jane looked her way, although she only really saw Lauren. Nope, not a one-time fluke. Cam clenched and unclenched her fists by her sides, failing at distracting herself from the visceral reaction. Jane waved and said, "Hello."

Cam bent down to give Tilly some belly rubs. "Ladies."

She still couldn't tear her eyes from Lauren, who shifted on her stool and offered Cam a slow smile. "Hi there."

It was the kind of smile that seemed to hold secrets, but also a trace of challenge. Did she give everyone that sort of smile or was it special for Cam? Did Cam want to know? No. No, she did not. She gestured to the computer. "What's so interesting?"

"You."

Charlotte's voice had a teasing edge that normally wouldn't bother her. In this context though, Cam's suspicion bloomed. "Dare I ask?"

Jane smiled with her usual sincerity. "Lauren is looking to bring the Rose & Crown into the twenty-first century, and Charlotte said you'd be perfect for helping with the food and drink menus."

Charlotte nodded. "And the updates to the inn. Since you oversaw the tasting room remodel, you know all the local people who do that sort of work."

"Including Dad, of course," Jane said.

Both Charlotte and Jane seemed thoroughly pleased with themselves. Cam looked at Lauren. She didn't seem pleased, exactly. Maybe hopeful. But also flirtatious. Cam had yet to glean whether it really was flirtation or just her demeanor. Either way, Cam's brain and body responded—a frustrating mix of defensiveness and desire that left her stomach in knots and her thoughts hazy.

"I—" She fumbled for an excuse. As if bored with the whole thing, Tilly retreated to her bed and curled herself into a ball.

"From what I hear, you're a genius when it comes to cocktails," Lauren tipped her head slightly and winked, "among other things."

Bloody hell, how much had they been talking about her? Way more than she was comfortable with, that's for sure. What was she supposed to do with that? "Genius seems a bit much."

"And humble. I like it." Lauren nodded and made a point of keeping her tone playful. Hopefully, her eyes didn't give away where her mind was because it was way beyond playful. In her mind, she was naked and under Cam, with Cam's hands roaming over her. Not to mention her lips. God, why couldn't she stop herself from going there every time Cam was within twenty feet of her?

Cam shrugged. "I mean, I do know how to mix spirits, but the other things might be a stretch."

"I think you're being modest," Jane said.

Charlotte folded her arms and nodded. "Totally modest."

Charlotte's delivery had more sarcasm that Jane's, but it probably had more to do with her friendship with Cam than the sentiments being expressed. At least Lauren hoped that was the case. "And I wouldn't be taking your help for nothing. I understand you're trying to launch a new brand of gin."

"Technically, it's already launched."

Lauren cringed on the inside, but her smile didn't waver. "Yes. Carriage House. Charlotte made me a G&T with it my first night here. It's quite good. More than good, actually."

"Um, thank you." Cam regarded her with what she could only describe as suspicion.

"But I understand you're looking to grow? Perhaps embark on a marketing campaign?"

Cam looked uncomfortable, although it was impossible to know if she disliked talking about her business or, as Lauren had started to fear, disliked her. "I would like to expand."

Lauren squared her shoulders, sliding into pitch mode. "So, I have a proposition for you. You help me spruce things up around here and I'll help you take Carriage House to the next level."

Cam narrowed her eyes and looked at Charlotte. "Is this your idea?"

Lauren looked at Charlotte as well, wondering how she'd answer, but before she could, Jane chimed in. "She suggested it, but I couldn't agree more. It's perfect."

She couldn't remember the last time she'd had such ready allies. Well, except for Anja, but they'd been friends for ages. It gave Lauren a warm, tingly feeling. Not something she had a lot of in New York. She pressed on. "I'm a professional, you know. I do marketing for a living."

Cam's gaze returned to hers. Was that disdain in her eyes? "I'll think about it."

Lauren resisted the urge to go for the hard sell. As often as it served her well in closing a deal, she had a feeling it would backfire with Cam. No, if Cam was going to work with her, she was going to have to come to it on her own. Well, perhaps with some nudging from Charlotte and Jane. "Of course. I can share my portfolio with you if you'd like."

"Portfolio?"

Lauren flashed her most confident smile. "Of my work. I've managed dozens of campaigns, mostly in the boutique hospitality industry, including brand management, print advertising, and digital collateral."

Cam didn't answer right away, making Lauren think perhaps she'd overplayed her hand. Eventually, Cam nodded. "Sure."

Point in her favor. Time to exit while she was ahead. "I'll email you. I'll also leave you and Jane to enjoy your lunch."

"You could join us." Jane looked at her with a smile. "We'd love that, wouldn't we, Cam?"

She didn't need to look at Cam to know Cam most certainly wouldn't love it. Which was okay. Annoying, seeing as she'd done nothing to provoke it, but okay. She could play this hand as well as the next. "No, no. You two enjoy. I've got work to do."

"You really are welcome," Cam said.

Whether it was guilt or curiosity, she didn't know. She'd take either at this point. "Thank you, but I'm good. I've got to make sense of the books before I can think about makeovers."

"Of course. Maybe next time." Jane didn't seem fazed by the interaction.

"Absolutely. Cam, Jane, I hope to see you again soon. Charlotte, I'll be in the office if you need me."

And with that, she made her exit. She really did need to sort through the books, figure out where money was coming and going. She'd already resigned herself to having to dip into her personal savings to do most of the work. She needed to make sure the Rose & Crown could sustain itself in the meantime. Because nothing would put a damper on a splashy rebrand more than bill collectors showing up to repossess the place.

❖

After lunch, Jane headed back to her office and Cam lingered. She had plenty to do, but she wanted to talk to Charlotte without Jane running interference. She took an empty stool at the bar and shook her head. "I can't believe you've thrown your lot in with her."

Charlotte rolled her eyes. "You make it sound like I made a deal with the devil."

"No, more like trying to get her into bed." She'd not given the idea any thought, but the possibility took root. "Oh, my God. Are you trying to get her into bed?"

Charlotte folded her arms and gave her a bland look. "Just because I'm poly, it doesn't mean I'm trying to get everyone into bed."

Cam raised a brow.

"I'm discerning. And ethical."

"We both know she's gorgeous."

Charlotte got a dreamy look in her eyes and sighed. "Yeah."

"See." Cam pointed at her. "You're proving my point."

The dreamy look vanished, and Charlotte was once again all business. "But also my boss, so off limits. I like her, Cam. She has good ideas and she asks my opinion, and I think she's going to make the Rose & Crown something special."

"It already is something special."

"It's barely staying afloat and you know it."

Cam frowned. "What happened to you wanting to buy it? The more she pours into it, the less likely she is to sell. Why would you help her with that?"

"Because maybe I'm realizing that buying a failing business isn't the smartest life goal."

Even if the statement held a kernel of truth, Cam didn't want to acknowledge it. "So, you're just going to give up? Work for her and take what you get?"

"It's more complicated than that."

"It seems to me anytime I tell you something is a terrible idea, you try to convince me it's complicated."

Charlotte pointed at her aggressively. "Because I'm right. You're so bloody black-and-white about everything. Life doesn't work that way."

It wasn't the first time they'd had this argument. Not about Lauren, of course, but about life and the seemingly infinite shades of gray Charlotte used to analyze and categorize things. Cam didn't like to think of herself as rigid, but she did prefer a simpler view of people and relationships and the world. She remained convinced that was the primary reason she and Charlotte didn't work out romantically. It made her sad, not because she still harbored feelings for Charlotte, but because it felt like such a gulf between them sometimes, even as friends.

Charlotte pulled her hand back and sighed. "Don't stew."

"I'm not stewing."

Charlotte gave her a look that said she knew otherwise. "You are. I'm not sure why you're so hell-bent on disliking her."

"It's not that."

"What is it? Talk to me." Any trace of anger had vanished, as though she sensed there was more to the situation than Cam let on.

In that moment, Cam remembered all the reasons she and Charlotte were best mates. Because even if they didn't see eye to eye on everything, Charlotte got her. Even more importantly, Charlotte cared about her enough to poke though her cool exterior to get at what really mattered. "I just have this feeling that everything is about to change. And I don't like it."

Charlotte reached over the bar and squeezed her hand. "Not all change is bad, you know."

"I know that. I'm not a dinosaur."

"Are you afraid that Carriage House is going to become more famous that Barrister's?"

"What? Where did that come from?" Cam tried to ignore the tightening in her stomach. "And what does it have to do with what Lauren is doing to the Crown?"

Charlotte studied her fingernails and didn't answer for an interminable length of time. "You're one of the smartest and most hardworking people I know."

Cam pointed. "Don't try to distract me with compliments."

Charlotte chuckled. "I'm not. There's a but."

"Oh, sure. Stroke my ego and then take it back."

"You're smart, but you're set in your ways. You have this amazing ambition, but you temper it, citing tradition or caution or some other bullshit."

Cam swallowed. They'd danced around this conversation in the past, but always managed to diffuse it before it went too far. "You're calling me a coward."

"I'm not and I refuse to let you shut me down by putting that word in my mouth. I think you're comfortable. There's nothing wrong with that. For some people, it's perfectly fine."

"But you don't think I'm one of those people."

"No." Charlotte looked her right in the eyes. "I think you're so much more than that."

Now that it was out there, like a bandage starting to fray at the edges, she couldn't leave it alone. "So, not only do I need to change, you think whatever Lauren cooks up is the change I need."

"Maybe."

"It feels risky." It felt a hell of a lot more than risky, but she didn't want to come across as dramatic on top of being stubborn and resistant to change.

"Yeah, but really, what do we have to lose?"

Cam didn't answer that question, not because she didn't have answers, but because she didn't like the ones her brain churned out with alarming speed. Images of some cartoon of a pub that served Marks & Spencer pies and chicken nuggets. "You have a point. She's going to do whatever she wants anyway. Being involved is probably our best chance to prevent the Rose from turning into some whitewashed Disney version of itself."

Charlotte smiled. Cam got the impression she'd already conceded the point Charlotte was poised to make. "And what about Carriage House? Will you accept her offer to help with the marketing?"

Cam shrugged. It might be a disaster, some feeble attempt to make her gin trendy. But it would be free, and probably demand less of her time than working with some actual marketing company. "I don't see where there's any harm. I don't have to use her ideas if I think they're terrible."

Charlotte leaned forward on the bar. "Do you really think they will be?"

The thing with terrible ideas was that some people invariably thought they were great. She wasn't willing to go for the lowest common denominator to boost her sales. And if that's what Lauren had in mind, they'd run out of things to talk about pretty quick. "We'll see."

"You know, your flexibility and open-mindedness are two of my favorite things about you."

"There's no need to be sarcastic." Cam tucked her tongue in her cheek.

The door to the pub opened and a couple walked it. Charlotte's gaze flashed over to them, then back to Cam. "I love you, you know."

Cam took a deep breath and rolled her eyes. "I know. I love you, too."

"I'll see you soon?"

From the looks of it, she'd just roped herself into spending quite a bit more time at the pub than usual. "I'm sure you will."

Charlotte moved down the bar to greet the new customers. Cam stood and looked at her watch. She'd taken a much longer lunch hour than she'd intended. Not that anyone was clocking her time, but she didn't want to abuse her position, or set a bad example. She offered Charlotte a parting wave and headed back to work.

On the walk back to the distillery, she turned over the conversation with Charlotte in her mind, as well as the one with Lauren, Jane, and Charlotte. In both cases, she'd come across as the curmudgeon. She'd never had a reputation of being carefree, but she wasn't crazy about this dour turn.

Despite her reservations, she'd meant what she said to Charlotte. Having her hand in whatever Lauren did to the pub made perfect sense. It was her best chance to influence the final outcome. The prospect of getting some free consultation on taking Carriage House to the next level made it a no-brainer. So, why did she still have this deep-seated reluctance in the pit of her stomach?

Even as she posed the question to herself, she knew the answer. She bristled against what Lauren represented, but it was Lauren herself that felt dangerous. Or perhaps more accurately, her reaction to Lauren. Yes, it felt like the Rose sat on the cusp of some sea change. But it felt like she might be thrown into that churn as well. And she had neither the time nor the inclination to go down that path.

When she got to the distillery, Cam started toward her office. She should sit at her desk and work through some invoices and contracts. But just the idea made her twitchy. Instead, she headed to the still room, bypassing the main area and heading to the smaller space she liked to think of as her lab. She had her sights on creating a small, limited run batch of gin blended specifically for the holidays. And even though that remained months away, now was the time to refine the recipe and all the details that went along with it. The process required intense concentration and brought immense satisfaction. Given how her day had gone so far, she could use some of both.

CHAPTER SEVEN

L auren picked up a tube of lipstick just as her phone rang. She looked at the screen, fully expecting to let it go to voice mail. Anja's name and number flashed at her. She might not be ready to face most of the people in her life, but she'd put off Anja long enough. "Hi."

"Oh, my goddess, she lives."

If it was anyone but Anja, she'd have found the hyperbole irritating. But it was Anja, so she snickered. "Breathing, even."

"I'm serious. I've been worrying about you. Are you going to tell me what the hell is going on?" Anja's tone was impatient, and Lauren could imagine her pacing around as she spoke.

"Do you want the short version or the holy hell, crazy drama filled version?"

"Uh, I want to know everything. You've been avoiding me for like two weeks."

Lauren took a deep breath, trying to decide what to lead with. "An uncle I hardly knew died and left me his pub-slash-inn so I came to England to deal with it."

"That's what you're doing in England? When you said 'some family business,' you made it sound like no big deal. I figured you were home already and buried in work."

Work. Ha.

"I can't believe you're in England and you didn't even invite me."

Anja, a professional photographer, had accompanied Lauren on more than a few of her trips, sometimes for work and sometimes just for fun. "I'm in the middle of nowhere. Seriously, a good three hours outside of London."

"I love the middle of nowhere. You know this."

She did. And under normal circumstances, she'd not have thought twice about inviting Anja to join her. But these weren't normal circumstances. Still, Anja was her best friend and hiding from her had been dumb. "I do know. I'm sorry. I threw everything together pretty quickly."

"I'm not really mad. I just miss you. I want to hear everything. And work. What are you doing about work?"

"I got fired." She closed her eyes, bracing herself for questions and righteous indignation and an ungodly amount of swearing.

"I don't understand," Anja said with almost eerie calm.

Since arriving in England, she'd pushed all thoughts of KesslerAldridge to the back of her mind. She'd mostly succeeded, too. More so than she'd expected. The reality of the situation, the injustice of it and her empty rage, flooded her mind. "I was accused of filing bogus expense reports and trying to sleep with Philip to cover it up."

"What?" Anja's voice pitched high, and in that one syllable, yelled over a thousand miles away, Lauren felt a trace of vindication.

She'd told Anja about Philip coming on to her, groping her and having to fight him off. Anja was the only person she had told. And despite Anja's rage, she'd supported Lauren's decision not to press charges, or even take it to HR.

Lauren filled in the more recent details—the paper trail someone had painstakingly created to make her look guilty, the look of regret on Eric's face, being escorted from the building by security. "Of course I know Philip is behind the whole thing, but I'm not sure how I'd be able to prove it."

"So you just left? You're going to let that motherfucker win?"

She knew Anja didn't mean it to come out as an accusation, but it felt that way. Lauren's stomach clenched, and some of her original fury boiled up, clearly suppressed more than subsided. "It literally happened the same day I met with the lawyer about my uncle's will. I decided to come here to regroup." She squared her shoulders even though Anja couldn't see and added, "And plot."

There was a long silence, and Lauren had a flash of panic that maybe she'd gone about this all wrong. That what had seemed so logical in her mind was in fact the worst possible way of handling her situation. That, in not fighting back immediately, she'd lost her chance, and with it, any hope of saving her reputation. There were few people whose opinion she trusted more than Anja's, professionally and personally. If Anja thought she was making a huge mistake, she'd have to pause and rethink everything.

"You shouldn't plot alone."

The air rushed out of her lungs all at once. The tension she'd not noticed between her shoulder blades loosened. Lauren flopped onto the bed. "I'm sorry I didn't tell you."

"Again, I'm not mad. But I'm here for you. I want to help."

"Thank you." So much more than her actual family, Anja was someone she could count on, no matter what.

"Does that mean you'll let me come out there?"

"Actually…" Lauren trailed off, letting the idea take shape. "I could use your help."

"Please tell me it involves Philip's untimely demise. Or castration maybe. I could get behind castration."

She'd need to deal with what she left behind eventually, but not today. "No. It's about the inn and the pub."

"Go on."

Lauren smiled at the intrigued delivery. Anja loved a project almost as much as she did. "I'm going to use the Rose & Crown to launch my own agency."

"I love a scheme as much as the next person, but I don't follow."

"What's been my most successful campaign to date?"

Anja didn't miss a beat. "Those posh hotels. Latour."

"Exactly. So much so that I decided to make boutique hospitality brands my niche when I strike out on my own."

"Right." Anja drew out the word, like she'd connected the dots but remained unsure of the result.

"I'm going to turn this place into a Latour property, in spirit if not literally. Then I'm going to sell it. I'll have the capital and the publicity I need to start my own agency. Revenge, served cold, just the way it should be."

Anja sighed. "Not as fun, but ultimately more satisfying. So where do I come in?"

"I'm starting from scratch here. This place has a website circa 1999 and nothing else. I need stills and video for web, social, everything."

"Oooh. That sounds fun. When can I start?"

It was Lauren's turn to sigh. "I need to do a little work first."

"Work?"

"Remember that place in the Catskills? Hazelnut Inn?"

"Yeah."

"Remember the before pictures they had in the bar for people to chuckle over while they drank their twelve-dollar IPAs?"

Anja laughed. "I do."

"That's sort of what I'm dealing with here. Only British, so like a million times older."

"Oh."

"It's not all bad. A lot of it is quite charming. But I've got to spruce it up some. And overhaul the menus in the pub."

"Is there anything you can't do?"

Lauren laughed, appreciating the implied vote of confidence. "Ask me after I pull this off."

"I don't doubt your abilities for a second."

"Well, that makes one of us." She possessed probably more confidence than most, but this project was a tall order. She preferred to think it was that and not the crushing blow of being fired that had her uneasy.

"I'm serious. You—shit, I have another call coming in. It's a client."

"Go, go. I'll call you this weekend. I still need to hear all about you."

"Will do. Love you, woman."

"Love you back."

Lauren ended the call and looked around. She'd called it home for close to a week, but being there still felt a bit surreal. Even the dog bed she'd brought in so Tilly could sleep in the same room as her felt more like a prop than anything to do with her actual life. She shook it off. Just another business trip. A slightly extended business trip, but the purpose and desired outcome weren't so different from the dozens of trips she'd taken in the past to visit clients. She'd helped them come up with new visions for their products and brands, and she'd do the exact same thing here. Only this time, she'd get to be the client, too. And the payoff would be twice as sweet.

Feeling energized, she finished getting ready, putting on her favorite lipstick and a spritz of perfume. Her meeting with Cam was in less than an hour, and she wanted to be waiting for her when she arrived.

Cam walked into the pub and found Lauren already waiting for her at a table in the corner. When she saw Cam, she stood. She looked like she was dressed for a business meeting. Not a suit, but a tailored blouse tucked into a high-waisted skirt and heels that managed to look utterly professional and sexy at the same time. Cam wished she'd put on something nicer than a plaid oxford and khakis, even if the idea of wanting to impress Lauren didn't sit well.

"Thank you for agreeing to meet with me." Lauren smiled and Cam was pretty sure the smile alone had gotten Lauren her way many times before.

"Charlotte convinced me. You can thank her."

The smile took on a mischievous gleam. "Oh, I already have."

Even with Charlotte's assertions there was nothing sexual simmering between them, the implied intimacy sent a ripple of discomfort through Cam. No, it wasn't discomfort. It was jealousy, plain and simple. And it drove her crazy. "I have no doubt. So, what exactly do you want from me?"

For a split second, something akin to desire passed through Lauren's eyes. It looked good on her and made Cam wonder what it would be like to have those eyes on her in bed. The image was so vivid, it sucked the air right out of her lungs. She coughed. Lauren raised a brow, more flirtation than concern. "I want your expertise on local customs, and I'd like you to consult on the menu. Mostly the cocktail menu, but Charlotte tells me you're quite a cook, too."

She should be bothered that Charlotte was talking her up like a prospective date, but she felt a little surge of pride instead. She'd bet money Miss Big City had a fancy modern kitchen and didn't even know what to do with it. "I guess it depends on what you have in mind."

"How so?"

"If you want to do overpriced, highbrow bullshit, you'll need to find someone else."

Lauren nodded slowly, the hint of a smirk playing at the corner of her mouth. "Are you always so frank?"

Cam shrugged. "It feels like a waste of time to be anything else."

"Here's the thing. If the Rose & Crown is going to attract people from out of town—people who will stay in the rooms and keep the place going—it's got to be something more than fish and chips and Sunday roast."

She didn't disagree, technically. "There's a lot of ground between that and twenty quid composed salads so tiny they wouldn't satisfy my ninety-year-old grandmother."

Lauren narrowed her eyes. "Do you have a ninety-year-old grandmother?"

Cam rolled her eyes. "No, but I could. That's not the point."

Lauren's expression morphed from suspicious to amused. "I could argue that it is, but I won't. I understand what you're saying. I don't want to alienate the local clientele. The idea is to bring in more customers, not swap one group with another."

"Even if that other pays more? I thought that was your whole mission." Cam's tone had more bite than she intended, but she couldn't walk it back now without undermining her own argument.

"You don't think very highly of me, do you?"

Was that some kind of trick question? If she knew one thing about women, it was not to fall for trick questions. "I don't know what you mean."

"Yes, you do. You think I'm some flashy city girl who's hell-bent on swooping in and changing everything on a whim without any thought or consideration for anything but what she wants."

She might have said something almost identical to Charlotte, but she knew better than to admit it and think they had any chance of working together. At the same time, flat-out denial would be lying and she made a habit of honesty.

"Do you know why I'm so good at my job?" Lauren asked before Cam could respond.

Cam hated rhetorical questions almost as much as trick questions, but this one felt like a gift horse and she wasn't about to look it in the mouth. "Why?"

"Because I know how to marry what's there with what people want. I pull out the best parts of something, enhance them, maybe add on something new. And then I tell a story that draws people in, makes them feel connected to something they've never touched or someplace they've never been."

It sounded pretty enough. But when push came to shove, it was still selling. "And you convince them to drop gobs of money on it."

If Charlotte had been there, she'd smack Cam on the back of the head for picking a fight. She wasn't trying to, but she couldn't seem to help herself. Something about Lauren got under her skin and drove her nuts. Some incomprehensible combination of annoyed and aroused.

She half expected Lauren to storm out or, at the very least, get huffy and defensive. Instead, she laced her fingers together and set them on the table. Cam got the distinct feeling she was about to be managed. "Do you market your gin?"

"Of course."

"And your new line? You market it differently from the original?"

It grated that Lauren was talking to her like she was a five-year-old, but she supposed she walked right into it. "Yes."

"How so?"

Cam resisted the urge to roll her eyes. She wasn't ready to confess just how little she'd managed to differentiate the two. "It has a bolder flavor profile, so we highlight that."

"And you're probably going for a younger audience, people more interested in adventure than tradition."

She didn't, but she should. Would. Hell. "Something like that."

"But at its core, it's the same high-quality gin you've been producing for a billion years."

"Not quite a billion." Cam smiled, trying to concede the point gracefully. "But yes."

"This is the same thing. I want to build on the history and reputation of the Rose & Crown, not destroy it. I want to share it with a wider audience and, in the meantime, provide an improved experience to the people who support it now."

At this point, she didn't doubt Lauren's sincerity. Or the fact that she knew a thing or two about marketing. But how could she preserve something she didn't understand, much less value? Maybe Charlotte was right. Maybe that's where she came in. Somehow, Lauren had gotten it into her head that working together would benefit them both. Maybe instead of fighting that, she could use it. If Lauren trusted Cam's opinion, Cam could keep things from spinning out of control. On top of that, she wasn't an idiot. She knew that more visitors in Netherfield could help her business and a dozen others trying to stay afloat. Even if those visitors weren't her cup of tea, their money spent just as good as the next person's. "Okay."

Lauren looked dubious. "Okay, you're saying yes?"

"Yes."

"Excellent. You won't regret it." Lauren stuck out her hand like they were closing a business deal.

Cam accepted, thinking there was every possibility she might regret it. Because beyond expecting to butt heads with Lauren, she was going to have to contend with the fact that she couldn't be around her without wanting to kiss her. And more. God help her, so much more.

CHAPTER EIGHT

Lauren had a million things she should be doing, from researching contractors to scoping out her competition. But she was starting to feel a little stir-crazy. Something about living and working in the same place maybe. She glanced at her watch. Charlotte should just be arriving for her shift. She'd pump her for some information and then venture out.

Maybe she'd take Albert's car for a spin and check out a couple of the neighboring towns, or maybe this wool farm Albert owned a stake in. That would be fun. Assuming that, by fun, she meant strange and unexpected.

Excited for what the day would hold, she pulled on jeans and a tank top, grabbed her denim jacket from the closet. Feeling silly wearing sneakers anywhere but the gym, she settled on ballet flats she could do a lot of walking in. She should probably invest in a pair of hiking boots since only the main roads seemed to be paved. The idea of a little retail therapy put an extra spring in her step as she headed downstairs.

She let Tilly out into the side yard for her morning business and headed into the pub. When she walked in, it was Jack who greeted her instead of Charlotte. "Hey, Jack. I wasn't expecting you until tonight."

"Charlotte switched with me. I've got me a date this evening."

The idea of her seventy-year-old bartender on a date made her smile. "Congratulations. Will you be bringing her here so we can meet her?"

Jack wagged a finger at her. "Not a chance. I'm inviting her to my place, making her a nice dinner."

Lauren bit her lip to keep from laughing because it would give him the impression she was poking fun. "That sounds like the perfect way to impress someone."

He offered a playful shrug. "We'll see."

"I'm heading out for the day. Feel free to call if you need me."

"You have yourself a nice time." He offered her a wave. "And remember, we drive on the left."

She offered a salute. "Thanks for the reminder."

She let Tilly in and gave her her breakfast, then let her into the pub so she could spend her day snoozing and greeting patrons. With a final good-bye to Jack, she headed to the tiny garage out back. After wrestling the garage door open, which took more time and strength than she cared to admit, Lauren opened the car door and paused. There was no steering wheel. Well, there was, but it was on the opposite side of the car. Right.

She closed the door and went around to the other side. She climbed in and took a minute to locate things like lights and turn signals and windshield wipers. Nothing dramatically different from a car back home. Not that she ever really drove at home. But she had her license and, really, how hard could it be? It wasn't like she'd be fighting her way through Manhattan traffic.

She turned the key in the ignition and, after some brief coughing, the engine roared to life. Even though she was expecting it, the sound startled her. She shook her head. Good thing she was by herself.

After a couple minutes of adjusting and acclimating to everything, she shifted the car into gear. Thank God it was an automatic transmission at least. Having to ask for driving lessons would be beyond embarrassing. She took her foot off the brake and eased it onto the gas. The car lurched out of the garage and she quickly returned her foot to the brake pedal. Okay, so this was going to take a little getting used to.

She didn't bother with GPS at first, figuring it would be easier to get used to the car and the driving, then worry about where she was going. As long as she avoided that crazy road into town that was way too narrow and half-covered with shrubbery. She returned her foot to the gas, more gently this time. The car crept forward. She smiled. Easy. Or as Mrs. Lucas would say, easy peasy.

After reminding herself for the tenth time to keep to the left, easy was no longer the word flitting through Lauren's brain. Did everyone have this hard a time or was it because she was so out of practice? At a stop sign, she took a second to close her eyes and take a deep breath. It was fine. She just wasn't used to feeling so awkward at something. She'd not crashed into anything, nor had she almost killed anyone.

She drove in circles for a while, familiarizing herself with the streets and lanes around the pub. There weren't that many of them to learn. With each turn, it felt a little easier—both the driving and the knowing where she was going.

More confident than when she started, she decided to track down the sheep farm. She pulled to the side of the road and searched it on her phone. She figured it would be a ways out of town, but it wasn't. It sat near the edge of the village and spread out to the fields and pastures beyond. Should she call first? Make an appointment? There was a wool shop, and according to the internet, it was open. Good enough for her.

Lauren propped the phone next to the gearshift and pulled back onto the road. It only took a few minutes to wind her way there. She passed the shop going slow enough to note how adorable it was, then realized there wasn't any sort of parking lot. She'd just need to double back and park on the street. Which would have been fine if there was a place to turn around. Or a cross street. Anything. But no.

A minute past the shop and she was at the farm. Or somebody's farm. The buildings ended abruptly, and all that remained in front of her were rolling hills dotted with trees and sheep. The road— another impossibly narrow road—was bordered by bushes on one side and a low stone wall on the other.

Lauren sighed and stopped the car. At least there wasn't any oncoming traffic to worry about. She'd just need to do a three-point turn. Or five. Or maybe seven. Again, no one was there to watch or make fun, so it didn't matter how awkwardly she went about it.

At point four, the back right corner of the car sank. With it, Lauren's stomach. She shifted into drive and pressed on the gas. Nothing. Well, not nothing. She felt the tires spin and heard that whirring noise of a tire stuck in something soft. Hell.

She tried again, even though she knew it was an exercise in futility. She banged on the steering wheel a couple of times, then climbed out of the car. It could be worse, really. There was much more of a ditch than she'd realized. She could have dumped her whole back end into it. This, in comparison, constituted a minor conundrum. Not that she was any better equipped to handle it herself. The image of her standing in the ditch, attempting to push the car, made her shudder.

She folded her arms and tapped her foot, considering her options. Surely there was a tow truck in town. She'd never called a tow truck, but it couldn't be all that complicated.

Lauren walked around the front of the car and reached in to grab her phone. She opened a browser, but nothing happened. She tapped reload and glanced at the signal strength. Nothing. She let her head fall back and sighed. Literally two minutes outside the village and nothing. Not that the signal in the village was anything to write home about.

She reconsidered the pushing option. No. Even if she was strong enough to move the car—and she had no idea how much strength such a thing would require—she'd seen enough movies where cars went rolling off with no one in them. No, she'd just walk back into town and call for help. She debated for a minute, then reached in to turn on the emergency flashers. Chances were good not a soul would come by, but it seemed like the thing to do. She grabbed her purse and started the trek.

Just shy of the wool shop, her phone winked back to life. Unfortunately, the search didn't yield any good news. The closest towing company, at least the closest one with an online listing, was three towns over. She could call them. It wouldn't be the end of the world. But she'd waste half her day waiting. Lauren decided to start with a call to Charlotte instead, to see if she had any better options.

Five minutes later, she had the promise of a lorry that could pull her out in under an hour. Lauren hung up the phone, relieved.

Charlotte made it seem like no big deal, like this sort of thing happened all the time. She considered going to the wool shop to pass the time, but it seemed rude not to be waiting when Charlotte's friend arrived. She made the short walk back to her car.

While she waited, she resisted the urge to check email or try to accomplish something on her phone. She looked around, really taking in the scenery. The rolling hills to her left were impossibly green, and the sheep, the kind that had black legs and faces and fluffy white bodies, looked almost too perfect to be real. Combined with the ancient-looking stone wall, the whole vista looked like it belonged in a picture book.

"People would pay good money to look at you," she said to the small cluster of sheep nearby. "Damn good money."

Cam held her phone in one hand and used the other to pinch the bridge of her nose as Charlotte relayed the call she'd gotten from Lauren. And the favor she was asking. "Calling in a tow will take all day. Couldn't you just zip out and give her a hand?"

"I'm not sure why you're nominating me to rescue her." Cam scowled, unsure whether her annoyance stemmed from being asked or from liking the idea of helping Lauren out of a jam.

"Because you can, because you're nice, and because it'll get you good gesture points."

Cam scowled even deeper. "I don't need good gesture points."

Charlotte sighed. Cam could feel her eye roll through the phone. "I do, or at least I want them. Do it for me?"

It was Cam's turn to sigh. "Fine. Where is she?"

"Just past the wool works. I think she was going to check it out."

At least it wasn't far out of town. She'd be able to get there, save the day, and be back at work in under an hour. "All right, then."

"You're the best."

"I know." Cam ended the call and shook her head. How did she let Charlotte talk her into stuff like this? Because Charlotte would do the same for her, anytime, no questions asked. They were pretty much family when it came to stuff like that. And even though Cam had a big family, Charlotte didn't.

She shook her head. It wasn't doing the favor for Charlotte that got her steamed up. It was the prospect of coming to Lauren's rescue, of spending even a few minutes alone with her. Because as much as Cam remained leery of Lauren, she was drawn to her, too. And being drawn to Lauren made her think about doing things she had no business thinking about.

Of course, she'd already agreed to working together, so she'd better get used to it. Maybe having Lauren feel like she owed her one would come in handy. Cam grabbed her keys and left her office. She passed through the still room, shouting to George that she'd be back. Fortunately, she left during the day often enough that he didn't even look up, merely lifted a hand in acknowledgment.

The drive took all of ten minutes. She saw Albert's car, slightly off the road, but no sign of Lauren. Maybe she was sitting inside. Cam passed the car and pulled in front of it. Not there. If Lauren had gotten up and wandered off, she was going to be bloody pissed off.

Cam put the truck into park and was just stringing together some choice words when she saw her. She must have climbed the low stone wall because she was in the pasture, on her rear end, surrounded by sheep. And from what Cam could tell, she appeared to be conversing with them.

Cam got out of her truck slowly, not wanting to startle the animals. Lauren either didn't hear her or was ignoring her because she didn't even look Cam's way. She was most definitely carrying on a conversation. The sheep seemed enthralled. Cam scratched her temple and waited a beat. Nothing. Eventually, she called out, "You all right, there?"

Lauren turned then, along with five black sheep faces. All of them looked surprised to see her. Lauren scrambled to her feet. "Cam."

"Were you not expecting me?"

"I..." She patted one of the sheep on the head and started toward the road. "I called Charlotte. She said she had a friend with a truck."

Of course she did. Cam closed her eyes for a second and sighed. "That would be me."

"Oh."

Could this day get any weirder? "Should I ask what you were doing sitting in with the sheep?"

Lauren glanced back at them and smiled. "I was waiting and I started talking to them and they came right over to the wall."

"Okay." Odd, maybe, but not completely crazy. "That still doesn't explain how you ended up on the other side of the wall on your arse."

"I took out my phone to take a picture, but then dropped it. I climbed over to get it and that one there," she pointed at one of the animals, who continued to watch them with mild curiosity, "bumped into me and I lost my balance."

In spite of herself Cam laughed. She would have expected Lauren to be dainty about that sort of thing, if not indignant. "And so you decided to stay and make friends?"

Lauren shrugged, like it was the most obvious thing in the world. "I was afraid for a second they might trample me, but they didn't."

Cam nodded. No, they wouldn't. "Sheep are pretty docile, especially if they don't feel threatened."

"So, that means they like me?" She had this hopeful look on her face that Cam found endearing.

"I think it does." She wondered vaguely if Charlotte intended this—not that she would rescue Lauren so much as she'd have a moment with her, break down some of the boundaries between them that Cam stubbornly clung to. Probably not, as she couldn't have predicted it would go this way, but still. The outcome remained the same. "You know, if I'm interfering with how you'd like to spend your day, I could just go."

Lauren's eyes got huge, like she'd forgotten herself for a moment. "No, no. Please get me unstuck. I'd be forever grateful."

"Forever, huh?" Once it was out of her mouth, Cam realized how casual, how familiar, the question came out. But it was too late to take it back.

Lauren offered her a slow smile that, just like during their meeting at the pub, seemed to hold more than a hint of flirtation. "Well, for a long time at least."

The smile, the comment, damn, the whole package, affected Cam more than she wanted it to. There was something about Lauren. Something that felt like more than garden variety attraction. She cleared her throat. "All right, then. Let's see what we can do."

Lauren sat on the wall, swung her legs around to the other side. Her expensive-looking shoes were caked with mud. She extended a hand and Cam took it instinctively, holding her steady as she crossed the narrow fosse. "It shouldn't be too bad. I didn't get myself all the way into the ditch."

Cam went to her truck and grabbed a length of rope. She looped it through the front bumper of the old car. "Get in and put it in neutral. Be ready to brake if you start rolling forward too quickly."

Lauren nodded. "Got it."

She sort of liked Lauren following her directions. She tied the other end of the rope to the hitch and climbed into her truck. Two minutes later, Lauren and her car were squarely back on the road. Cam undid the rope while Lauren beamed at her.

"I really can't thank you enough," Lauren said.

"Happy to help." Which wasn't untrue. She didn't have a hero complex or anything, but lending a hand to a friend or neighbor in need was what she did, what anyone in town would do. And whether she liked it or not, Lauren now qualified—as a neighbor, at least.

"I hope I didn't pull you away from anything important."

Cam chuckled. "Just my sales figures."

"Oh, I'll need to look at those as part of your marketing plan."

Cam had a mental image of sitting in her office with Lauren, shoulder to shoulder. It had a certain appeal. She should probably stop pretending it felt otherwise, at least with herself. "Sure."

Lauren pointed at her, but it read as friendly rather than accusatory. "Since you're here, we should go ahead and schedule a meeting."

They might as well get on with it. "Sounds good."

Lauren pulled her phone from her pocket. "I'm pretty open, as you might imagine. What about you?"

"I'm flexible. How's tomorrow afternoon?"

"Perfect. Do I get to come to the distillery?"

In spite of herself, Cam felt a surge of pride. "I'll give you the grand tour."

"I can't wait." Lauren clapped her hands together and seemed genuinely delighted by the prospect. It made Cam like her just a sliver more. She sighed. The slivers were starting to add up.

"Three o'clock work for you?"

"Yep." Lauren punched something into her phone.

"Come to the guest entrance and we'll start in the tasting room."

"Do I get to taste things?"

"I'd be disappointed if you didn't."

Lauren's eyes sparkled with mischief. "I'd never want to disappoint."

The semi-flirtation left Cam feeling awkward and tongue-tied. The need to escape moved to the forefront of her brain. "You're okay from here?"

Lauren smiled. "Well, I still need to turn around. Maybe you could stick around to make sure I don't land in the ditch."

Cam pointed up the road. "There's a driveway up the road just a bit."

"Seriously?"

Cam shrugged. "Follow me."

Lauren offered her a casual salute and got into her car. Cam drove up the road, turned around, then waited for Lauren to do the same. Lauren offered her a wave, then drove ahead. Something resembling reluctance settled into Cam's chest. She shook it off and headed back to work. Each encounter with Lauren left her less sure what to make of her, or the situation.

No, that wasn't entirely true. She was sure about a couple of things. One, she was looking forward to tomorrow very much. Two, looking forward to it and letting her guard down were likely going to get her into trouble.

CHAPTER NINE

Cam watched Lauren, telling herself for the tenth time she didn't care about Lauren's opinion. But of course that wasn't true, and arguing with herself about it offended her sensibilities even more than caring in the first place. The whole thing was pathetic.

She cleared her throat. "The three main stills are here. This is where we produce all of the Barrister's for market."

Lauren angled her head and narrowed her eyes. "How old are they?"

"Victoria is the oldest. Not an original, but she's been working since 1920." Cam pointed to the oldest still. She wasn't the largest, but she remained Cam's favorite.

"Wow."

"Elizabeth came online in 1957, after the war. And my father put in Mary, the big one here, the year I was born."

"Are all your stills named after queens?" Lauren folded her arms. That stance, combined with her jeans, hiking boots, and flannel shirt, made her look casual and approachable. It almost allowed Cam to forget her first impressions. Almost.

"I'll point out I had nothing to do with that. If you'll follow me." Cam led the way to her blending room, home to the two small stills and all her books and bottles and jars.

When Lauren entered the room, her eyes got big and she turned a slow circle. "Is this your laboratory?"

Cam smiled, allowing herself to be pleased by Lauren's reaction. "It is."

Lauren's arms crossed again, but this time her eyes held a playful glint. She pointed at one still, then the other. "And what are their names?"

Cam tucked her tongue in her cheek, feeling silly for a moment about naming stills in the first place. "Edith and Henry, after my great-great-grandparents who founded the company."

"I wouldn't have pegged you for the sentimental type." Lauren's posture didn't change, but her eyes softened. It was disarming and had the potential to do some serious damage.

Cam lifted a shoulder. "Only about gin."

Lauren laughed, the sound far sexier than it had any right to be. "I can tell you mean it."

"To tell the truth, I'm not sentimental about gin at all. Gin is science and logic with occasional flashes of brilliance. I'm sentimental about family."

"That's really sweet." Despite the enthusiasm of her words, Lauren looked away. It was subtle, but the shift was there. A cooling in her demeanor.

"Family is everything in this company. We've stuck together and kept it going for five generations and through two World Wars."

Lauren nodded. "That's remarkable, truly. Now, tell me what you do in here. I want to know everything."

Maybe the abrupt change of subject didn't mean anything, maybe it did. Either way, it was none of her business. Even if the shadow that passed through Lauren's eyes made Cam want to sweep her up and kiss away whatever had put it there. "I used these smaller stills to make individual distillates that I can blend and play with. It's far more efficient than making a whole batch of every combination I want to try."

"That's brilliant. Will you walk me through your process? I've learned about wine and beer, but I know nothing about distilling."

It was Cam's turn to narrow her eyes. "How much detail do you want?"

Lauren laughed again, driving any lingering sadness or coolness from the room. "Everything. I can seriously nerd out on this stuff all day."

"Okay, but I have a feeling I can max out even the nerdiest person when it comes to making gin. Don't say I didn't warn you."

"I accept full responsibility for the ensuing lecture. Lay it on me."

If befriending sheep had softened her distrust of Lauren, the enthusiasm for gin might be enough to make Cam like her in earnest. "Barrister's is a London dry gin, which means it can only contain natural ingredients and has to include juniper. It also means the gin we sell has to be distilled all together. No mixing or steeping things after the fact."

Lauren nodded, giving every impression of genuine interest. "Does it have to be made within so many miles of London? Like Bordeaux or champagne?"

"No. Anyone anywhere can slap that label on if they follow the rules."

"That's too bad." Lauren tipped her head to the side. "You said Barrister's is London dry, but not Carriage House. Is it different?"

"Technically, Carriage House is a distilled gin because it has other botanicals blended in after distilling." She gestured to the shelves. "Things like this."

"How do you know what things will go together?"

"A little bit is instinct. A lot is experience, trial and error."

Lauren nodded. "There have to be a billion combinations."

"There probably are. But there are categories of things. That narrows it down a bit."

"What do you mean?"

Genuine interest notwithstanding, Cam tried to give the short version of the answer. "Botanicals, spices, citrus. You pull one or two from each category to get good balance. If you go too crazy on one, it tends to go sideways."

"Oh, that makes sense."

"We can sample them, if you want, then blend up a batch for you."

"Really?" Lauren's eyes got big and she seemed utterly delighted. It made Cam want to show off. And maybe, just a little, spend more time with her.

"Absolutely." She gestured to a stool at her worktable. "Have a seat."

Lauren perched herself, propped her elbows on the table, and leaned forward. "Should I be taking notes?"

Cam chuckled. There was a chance Lauren was humoring her, but she pushed the notion aside. "There won't be a test, I promise."

She poured a few mils of her base gin into a pair of small stemmed glasses and slid one in front of Lauren. Lauren raised a brow. "Are you going to tell me what I'm sampling?"

"Of course." Although the idea of blindfolding her and being able to watch as the flavors and aromas played across her palate had a certain appeal. "This is technically gin. It's distilled with juniper and coriander, along with a couple of things to enhance and fix the flavor compounds. It's the base I add all the other flavors to."

Lauren took a sip, made a face.

"It tastes like cheap gin, right?" Cam asked.

She smirked. "That's what I was thinking, but I didn't want to insult you."

Cam laughed. She couldn't decide if she admired the honesty more, or the restraint. "I appreciate the concern, but if I were putting this on the market I'd be in trouble. This has zero personality."

"So, we're going to give it personality?"

"We are. First up, the botanicals." She walked Lauren through the teas and roots she'd distilled individually. They smelled and sampled. Lauren's enthusiasm exceeded Cam's expectations. Her eyes lit up, she exclaimed over how distinct everything was, and she cringed and flailed her arms over the taste of wormwood.

"Sorry," Lauren said.

"Don't be. I should have warned you it's a bit funky." Cam got them each a glass of water. "How about we do citrus next? Much more predictable."

"Yeah, lemon and lime are more my speed."

Cam led with those, then bitter orange, grapefruit, and lemongrass. She made a mental note that Lauren seemed especially fond of the pink grapefruit. Spices came next—cassia, nutmeg, and pink and black peppercorns. "And now for the bonus round."

THE INN AT NETHERFIELD GREEN

Lauren quirked a brow. "Bonus round?"

"Things less typically associated with gin, but that I think add a little something extra."

Her eyes lit up. "Like what?"

"Let's see if you can guess." She poured a taste of rosebud.

Lauren sipped, smacked her lips together a few times. "It's floral. Roses? Rosewater?"

Cam nodded. "Well done."

Lauren successfully guessed fennel seed and chamomile, but was stumped by the final one. "It's familiar. That's what's driving me crazy. I know I know that flavor."

Cam expected her to get petulant, or perhaps grow bored of the whole thing. But she insisted on another taste. "Try closing your eyes."

Lauren obeyed without a second of hesitation. It was sweet and trusting and, God help her, a total turn-on. She took the glass Cam handed her and took a sip. "It's grassy, but not grass." She sighed. "I give up."

Cam smiled, unable, really, not to. "It's asparagus."

Lauren slapped her palm against the table. "That's it. I knew I knew it. But to have it like that. So weird."

"It's a bit out there, even in my quirky world."

"It's good. Funky, but good."

The fact that Lauren appreciated distilled asparagus did something to Cam. She couldn't put her finger on exactly what, but it managed to be both reassuring and disquieting. "When you blend it, you don't really pick up that it's asparagus, but it brings a certain smoothness. It's hard to describe."

"Do you use it in Carriage House?"

Cam folded her arms. "That's proprietary information, Ms. Montgomery."

Lauren mimicked the gesture. "Oh, well, we can't have you spilling proprietary information."

Part of Cam couldn't believe they were bantering like this, but at the same time, it felt completely natural. She might not be ready to admit to liking the woman, at least not out loud, but it clicked now why everyone else seemed so keen on her. "I'll make you a deal."

Lauren kept her arms crossed, but angled herself and gave Cam a side-eye. "Go on."

"I promised to mix you up a small batch of your choice. I'll also make you one with asparagus."

Lauren grinned. "Two bottles of gin? Sold."

"Okay, tell me what you want. You should pick three to five total, and at least one from each category. Bonus category is optional."

She tapped her fingers together. "And you're going to make me something with asparagus?"

"I will."

"Excellent. I want," she paused and squinted at the bottles and jars on the shelf, "chamomile, grapefruit, lemon, and pink peppercorn."

Cam grabbed a pencil and scribbled her preferences. "That sounds good."

"Yeah?" Lauren watched Cam stare at the list of ingredients. She'd picked her favorites, but had no idea if they'd go together. Cam furrowed her brow, and Lauren imagined her trying to find a nice way to say it would be terrible. But then she jotted down a series of numbers and offered her a smile.

"It's going to be delicious. Bright and citrusy. It'll make great gin and tonics."

She had to believe Cam wouldn't make a bottle of something she knew wouldn't taste good. "Okay, good. I'm going to trust you."

"You should. I'm very trustworthy." Cam winked at her and Lauren tried to ignore the flutter of delight in her chest and, well, lower than her chest.

Cam grabbed a bottle and set a funnel in it. She had this tall, thin beaker that she filled with the different flavor components—all different amounts. "How do you know how much of each to use?"

"Practice."

Once she'd added all the components to the bottle, she topped it off with the base she'd described when they started. Then, without any notes, she did a second bottle, using different elements. When both were done, Cam capped them and gave them a gentle shake.

Then she poured a sample for each of them. Lauren tasted hers first. Not that she expected it to be terrible, but it was better than she expected. Cam's descriptors were spot-on. She sipped Cam's next. It was good, really good. But what got her was how different they were. "Wow. I love mine, but there's something about this one. It's so," she searched for the right word.

"Savory?"

"Yes." That was exactly it. "I bet this would be amazing in a dirty martini."

"You're getting the hang of this."

Cam smiled and, if she didn't know better, Lauren would swear she was flirting with her. Hell, maybe she didn't know better. Things with Cam felt more confusing by the day. Maybe confusing wasn't the right word. Incongruous. One second Cam seemed to barely tolerate her, and the next she was convinced Cam was on the verge of kissing her. Since her feelings sat pretty squarely in the kiss-me-please category, her confusion had mostly to do with Cam's feelings. Compared to how they started, she could hope—argue, even—this was progress.

"What?" Cam regarded her with a look of suspicion.

"Nothing. Just thinking about dirty martinis."

"Shall we make a few cocktails?"

Lauren wasn't sure if it was the twenty or so sips of pure alcohol or the fact that Cam finally seemed relaxed around her. Whatever it was, she liked it. And she didn't want the afternoon to end. "Absolutely."

Cam led them back through the main distilling area to the tasting room in front. She gestured to a small card on the bar. "These are the specialties of the house, but I'd be happy to make you something else if you have a request."

Lauren perused the menu, expecting a staid list of classics. Instead, the list of six cocktails featured a surprising array of spices, herbs, fruits, and flowers. There wasn't one in the bunch she wouldn't try. "Did you create all these?"

"You sound surprised." Cam smiled and there was a hint of smugness in it. Not arrogance, really, just a flash of I told you so.

The kind that passed between friends, or people who were more than friends.

"Not surprised, just..." she searched for the right word. It didn't help that her brain wasn't working right.

"Surprised."

Cam was teasing her. How delightful was that? Totally made up for being caught without a good comeback. "Okay, maybe a little."

"Admit it. You think I'm some uninspired, provincial stick-in-the-mud."

Lauren frowned. "I don't think that at all."

"No? You blow in from New York City, all fancy shoes and big plans to change everything. And I'm the one who wants things to stay the same."

Cam's eyes flashed, but it was impossible to tell whether the spark came from annoyance or desire. Could it possibly be desire? Lauren couldn't help but imagine that fire directed at her in a completely different setting. One that involved Cam in her bed, on top of her, inside her. Her imagination was getting the better of her. Cam was just starting to tolerate her.

Lauren let out a sigh. "You really don't like me, do you?"

"Don't look at me like I just ran over your puppy. I don't dislike you. We don't see eye to eye on things. You know that."

Lauren swallowed, shook her head. She needed to get Cam out of her head, out of her system. Unfortunately, she knew of only one surefire way of doing that. And if Cam knew what she had in mind, she'd probably blow a gasket. "I was hoping we'd moved past that. I enlisted your help because I want to do this right, and because I think we both stand to benefit."

Cam seemed to relent then, or soften maybe. "You're right."

"Right about what? I want to make sure I understand what you're conceding." She added a wink so Cam would know, hopefully, she was being playful.

"Working together is in both our interests."

Lauren sighed. "And I don't think you're provincial. Or a stick-in-the-mud."

Cam raised a brow. Like Lauren's wink, it felt playful. She hoped. The tiff, or whatever it was, seemed over. "Sure."

"I'll take it." She returned her gaze to the menu, wanting to get them back into Cam's comfort zone. "Now, I want you to make me all of these, but I'd end up under the bar if you did, so surprise me."

"It would be my pleasure."

And just like that, the tension dissolved and Cam's confident smile was back. Had she imagined it? Or had she gotten so far ahead of herself that anything short of making out with Cam was a disappointment? She'd probably never know. Better to focus on the now, on the future, anyway.

Cam pulled out a pair of cocktail shakers. After filling both with ice, she started adding different things to them. Sometimes by the jigger, sometimes just a drop or two. She did it all from memory. Watching her work was impressive. It also happened to be sexy as fuck. Her hands were deft, and the look of concentration on her face suited her. Lauren knew without a doubt she would bring that confidence, that concentration, to the bedroom. What were the chances they'd end up there before it was all said and done?

Just the idea of it turned her on. When was the last time that happened? Too long. Way too long. She cleared her throat in an attempt to clear her mind. "What are you making me?"

Cam grinned. It might have been the first truly genuine smile she gave Lauren, and damn, did it pack a punch. "I'm starting us with the elderflower-infused Tom Collins and the charred citrus and rosemary gimlet. They're two of my favorites and both on the lighter side. I figured if we shared, I might talk you into trying a couple more."

"You might have to roll me back to the inn, but I'm finding it hard to tell you no."

Cam glanced up from her work. Lauren held her gaze, willing something to spark, to catch hold. "I'll go easy on you," she said after a moment.

It lasted only a second, but Lauren was pretty sure she hadn't imagined it. Not wanting to press her luck, she offered a shrug. "I'm game for whatever you're serving up."

The Tom Collins came first. In Lauren's prior experience, the drink was basically overly sweet lemonade laced with gin. Cam's drink tasted nothing like that. The lemon was fresh, tangy enough to make her cheeks pucker, but softened by the elderflower. The gin was there, but it complemented the other flavors instead of leaving a boozy aftertaste. It was the kind of cocktail that would be good with brunch, or on a warm afternoon spent lounging in the sun. "Wow."

"Thanks. Keep sipping that and I'll finish the second round." Cam smiled again, the same genuine smile as before.

Why hadn't she thought of this angle sooner?

They sampled something with cucumber and basil, a gin and tonic with her gin and twist of grapefruit peel, and finished with the dirty martini. By the end, Lauren's crush on Cam had taken on a life of its own and she was on the drunk side of tipsy. She lifted both hands. "Unless you want to carry me home, I think I need to stop."

A look passed through Cam's eyes. A look that said Cam would be perfectly happy to carry her home and right up to bed. Even in her fuzzy state of mind, Lauren knew, this time, she wasn't imagining it. Unfortunately, it passed, leaving something more innocuous behind. "How about we get you some food?"

"I know just the place. Will you join me? My treat to thank you for teaching me so much." Did she sound too eager? Hopefully not.

"I wish I could, but I already have plans."

"Oh."

"I'd love a rain check."

Cam seemed sincere, so Lauren swallowed her disappointment. "Deal."

"I will walk you home, though."

Lauren waved a hand. "You really don't need to. I'm not that far gone. Yet."

"I insist. Let me be chivalrous."

She'd never been one for the chivalrous type, but she'd never been one for the small-town, old-fashioned, reticent type either. "All right. Can I help you clean up first?"

"Not at all."

Cam came around from behind the bar and held out her arm. Lauren slid off the stool, trying to look steadier on her feet than she felt, and slipped her hand around Cam's bicep. It wasn't super muscular, but solid and strong. Lauren tried not to think about Cam shirtless, or what it would be like to be scooped up in her arms, cheesy movie heroine style.

They walked back to the Rose & Crown in a semi-comfortable silence. When they got there, Lauren reluctantly let go of Cam's arm. "Thank you for today. I had a lot of fun. And I learned so much."

"You were a very eager student."

Lauren wanted to make a comment about being an eager student of an entirely different sort, but she resisted. Cam didn't strike her as the kind of woman who wanted to be chased. "So, next time we'll talk about my menu and your marketing?"

Cam nodded. "That would be terrific."

"Great."

It was kind of embarrassing how badly she wanted Cam to kiss her. She told herself it was the gin talking even though she knew it wasn't true. "You know where to find me."

"And you're sure you're all right?"

"Never better. Thanks for walking me home."

Cam nodded again. "Make sure you eat something."

"I will." Was she imagining it or was Cam lingering? Stalling, even?

"Right. Well, have a good night."

Definitely lingering. How delightful. "Good night."

Cam nodded a third time, then left without making eye contact or uttering another word. Lauren watched her go, enjoying the way her pants fit and her purposeful stride. She indulged in a sigh, then headed in to see what Mrs. Lucas had cooked up for dinner.

CHAPTER TEN

Cam left Lauren, annoyed by just how churned up she felt. They'd had a perfectly nice day, one where she hardly thought about how much she wanted to kiss the curve of Lauren's neck. Or sit Lauren on her worktable and let her hands creep up Lauren's shirt. They'd arrived at something resembling mutual respect, and then she had offered to walk Lauren home. And Lauren had given her those bedroom eyes, and it was all she could do not to drool all over her.

It was demoralizing. It was pathetic. It was a total turn-on. And perhaps worst of all, it was proving more irresistible by the day.

She went back to work to clean up from their tasting, but found Dev had beaten her to it. She tracked him down to say thank you, then retreated to her blending room. Once there, however, she could swear Lauren's perfume lingered in the air. Whether real or imagined, it sent her imagination into overdrive and sent her seeking the dull safety of her office.

She went back to the sales figures she and Sophie had gone over a couple of weeks prior. They weren't bad, but they really could be better. Truth be told, she wasn't opposed to some concentrated marketing efforts. She simply didn't know what that should look like. If Lauren's ideas were halfway decent, maybe all this would be worth it in the end.

She made some sales projections based on their current trajectory, then sketched out some more aspirational goals. Sophie's comment about being in more pubs came back to her, and she made a note that she wanted to focus there first. Because even though she was no expert, she knew that having a customer request her product in their favorite shop was the best—not to mention free—publicity she could get.

Six o'clock finally rolled around and she shut off her computer. She made the rounds of the building, checking on things that didn't require checking. The ritual soothed her, though, and helped her brain transition out of the workday. She bid the remaining staff good night and walked home, not bothering to stop in at her place before heading to her parents' house.

Sophie and Jane were already there when she arrived and the table was set. She washed her hands before giving her mum a kiss on the cheek. "Anything I can do to help?"

"Not a thing. We're just about ready."

Everyone settled into their usual spots at the table and started passing dishes. Cam hadn't sampled nearly as much as Lauren, but she was looking forward to a hearty meal. She added a second slice of roast beef to her plate before handing the platter to Sophie.

"How was your afternoon with Miss Montgomery?" Sophie's tone was innocent, but her face was anything but.

Cam glanced over at Jane, who regarded her with a raised brow, then her parents. Fortunately, they didn't seem to pick up on the subtext. "It was very productive."

Jane tipped her head. "Wait. I thought she was trying to convince you to help her. Does that mean she succeeded or that you resisted?"

Sophie smirked. "Cam already agreed to help her. Today was about showing off."

"I wasn't showing off." Cam scowled. She was but wasn't going to own it, especially to Sophie. "If anything, I was showing off our products."

"You two looked awfully chummy in the tasting room," Sophie said.

Sometimes it was so damned inconvenient to have her sister working at the same company. "I made her a couple of cocktails. I'm not sure how you got chummy from that."

Sophie pointed at her, then made tiny circles with her finger. "You were smiling."

"Our gin makes me smile. Getting someone new to appreciate it makes me smile. Besides, she agreed to help with marketing."

Sophie leaned forward and propped her chin on her hand. "Do tell."

Cam looked around the table. Her father was spooning potatoes onto his plate, but all other eyes—Sophie, Jane, Kitty, her mother—were trained on her. "She's a marketer. As in, does marketing and advertising for a living. She's going to come up with a marketing plan for Carriage House. I might use it, I might not."

"A barter." Jane smiled. "That's a wonderful idea."

She could always count on Jane to stay positive and assume the best of a situation. "Thank you."

"So, it's a business arrangement and nothing more. That's what you're saying?" Sophie did not look convinced.

"It's all Charlotte's doing, if you must know. She cooked up the idea and roped us both into it. Right, Jane?"

Jane nodded. "Something like that. It makes perfect sense, though. Lauren needs help and so do you."

"What exactly are you planning to do for her?" Sophie made the question sound suggestive, if not downright lascivious.

Cam glared. It was one thing for Sophie to tease her about chasing women, it was another entirely for her to do it in front of their parents. "I'm going to create a cocktail menu for her, offer input on whatever she has in mind for the inn."

"And you're qualified to do this how?" Sophie looked at her like she'd said she was helping Lauren build a rocket.

"I assume you mean the inn part and not my knowledge of mixology."

"Obviously."

"I don't know, but she seems to think I know what will lure tourists. I'm not about to disabuse her of that notion if it means I get a say in how much gets changed."

"You did design the whole tasting room," Jane said.

"And we get so many more visitors than we used to," Mum added.

"Thank you. It's nice to know some of my family thinks I have something to contribute."

Sophie finished chewing a bite and pointed at Cam with her fork. "I'm not denying you've got things to contribute, I'm only trying to sort out whether some of those things are in the bedroom."

"Sophie." Jane's voice was scolding.

"What?" Sophie gave Jane a withering look. "You're honestly going to tell me it didn't cross your mind?"

Jane, bless her, looked truly scandalized. "No. It did not."

Cam dared a glance at her mother, then her father. Both appeared mildly curious. "Could we change the subject, please?"

"Who's going to do the work at the inn?" Mum asked.

"I don't know. I don't even know what she has in mind." She knew where this was going and she didn't like it.

"You should suggest your father," Mum said.

Cam closed her eyes. She should have known this was coming. Her father had taken up handiwork after retiring, and since there were no contractors based in town, he'd taken to doing odd jobs for people. He was quite good, actually, but the idea of entwining her life with Lauren's even more than it already was sent a ripple of discomfort through her.

"That's a great idea." Sophie offered a smile laced with mischief.

"Like I said, I don't know what she has in mind."

Her father waved his hand. "You know what I can do. Don't get me roped into anything above my weight class and I'm happy to help."

"Thanks, Dad." She sighed. She might grouse from time to time, but she had a great family. Even Sophie, with all her instigating. She could count on them for anything, including unwavering support.

That support included the launch of Carriage House. As much as she wanted it to do well for herself, she wanted to make her family proud. And give the company a financial boost. Whether she liked it or not, working with Lauren gave her a good shot of doing exactly that. She wasn't going to waste it.

❖

After spending the day with Cam at the distillery, Lauren set aside an afternoon to start working on the marketing campaign she promised to deliver, starting with some heavy-duty research. She made herself a pot of coffee, booted up her laptop, and got to it. Recent marketing campaigns, industry statistics, any sales figures that were public—she went for it all. She scribbled notes, copied and pasted things into spreadsheets. She absorbed information until her head swam with it.

She sat back in her chair and tipped her head from side to side, trying to work out some of the tension that had settled at the base of her neck and between her shoulders. She glanced at the clock. More than three hours hunched over the computer. She shook her head. Some habits, it seemed, stayed with a person.

Still, it had been a productive three hours. She knew more about the premium spirit industry than she probably cared to, but couldn't bring herself to be bothered. In truth, she liked the research, almost as much for learning something new as for getting a business edge. It had served her well with clients, even if her colleagues thought it overkill. It showed she cared, was invested. A clever idea might win a client, but that investment was what earned their trust.

Cam was no different. Maybe she wanted to impress her, but it was mostly about doing a good job. And since gin was not in her wheelhouse, she needed to study up. Fortunately, she'd learned high-end alcohol was a distant cousin to the hospitality industry. Customers tied brand to lifestyle and, by extension, identity. That set the stage for building brand loyalty, and that was one hundred percent in her wheelhouse.

Her biggest challenge, aside from Cam's skepticism, might be the brand itself. Or, perhaps more accurately, the lack thereof. She'd tried to free-associate ten words with it and had only come up with three. And they weren't even a good three. She might be wrong, but she had a feeling Cam wouldn't do much better.

A challenge, but not an insurmountable one. Some days, she preferred starting with a blank slate. It meant less mess to undo and overcome. All she'd need to overcome was Cam.

Lauren sat up straight, a second wave of energy zipping through her. She regretted not installing a white board first thing, or ordering any oversize sketch pads. Undeterred, she grabbed a notebook and a set of colored pencils. She closed her eyes for a count of ten. When the time was up, she went to work, jotting words and doodles as fast as her hand would go.

Her ideas wound themselves into concepts, and she settled on four distinct themes—not entirely different, but each unique. She ripped the pages from the notebook and started fresh, refining each one into a draft she could show Cam. She nodded as she worked. She already had a favorite, but really, any of them could work.

She missed this. Work in general, but especially the burst of creative energy in the beginning, when possibilities stretched out in front of her like an endless horizon. The only thing better was presenting the finished product, watching the client's face and knowing she'd completely nailed it. She imagined that moment with Cam—satisfaction and excitement mixed with just a hint of awe. God, did she want to see that look on Cam's face. If she and Cam never made it into bed, that would be the next best thing.

The knock on the door jolted her back to the present. "Come in."

Mrs. Lucas popped her head in. "Are you all right, dear?"

Lauren dropped the pencil, distracted enough to notice how badly her hand had begun to cramp. "I'm fine. Why wouldn't I be?"

"It's eight, dear. You always come in for dinner by seven or so."

She looked at the clock, more instinct than not believing the assertion. "Wow. I completely lost track of time."

Mrs. Lucas shook her head. "You work so hard. I don't know if it's your age or your big city ways."

Lauren chuckled. In New York, calling it quits by eight was a good day. On more than one occasion, she'd spent the night in her office, taking a shower in the company gym and sending her assistant to her apartment for a fresh change of clothes. She might miss the work, but she didn't miss the hours. Should that worry her?

"Are you sure you're all right?"

"Yes, yes. Thank you for checking on me. I'm coming now." She didn't have the heart to tell Mrs. Lucas she'd probably put in another two or three hours after dinner.

"I did beef for the Sunday roast and there's a bit left. Shall I do you a plate of that?"

"That sounds lovely." It did, but she'd eaten more meat in the last three weeks than the three months prior. She mentally bumped menu overhaul to the top of her personal to-do list.

Mrs. Lucas turned, not waiting to see if Lauren agreed or followed her. "You go relax. I'll bring it out to you."

Lauren's heart softened at the maternal tone. She couldn't remember the last time she'd been clucked over like that. Mrs. Lucas bustled into the kitchen, and Lauren headed for the dining room. The pub had all of seven people in it, counting Charlotte. She didn't even bother suppressing a sigh. Tilly loped over to say hello. She'd proved herself to be affectionate but not overeager—exactly the type of dog Lauren would choose were she inclined to get one.

She caught Charlotte's eye. "What are you still doing here?"

"Jack was feeling a bit under the weather, so I offered to cover for him."

The explanation, delivered casually like it was the most obvious answer in the world, made her smile. She'd been here a few weeks, but the easygoing, almost familial way, everyone seemed to go about things still caught her off guard. It was so far removed from her own experiences—at work or with her family. "That's nice of you."

Charlotte shrugged off the compliment. "I haven't seen you all day. What have you been up to?"

"Learning about gin."

Her brow lifted. "A day at Barrister's?"

Lauren's mind went to her afternoon at the distillery. And to Cam. "I wish. No, I was doing research. Much less fun."

Charlotte folded her arms and leaned forward on the bar. "What kind of research?"

She wouldn't show her ideas to Charlotte. First look was something always reserved for the client. But that didn't mean she couldn't pick her brain a bit. "What do you think about Carriage House?"

Charlotte gave her a curious look. "What do you mean? Like the taste? It's hands-down my favorite gin."

Lauren smiled. "Can't disagree with you there. I'm thinking more about its image, the brand."

Charlotte pointed at her. "Ah. You're working on the marketing thing."

"I am. But I can't build a marketing plan unless I know what I'm marketing."

"And really fucking good gin isn't enough to go on?"

Lauren laughed. "No, it's not. Because, technically, Barrister's is really fucking good gin, too."

"A close second in my book, but I know what you mean."

"Right. Okay. So, when you think of Barrister's, what do you think? Not the taste, but the brand, what it stands for."

"Oh, I see." Charlotte nodded. "Um, classic. Traditional, but not in a bad way. Classy but not pretentious."

"Exactly. That's the brand. And, for Barrister's, it works perfectly." Lauren tapped on the bar with her finger. "But what about Carriage House?"

"More modern. What's the word Americans use? Hip."

Lauren nodded. "Do you get that from the brand or just by comparing it to Barrister's?"

Charlotte frowned. "Just by comparison, I guess."

"Don't feel bad. That's important for me to know. The whole point is giving Carriage House an identity of its own." Again she thought of a blank canvas.

"What did Cam say when you asked her?"

Lauren lifted a shoulder. "I haven't asked her yet."

"But you're going to?"

She thought about so many clients she'd worked with in the past—well-intentioned but way too close to the products they'd created. She really hoped Cam wasn't like that. "Yes. In the end, she's the one making the decisions. But I want to give her something to respond to. I want that something to come from more than my own impressions."

Charlotte nodded slowly. "You're really good at this, aren't you?"

Lauren angled her head. "Marketing?"

"Yeah. I mean, I understand it's your career and all, but you don't just do it. You kill it. I can tell."

Something about the compliment made Lauren feel sentimental. Like she'd lost track of how much she loved her work in the train wreck of the last few weeks. She had this urge to give Charlotte a hug, but thought better of it. "I have my moments."

"I'm glad you're here. The pub needs someone like you. And even if she's not quick to admit it, Cam does, too."

Lauren let Charlotte's words sink it. She'd been so focused on what she needed—to pull herself together, get a win, get back on her feet—she'd not really given a lot of thought to being what anyone else might need. A little knot in her chest loosened, and she smiled. "Thanks."

CHAPTER ELEVEN

After being cooped up in her office, the prospect of a day out brought even more excitement than usual to Lauren's morning. Even better was the goal of scouting new things for the inn. Charlotte offered to be her guide, and she readily accepted. Not only was shopping more fun with a friend, she really wanted to get to know Charlotte better. And doing so outside of their working relationship seemed like the perfect way to do it.

Lauren made a wish list of things she wanted and tried to keep her expectations low. She liked to think she had a good eye for design. She'd decorated her apartment on her own and considered the result stylish and modern, clean but not impersonal. Designing twelve rooms, though, felt more than a little daunting. On a shoestring budget. And a tight timeline. And with little more than the internet at her disposal.

She'd just have to tackle it like any new project—commit to a concept and then break each component down to its essential function. That's how she landed accounts, how she won over clients, and the way she accomplished pretty much everything in life. And it had always worked. Well, almost always.

She finished getting dressed and pulled her hair into a ponytail. She squared her shoulders and checked her reflection in the bathroom mirror. Out of nowhere, Cam's face came into her mind. Okay, maybe not out of nowhere. She'd been thinking about Cam a lot. They'd spent, not a ton of time together, but some. And each time they did, she found herself liking Cam more and more.

Given the strength of her attraction to Cam, liking her on top of it felt like the slippery slope to a full-blown crush. Not that there was anything wrong with a crush in principle. The problem was that Cam seemed so far on the other side of things. Still, spending time at the distillery had helped on that front. Maybe it was feeling in her element, having something she loved to focus on. She'd let her guard down for sure. It had been nice. It had been sexy, too.

Lauren sighed. No time for daydreaming. She had rooms to decorate and a deadline on the horizon.

She headed downstairs and let Tilly out. They'd established quite the routine, and Lauren found it soothing, charming even. Once Tilly was fed and set for the day, Lauren let herself out the back door. As if on cue, Charlotte turned the corner. Her hatchback was bright blue and had to be at least ten years newer than the car she'd inherited from Albert. Bigger, too. It wouldn't hold furniture, but they'd be able to fit lots of odds and ends into it. And the best part—Charlotte would be driving. After her misadventures on the way to the sheep farm, she'd been hesitant to venture out behind the wheel.

"Morning, lovely," Charlotte said when Lauren climbed into the passenger seat.

"Good morning. I'm so excited for today. Thank you again for coming with me."

Charlotte shrugged. "I enjoy a nice poke around a shop."

"A woman after my own heart. Which is why I'm doubly glad we're going together. You can show me all the good spots."

"Don't get too excited. There aren't that many spots to be had, at least not close by."

"I'll take what I can get. And anything I can find locally should make Cam happy. I'll need that to balance everything I buy online."

Charlotte turned at the corner, taking them in a direction Lauren had yet to explore, and laughed. "You seem to have her figured out pretty quick."

"On some fronts, at least." Too bad she'd yet to figure out the one at the forefront of her mind—why she was so damned attracted to a woman who seemed to barely tolerate her.

"She's a total cream puff underneath, but her exterior can be a bit tough."

Lauren thought back to the first real conversation she had with Charlotte, the one where Charlotte owned her and Cam had been in a relationship. What was the phrase she'd used? Ages ago. "Does that come from personal experience?"

Charlotte gave her a bit of a sideways glance. "How much do you want to know?"

Well, the answer could nip her crush in the bud or it could fan the flames. Either way, she preferred working with more information rather than less. "As much as you're interested in sharing."

"Right, then. Well, we were an item for a little while. We were much younger. Early twenties."

"How did it end?" The question was out of Lauren's mouth before she had a chance to filter herself. Charlotte didn't seem bothered, fortunately.

"Cam is pretty traditional. I am not, at least when it comes to relationships."

Lauren smiled. "No desire to be tied down?"

"Oh, I love being tied down, or up." Charlotte glanced her way long enough to offer a wink. "I also think it makes no sense to say you're only going to have sex with one person for the rest of your life."

"Oh." Anja was poly, a fact that Lauren found infinitely fascinating. Even if it wasn't for her, she could see the appeal.

"Too much?"

Lauren smiled. "Not at all. I was just thinking of my best friend, who has a similar approach to things."

"That's a relief. I'm not closeted about it, but there are still plenty of people who think I'm a slut." Charlotte crinkled her nose. "Presuming, of course, that being a slut is a bad thing."

Lauren laughed then. She knew she'd liked Charlotte, but something about this exchange took things to a whole different level. Like they were sharing intimacies. "I am not one of those people."

Charlotte lifted her shoulders and let them fall. It seemed to Lauren like a gesture of relaxation, which made her glad. "Do you think you and Cam will—?"

She cut herself off, as though realizing she shouldn't ask, or maybe more accurately, didn't want to know the answer. Lauren chuckled. "I'm pretty sure Cam hates me."

"Stop. She does not." Charlotte's words were emphatic, but her body language said something different.

"You don't need to sugarcoat it. She's been quite clear." Lauren flashed back to the day at the distillery. "I'm winning her over, though."

Charlotte glanced at her sideways. "I might be overstepping, but I think part of the reason she's resistant is because she finds you attractive."

It would be fun to take that at face value, assume all she had to do was wear down Cam's initial defenses and then they could—what? Sleep together? Date? That was the problem. She wasn't sure. All she knew was that she couldn't seem to get Cam out of her head, a fact that proved especially difficult at night, when she was tucked in all alone thinking about how long it had been since she'd shared her bed with a woman.

"Was that too far? I'm sorry."

Lauren snapped out of her thoughts to find Charlotte regarding her with concern. She shook her head. "Not at all. I was just trying to decide if you were right and, if so, what I wanted to do about it."

At that, Charlotte offered her a smile that was full of mischief and reminded her so much of Anja it gave her a pang of missing her. Maybe she could get Anja to visit sooner. She'd angle for that. In the meantime, she had a delightful new friend and shopping to do.

It didn't surprise Cam that Lauren had already worked up some ideas for a marketing campaign. From what she'd seen so far, Lauren went about everything like a tornado—unbridled energy that seemed to sweep up everything in its path. But she'd not expected a formal business meeting, set up via email and with all the professional courtesies. Nor had she expected Lauren to walk in like she was taking a meeting on Fifth Avenue.

But that's exactly what she got. Cam got to the pub a little early to see Charlotte and Lauren stride in from her office with an oversize portfolio. Not that she had a lot of experience with such things, but all Cam could think was that she looked like a power femme on a mission. She'd been so obvious in staring that Charlotte had to elbow her in the ribs. There'd be teasing about that later for sure. Lauren even shook her hand and thanked her for coming in before gesturing to a table near the window.

Once they'd settled in, Lauren folded her hands and rested them on the table. So confident, so calm. Cam wiped her own hands on her trousers and tried not to fidget.

Lauren didn't waste time on small talk. "I've worked up a few ideas, but I'd like to start with your thoughts."

She thought about how amazing Lauren looked in that tight skirt and fitted blouse, all business. She thought about how badly she wanted to kiss Lauren, to pull the pins from her hair and watch it tumble around her shoulders. But she was pretty sure that's not what Lauren had in mind. "About Carriage House?"

"Yes. When we talked initially, you said you thought of it as the younger, more modern sibling of Barrister's."

She thought back to that initial conversation. She'd found Lauren beautiful then, too, and had given more than a passing thought to kissing her. "Right. I want it to appeal to everyone, obviously, but the target is a younger demographic. People not already drinking Barrister's."

Lauren pointed at her. "Exactly. New customer base. And given the cocktail renaissance sweeping the twenty-something crowd, the timing couldn't be better."

Cam winced. "You aren't going to suggest Jet Skis, are you? Or sports cars? I'm not sure I could handle that."

Lauren huffed and gave her a stern look. It was far sexier than it had any right to be. "Do you really think so little of me?"

"No, she thinks that little of anyone under the age of thirty," Charlotte said from her place behind the bar.

Lauren raised a brow, seemingly amused.

"Okay, that part might be true." She might be only a few years removed from her twenties, but she'd felt like a serious adult for as long as she could remember, and she didn't have a lot of patience for the reckless or the rowdy.

Lauren sat up straighter and squared her shoulders. "The goal is to sell, not become a sellout. We're not going to do anything you can't feel good about."

Cam sighed. It was one thing for Lauren to be beautiful. But every time she turned around, Lauren had to go and surprise her with some other appealing trait—being nice, having integrity, caring about her opinion. It was making her damn near irresistible. "I appreciate that."

"Now, tell me how you think of Carriage House. Four words."

"Four?"

Again with the stern look. "Four."

"Fresh. Bright. Modern." Cam paused, suddenly self-conscious. Was this even what Lauren meant? Or was she completely off the mark?

"Those are really good." Lauren smiled at her encouragingly.

"I'm not sure I have a fourth."

"That's okay. I think you're right on the mark. I'd add sophisticated, but accessible."

Cam nodded slowly. She'd never have come up with either of those, but they rang true. "Yes. That's perfect."

"Great. Thank you for indulging me. I wanted to make sure we were on the same page before I started pitching you ideas." She opened the portfolio she'd come in with. "I've worked out four possible concepts."

She'd expected some general thoughts, maybe an idea for a print ad or the website. But Lauren pulled out four large pieces of paper, complete with sketches, color palettes, and tag lines. Not a Jet Ski to be had. "Wow."

"If there are elements you like from more than one, we can potentially combine, but I don't want to try to send too many messages at once, if that makes sense. It just waters everything down."

"It does." She liked the analogy. And even if she'd hated the concepts, she would have appreciated the work Lauren put into putting them together. But she didn't hate them. She liked them, the whole lot.

"Is there one that immediately speaks to you?"

Visually, Cam had a favorite. The imagery included a group of friends at a dinner party—not formal, but not pizza and dungarees either. The eight or so people were racially diverse and sharply dressed and one of the couples appeared queer. They probably couldn't use that exact photo, but it spoke to the vibe she wanted. The colors that went with it—mostly greens with a splash of dark blue—suited her existing logo and label. Still. She wasn't sure she was supposed to just pick one. "Yes, but I'd love it if you'd explain each of them to me."

Lauren smiled, slow and satisfied. It was the tiniest crack in her professional poise and sexy as hell. "I'd be happy to."

"All right. Tell me about this one." Cam pointed to the one she considered a little too manly—not too manly for her, but for an overall identity for Carriage House.

Lauren tipped her head back and forth. "This one is geared toward the twenty-something guy, the one who sports a lumberjack beard but designer shoes. I think you could get a lot of traction with this, with a share of the market that buys a lot of alcohol."

"But?"

"But I think it's a little too narrow. And since we aren't looking to launch a multi-faceted campaign at the moment, it might not be the way to go."

"Makes sense." Cam wouldn't have used those words, but her sentiments were the same. "What about this one?"

Lauren walked her through one that was more feminine and one that had a real city vibe. Each time, Lauren detailed what she considered the pros and cons. Until they got to the last one. It didn't take long for Cam to see it was Lauren's favorite as well.

Excitement bubbled out of her like a proud parent talking about her kid. The fact that Lauren's enthusiasm came from talking about her work resonated with Cam. Having the subject matter be her gin, the closest thing she had at this point in life to a child of her own, stirred something else. Affection, maybe. Paired with the attraction she couldn't seem to shake, it left her wanting. She shook her head, a physical gesture to deny just how potent it was.

"You don't like this one." Lauren's smile remained, but disappointment shone in her eyes.

Cam shook her head more emphatically. "No, I love it. I think it's the one."

"Really? Because you're frowning." The disappointment gave way to suspicion.

"I, uh, was getting ahead of myself. This is definitely the one." Cam tapped the piece of paper with her finger.

Lauren seemed to take that answer at face value. She nodded slowly. "I agree. It's the one I'd have picked, too."

A tendril of hair had escaped Lauren's updo, and Cam fought the urge to take it between her fingers, tuck it behind Lauren's ear. "So, why did you show me the others?"

"Because it's your brand and your decision."

There was a hint of mischief there. Yet another crack in the rigid professionalism. "But what if I'd chosen one of the others?"

"You wouldn't have," she said with a wicked grin. "I wouldn't have let you."

Cam chuckled because she knew it was true. It didn't surprise her that Lauren had that kind of influence or confidence. What surprised her was how much she liked it. "Fair do's."

"Excellent. I'll work up a more comprehensive package and we can discuss photography, design, and the media channels you're going to start with. Oh, and a website. I think we should build a whole new web presence, linked to Barrister's but not a child of it."

And just like that, they were back to business. Or maybe they'd never really left. She hated not knowing if Lauren shared her feelings, which left her even more off kilter than being attracted to Lauren in the first place. "Is this part of my package or will it cost extra?"

"About that."

Cam braced herself. "Yeah?"

"I hear you're good at DIY stuff. Finishing furniture and whatnot."

Cam glanced across the pub at Charlotte. She'd made a show of keeping busy, but clearly had been eavesdropping because she looked up and shrugged. Cam said, "It's a hobby. I'm no expert."

"But you've done it before."

"A handful of times." Where was she going with this?

"How would you feel about an addendum to our arrangement?"

How did this woman manage to make a mundane negotiation sound sexual? Or was it just her? Again, hugely frustrating. "What are you proposing?"

"I picked up a few pieces of furniture and could use some help refinishing them."

"You did?" Lauren did not strike her as the do-it-yourself type.

Lauren offered her a shrug and a coy smile. "I'm going for authenticity."

Cam chuckled. Well played. "And if I help you, you'll make me a website?"

"Seems like a fair trade."

As far as Cam was concerned, she was getting the far better end of that arrangement. But if Lauren thought it was fair, who was she to argue? Cam stuck out her hand. "Deal."

Lauren shook her hand and beamed. "I promise you won't be disappointed."

No, she didn't figure she would.

CHAPTER TWELVE

C am stood in the center of the tiny garage and surveyed the assortment of mismatched chairs and a small table Lauren said she wanted to use as a writing desk. "I can't believe I let you talk me into this."

Lauren planted her hands on her hips. "You're the one who said she was handy."

She hadn't, actually. Charlotte had. "I am."

"Which is really good because I am not."

"Wait. What do you mean?" She'd agreed to help refinish furniture in exchange for a new website. That had somehow expanded to include a professional photo shoot for Carriage House and carpet removal in two of the rooms at the inn. In both cases, she figured Lauren had experience but wanted help.

"Other than assembling some IKEA furniture in college, I've never DIYed anything in my life."

Surely she was joking. No sane woman would tackle a project like this if she literally had no idea what she was doing.

"But I have above average intelligence and I work out."

Cam looked Lauren up and down. She wouldn't argue with the part about working out. No, with her lean legs and toned arms, Lauren appeared to have that part in spades. She was smart, too, from what Cam had seen. Maybe a bit of a know-it-all, but smart. "But you don't know what you're doing."

Lauren shrugged. "That's why I have you."

This had disaster written all over it. Even if Lauren let her take the lead—which seemed unlikely, even given the circumstances—projects like the ones she had in mind could go sideways quickly. Technically, that wasn't her problem. "Does this mean you're going to follow directions?"

Lauren smirked. It was a good look for her. "I am capable of that, you know. I've worked for someone else my whole career."

Despite the playfulness of the comment, a shadow passed through her eyes. Cam wanted to ask her about it, get her to open up. That would make things personal, though. Getting personal with Lauren seemed even more hazardous than a novice operating power tools. She cleared her throat. "Right, then. I'll be happy to boss you around."

The shadow passed and Lauren grinned in earnest. "Excellent. I mean, really, how hard could it be?"

"Famous last words, woman. Famous last words." She attached a circle of medium grit to the sander and demonstrated the proper motions and pressure. Lauren nodded and had a look of intense concentration on her face. Cam took her level of focus as a good sign.

"Got it," she said.

"For the chairs you're painting, and the legs of this table, you don't have to be super precise. The top of the table is where it really matters."

"Right. That makes sense."

She liked Lauren agreeing with her. Maybe this wasn't a terrible idea after all. "It makes the job a lot easier. Smoothing out a nice flat surface is far simpler that getting into all the crannies."

"I read that on Pinterest. That's how I decided what to paint and what to stain."

"What's Pinterest?" she asked before she could help herself and regretted it the moment the question was out of her mouth.

"It's like an online pin board where you can collect ideas for—oh, never mind."

Cam lifted both hands, sorry her thoughts were so transparent. "What? I was listening."

"Yeah, but you should have seen your face. It was super judgy."

Was it? Maybe a little. She'd need to be more careful. Nothing seemed to get by Lauren. It was irritating, but also impressive. "Simply curious, I swear."

"Likely story."

Cam handed her the sander. She didn't want to start an argument. Not that this seemed in any real danger of turning into an argument. No, this back-and-forth sat on the cusp of something more dangerous—the kind of flirty banter that would end in her kissing Lauren. As appealing as that was, it couldn't possibly end well.

"So, we sand now?"

Cam cleared her throat. "We sand."

Lauren hit the power button. When it began to vibrate in her hands, she jumped and let out a yelp. To her credit, she didn't drop it. She looked at Cam and, instead of looking embarrassed, she laughed. Like, really laughed. If Cam thought she wanted to kiss her before, she'd been mistaken. The desire jangling though her right now, that's what it felt like to want to kiss someone.

"You all right?" Cam asked.

Lauren nodded.

"Don't forget this." Cam reached over and pulled the mask into place.

"Thanks." The word came out muffled, but the sentiment was clear.

Cam pulled on her own mask and gestured for Lauren to get started. She brought the sander down to the seat of the chair and went to town. She didn't flinch or hesitate. She wasn't entirely graceful about it, but for her first time, it wasn't bad. Cam went to work on the legs of the table, alternating between a sanding block and a steel brush.

She told herself she needed to keep an eye on Lauren, make sure she didn't hurt herself or get too carried away with the sander. The reality was that Cam couldn't stop staring. Her eyebrows furrowed in concentration behind the safety glasses. The way the oversize T-shirt that read "Fine like wine" left one of her shoulders exposed. The way she'd pulled all her hair into this messy bun that made Cam's fingers itch to tug it free.

Lauren glanced her way and shut off the sander. She pulled the mask down with her free hand. "What? Am I doing it wrong?"

"No, no. Not at all."

"Why are you giving me a funny look, then? If I'm not doing it right, I want to know. How else will I learn?"

The adamant tone made Cam smile. It also made her all the more embarrassed to have been caught staring. "You're doing great. I was just watching."

Lauren narrowed her eyes.

"I swear."

"Okay." Lauren put the mask back in place and restarted the sander.

Cam resisted the urge to shake her head. She needed to get a grip. If she and Lauren were going to spend time together—and it seemed like they'd agreed to spend all sorts of time together—she needed to not act like a complete fool. She definitely couldn't let on just how much Lauren had been creeping into her thoughts, even when they weren't together. She resumed sanding, putting more muscle into it than was perhaps necessary.

Maybe she could rope Charlotte into some of their meetings. The buffer of a third person might help, and she trusted Charlotte's opinion. Although if Charlotte caught wind of Cam's attraction, Cam would never hear the end of it. That might prove even worse than all this alone time with Lauren.

What a mess.

After thanking Cam and wishing her a good evening, Lauren returned to the garage. She surveyed their progress and smiled. Thanks to Cam's knowledge, not to mention her power tools, they'd accomplished more than she'd hoped. She just needed to let the first coat of paint dry and she could put on the second. If she did that tonight before bed, they'd be able to tackle the floors the next time Cam came over.

She'd not admitted as much to Cam, but she was a bit nervous about them. In her world, that was the sort of project one left to the experts. But her funds were running uncomfortably low, and Cam had insisted they could do it. The thing was, she trusted Cam. That might be the real kicker. What had started out as a barter of services had turned into much more. Friendship, maybe, however unlikely that might have seemed in the beginning.

Of course, that wasn't even factoring in the attraction. She tipped her head back and forth. Yes, the attraction complicated things. On top of everything, it seemed to be waxing instead of waning. At the rate things were going, she wouldn't be able to keep ignoring it and hoping for the best.

Lauren shook her head. She'd worry about that later. Now, she needed to clean up for her talk with Mrs. Lucas about the pub menu. She headed in the side door and to her room, or rather, her new room. She'd decided to move into the small apartment downstairs where Albert had lived. Although the idea made her uncomfortable at first, it was the right decision. Not only did it include a small kitchen and sitting area, her being there freed up a guest room she hoped to have booked before too long.

She'd resisted the urge to redecorate it completely, but new bedding and some throw pillows made it feel more like hers. Oh, and a matching bed for Tilly. She'd ordered a fancy memory foam one online and Tilly had taken right to it. Yes, her snoring had gotten worse, but Lauren couldn't bring herself to be bothered.

She stripped off her dusty clothes and headed into the bathroom. She set the water fairly cool and stepped under the spray, appreciating the jolt to her senses as much as ridding herself of the sawdust that had settled onto every inch of her. While she lathered and loofahed her body, her thoughts drifted to Cam. Wondering if Cam was in the shower right now, too. Wondering what it might feel like to slide soapy and slippery fingers over Cam's skin.

The arousal didn't surprise her at this point. She'd come to accept the fact that she couldn't think about Cam without getting turned on. Most of the time, she ignored it, if for no other reason than being turned on all the time was ridiculously distracting. Other times, she indulged it, let her imagination roam. Thinking about what it would be like to act on it, to have her desire reciprocated.

Today, she indulged it.

Lauren adjusted the temperature of the water, closed her eyes, and let her hands move over her body. Her nipples were already taut, hard peaks that stiffened even further under her touch. She grazed a hand over her stomach, down her thigh.

Cam's hands, she'd noticed, were a little rough. For all her corporate leanings, Lauren had a thing for rough hands—what they symbolized as much as how they felt. They'd create friction against her skin, especially where it was softest.

She slid her hand back up, pressed two fingers to her swollen clit. The sensation, paired with images of Cam, made her groan. She angled her hand, pressing her fingers inside. Her whole body clenched, and she braced her free hand on the shower wall.

What would it be like to have Cam behind her, one hand around her waist, the other fucking her? She let her head fall forward, rested it against the cool tile. Cam would cup her breasts, pinch her nipples. She'd whisper in Lauren's ear, telling her what she wanted, telling her she was beautiful.

Lauren rocked against her hand, longing for Cam and longing for release with equal ferocity. The orgasm tumbled over her and threatened to make her knees buckle. She kept her footing, barely, and blinked her eyes open. The bright light of the bathroom and the cool water sluicing over her brought her back to reality more harshly than she would have liked. "Fuck."

She finished her shower and shut off the water. By the time she'd dried off, her pulse had slowed, the throbbing in her clit subsided. She padded into the bedroom in search of clothes. Between the physical labor and the orgasm, she had half a mind to crawl into bed. But it was the middle of the afternoon. The sun was shining and she had things to do.

Lauren dried her hair and pulled it into a ponytail. She pulled on jeans and a tank top and slid her feet into sandals. As she left the room, her stomach rumbled, and she was grateful the next item on her agenda involved food.

CHAPTER THIRTEEN

Lauren spent the rest of her day on non-physical tasks— scoping websites for both inspiration and market analysis. She stayed up way too late, but slept well and woke up full of energy. She showered and dressed, humming with a mixture of enthusiasm and confidence. Even with so much still to do, it already felt like things were coming together.

She bounced into the pub, excited to show Charlotte the draft of the new menu before tackling the dreaded carpet project, but came to an abrupt stop when she realized Charlotte wasn't alone behind the bar. Sidled up next to her, looking very cozy, was Cam. "Hi."

Cam took a step to her left, putting space between herself and Charlotte. If they'd looked a little guilty before, the shift only reinforced the idea they were up to something. "Good morning," Cam said, her voice stilted.

"Morning, Lauren." For better or worse, Charlotte seemed unfazed by the whole thing. "Cam just stopped by with some samples of what she's working on. Do you want to give them a try?"

She was torn. Yes, she wanted to try anything Cam was cooking up. Yes, she wanted any opportunity to be in close proximity to Cam. But even though they'd settled into being friendly, she still got this undercurrent of antagonism from Cam, which left her feeling like an awkward teenager with a crush. Even with the time they'd been spending together, Lauren couldn't put a finger on where things stood between them. "Sure."

Lauren walked up to the bar. Charlotte pulled out a stack of shot glasses, and Cam poured from a small bottle into three of them. "This one is infused with cardamom. I thought it might be a nice small batch run for the holidays."

Lauren sniffed it before taking a sip. The flavor matched the aroma—warm and inviting. "Oh, that's good."

Cam smiled, causing Lauren's pulse to kick up a notch. "Thank you."

"What would you make with it?" she asked, unable to think of anything.

"I'm still working on that. A martini, maybe with star anise." Cam tapped a finger on the bar.

"And what about something with ginger beer and lemon?" Charlotte said.

"I love the way you two think." She really did. Lauren loved a good drink as much as the next person, maybe even more, but she couldn't come up with ideas for what flavors would go together. Her brain didn't seem to work that way.

Charlotte tipped her head toward Cam. "She's the real genius. I just stand here and look pretty."

"You're very pretty." Lauren pointed at her. "But you're a genius in your own right, too."

Charlotte bobbed a curtsy. "Thank you."

"Speaking of, I have a draft of the new menu. Mrs. Lucas helped me come up with a couple of things, and I found a bunch of gastropub fare online."

"Ooh, fun," Charlotte said.

Cam made a face.

"What?" Lauren asked. "Why are you scowling?"

"She thinks gastropubs are going to be the demise of English culture."

Lauren looked at Cam and raised a brow. "Seriously?"

Cam rolled her eyes. "She exaggerates, but I mostly think they're pretentious and overpriced."

A trio of men walked in and Charlotte stepped away to take care of them. Lauren looked down at the menu she'd been so thrilled with just a minute ago. Was it pretentious? Maybe a little. She'd been so focused on adding variety, making it more modern, she'd not thought about the possibility of taking it too far the other way.

"Come on. Let me see." Cam held out her hand.

"So, here's what I'm thinking." Lauren reluctantly gave Cam the piece of paper.

Cam took it and skimmed the list, feeling her lip curl with each item. "This is rubbish."

"What do you mean?" Lauren folded her arms, looking as offended by the comment as Cam felt about the menu. "What's wrong with it?"

"I don't know what half these words mean. And I don't want to know."

"Come on. You're being dramatic."

"I'm not." Cam pointed at her, not trying to rein in her frustration. "What the hell is gazpacho?"

Lauren shot her an exasperated look and showed no signs of backing down. "It's a cold tomato soup. I thought it would be nice to lighten things up a bit, especially in the summer."

"Ten quid for cold soup? Are you bloody insane?"

Lauren uncrossed her arms and squared her shoulders. "The price points aren't set. I'm looking for feedback on the concept."

Cam gave her bland look.

"And you aren't a fan."

Cam rolled her head from side to side, trying to work out some of the tension that had suddenly taken root in her neck. "You want to bring in tourists, city folks. I get that. But this? This is too much. This is selling out."

Lauren took a deep breath, and Cam got the feeling she was making an effort to remain calm. "I've already said that isn't my intention. What, or maybe I should be asking who, exactly, you think I'm selling out by putting gazpacho on the menu?"

Cam fumbled for the right words. Again, they eluded her. How could she explain this visceral reaction she had to the idea of everything changing, the idea of the Rose & Crown being anything other than what it was now? It was about her, yes, her own sentimental attachment to the place. She could own that. It was more, though. It was thinking about Albert and his chums, all over the age of eighty. Albert wasn't the first of them to die. Those that remained still came to the pub more days than not. If the place was full of twenty-somethings who'd pay ten quid for a bowl of mush, where would that leave them? And the women who came in a couple of nights a week to get away from their husbands? And the people who worked at the distillery and the sheep farm? Where would they go to relax and share a pint at the end of the day?

She realized that Lauren was staring at her, waiting for an answer. She cleared her throat. "The pub is special, it's…" Cam could feel herself getting emotional, knew it was written all over her face. She huffed out a breath. "It's complicated."

Lauren's whole expression changed. Cam expected to be pulled into fisticuffs, but instead of glaring or yelling or rolling her eyes, Lauren's face softened. "Tell me. I want to understand."

Cam opened her mouth, closed it. She opened it again. "Villages like this one are going extinct."

"I get that. I really do. I'm trying to prevent that, to bring people and money and life here."

"But if those people are very different, the ones who live here are going to get lost in the shuffle. If the pub is full of fancy people and fancy food, the people who live here won't go there anymore. And there isn't anywhere else for them, for us, to go."

"Oh, my God. It's gentrification. That's what you're afraid of."

Cam narrowed her eyes. She was pretty sure that's what Americans called social cleansing. "Maybe. What does that mean to you?"

Lauren closed her eyes and shook her head, and a sense of foreboding rose in Cam's chest. When Lauren opened them, she looked squarely at Cam. "It means you're absolutely right. I didn't even realize I was going down that path and, honest to God, it's the last thing I want."

The apparent about-face caught her by surprise and was enough to make her dizzy. "So, what does that mean for the menu?"

Lauren shrugged, then smiled. "It means we scrap it and start over."

Could it really be as easy as that? "What's the catch?"

Lauren looked at her with exasperation. "Why do you assume I'm going to be difficult?"

"I—" Cam held the denial on the tip of her tongue. She did assume Lauren would be difficult. Saying otherwise would be a lie. "I don't know."

"Don't you?"

God, this woman didn't let up. Which, to be honest, Cam respected. "You're very big city." She paused, sighed. "Very corporate."

Lauren nodded slowly, as though trying to decide whether to be insulted. "I'll give you that. For the record, though, corporate is a means to an end more than an inherent inclination."

"Inherent inclination?" Cam chuckled even though she was certain Lauren hadn't meant to be funny.

"I want to open my own agency, but I need the experience and reputation of an established one if I expect anyone to take me seriously."

"Huh." Cam had no desire to strike out on her own, but she could appreciate leveraging the reputation of a known entity. She'd never have gotten Carriage House off the ground without the Barrister's name behind it. Not to mention the production facilities.

"What? Are you judging me for that too, now?" She looked, not insulted, but maybe resigned.

"No. The opposite," Cam said.

"Really?"

She tried to soften her stance without backpedaling completely. "Really. I think that's admirable."

"But you still think I want to change everything for the worst."

"Not the worst." How was it that Lauren swooped in with her crazy ideas and Cam was the one who came off looking like an ass?

"And you admit some changes are needed?"

Cam rolled her eyes. "We've already established that I do."

"But I still want to preserve what works, what's good."

Did Cam believe that? Did she want to? She'd been dead set on holding her ground, trying to convince Lauren not to change things, or not change them very much. But when it came down to it, compromise was probably as good as she was going to get. She liked compromise, generally. And there was the matter of keeping the pub in business. "Okay."

Lauren raised a brow. "You finally believe me or you're tired of fighting with me?"

"I believe you."

"Good." Lauren looked satisfied. "Now, do you have any ideas about the menu?"

"Salads, maybe? And sandwiches? Stuff a reasonable person would eat."

"See, now we're talking. I'll go back to Mrs. Lucas and see what we can come up with."

Cam nodded, relieved but also something else. Something slipperier. Something that resembled admiration.

Lauren looked at her with doe eyes that made Cam feel like a heel. "So, you're not mad at me?"

Cam felt her shoulders slump. What was it about Lauren that brought out the most abrasive parts of her? "Of course I'm not mad."

"Good." Lauren grinned. "Because, you know, we've got a lot of work to do today."

"Right." Cam chuckled. She might not get Lauren entirely, but one thing was for certain, Lauren never failed to keep her on her toes.

Lauren attempted to wipe the sweat from her brow, but only succeeded in smearing gritty carpet dust across her forehead. This might be the worst idea she'd ever had. And she'd had plenty of terrible ideas.

"What?" Cam looked at her over a large piece of brown carpet.

How did Cam manage to look so good doing such utterly disgusting work? Lauren could only imagine how frightful she must look. It wasn't fair. "I'm having a moment of regret."

"Nonsense. We're almost done."

That part was true at least. Albert had gotten it into his head in the late eighties that carpet would appeal to lady guests, but never got farther than two rooms. Hearing the story from Mrs. Lucas was the first time Lauren said a prayer of thanks for Albert's tendency to start things and never finish. Unlike his haphazard upgrade of the electric or rigging some of the plumbing, this was actually going to save her money and time.

Lauren smiled. "I have to say, you are quite good at it. Have you done this a lot?"

"What? Trade manual labor for professional favors?"

Cam lifted a brow and, truthfully, it was all Lauren could do not to swoon on the spot. There was nothing suggestive or sexual about the comment. She was pretty sure Cam didn't even mean a lighthearted double entendre. Neither of those things kept her mind from thinking about trading all sorts of favors. "Um."

"I was kidding." Cam looked at her with a mixture of confusion and alarm.

"Sorry, sorry. I don't know where my mind went." Or at least not that she was telling. "I meant pulling carpet."

Cam smiled like she knew that's what Lauren meant all along. Like she was teasing her. Was that possible? "I did it at my place. My aunt had put carpet in the bedrooms and the bathroom when she lived there."

Lauren made a face before she could stop herself. "The bathroom?"

"Right? Utterly disgusting. It was one of the first things I changed."

She realized she knew absolutely nothing about where Cam lived. "Is the house yours now? Or sort of a family thing?"

"Both, in a way. I live in the carriage house at the edge of my parents' property."

"Nice." She'd grown up with money, but not carriage house kind of money. She'd not gotten the wealthy estate vibe from Cam. Interesting.

"Don't get the wrong idea," Cam said, as though reading her thoughts. "It's not some grand manor or anything. Just old enough to need a place for the carriage and horses."

Lauren chuckled at the ferocity of Cam's tone. "You seem horrified by the idea that I might think you come from money."

Cam shrugged. "It's more of a thing here, the upper class. Most of us who don't come from it want nothing to do with it."

So different from her parents, who strove for money and status above all else. She'd share that with Cam one day, maybe. "I promise I don't think you're gentry."

Cam shook her head and actually shuddered. "Please."

Lauren connected the dots of Cam's story. "Wait. Carriage House. Is that where you got the name for your gin?"

Cam lifted a shoulder as though she might be embarrassed by it. "Maybe."

"You really are sentimental."

"I am."

Cam's embarrassment seemed to fade, leaving this kind of openness, this authenticity, that did something to Lauren. It made her sentimental in return, maybe. Something she couldn't afford to be when it came to Cam. She finished rolling the chunk of carpet they'd cut and shoved it against the wall. "I like it. Tell me about your house."

Cam freed the final piece of carpet from under the baseboard. Lauren moved to the end and they started rolling it together. "My grandparents converted it to a house for my great-aunt, who never married. When she passed away, I claimed it."

"Did you have to fend off your sisters?"

"Jane is the oldest and married, so she didn't want it. I'm the next oldest, so it was mine by rights."

"Does that really work with siblings?"

"It didn't with yours?" Cam gave her a quizzical look.

"Only child."

"Right. Sorry. I shouldn't have assumed."

She'd wanted a sibling for most of her childhood. The longing had faded, helped along by her general preference to steer clear of her parents. Not that she never wanted to see them.

"Hey. You okay?"

Second time she'd been caught with her thoughts wandering. At least this time wasn't about getting Cam into bed. She smiled brightly. "Totally fine. Let's get this done."

They worked together in silence for a few minutes, carrying the carpet down the stairs and to the skip out back. Lauren wiped her brow and again realized she was just making things worse. She was glad she hired a professional to do the sanding and refinishing of the floors.

"We could do the drinks meeting there, if you'd like," Cam said.

It took Lauren a moment to understand her meaning. "Oh, at your house? I'd like that."

"I mean, I need to prove I'm not some upper crust poser."

"Yes, I need hard evidence." Lauren didn't think for a second Cam was that at all, but she wasn't about to turn down an invitation to her house. Whether or not it led to anything, it felt like a step closer to being, well, close. As much as she might want to get into Cam's pants, being her friend was the more important part. And spending time in Cam's place felt a whole lot friendlier than a meeting at the pub or the distillery.

"Monday, perhaps? In the afternoon? The tasting room will be closed, so I can finish with work by three or so."

Lauren smiled. "Sounds perfect."

"Good."

Cam nodded as though they'd just settled some important piece of business. Not exactly the flirtatious or suggestive vibe Lauren might have hoped for, but she'd take what she could get. At least for now.

CHAPTER FOURTEEN

Lauren spent the morning in her office, emerging only after her stomach reminded her at one she'd skipped breakfast. She sneaked into the kitchen to make a cheese sandwich and decided to take it out to the bar so she'd have some company. The pub had four whole patrons, only two of which were eating. Tilly trotted over to say hello, and Lauren bent down to scratch her ears. She gave Tilly a bite of her sandwich before pulling up a stool across from Charlotte.

"How's it going?" Lauren asked.

Charlotte smiled. "All right. You?"

"Lamenting the cost of new furniture." Lauren shrugged and took a bite.

She winced. "I'm sure. What are you going to do?"

Lauren wiped the crumbs from her fingers. "Suck it up. We're only going to get one chance to make a new first impression."

"Right, right. You've got a point there."

"It's going to look great, though, and that's what matters." At least that's what she kept telling herself.

"Cheers to that. What are you up to this afternoon? More work?" Charlotte asked.

Lauren smiled. "I have a meeting with Mr. Crawley about a few projects, and then Cam is walking me through the new drink menu, complete with samples."

Charlotte nodded appreciatively. "You're in for a real treat, I'm sure."

"She's really that good, huh?" Lauren thought back to her afternoon at the distillery. Cam had only served her drinks made with gin, but they'd been off the charts delicious.

"She is. It's like she knows things, senses what will work, in ways us mere mortals can only appreciate after the fact."

Lauren laughed because she sensed Charlotte wasn't joking. "I'm looking forward to it. Seeing her place, too. It feels like even more of a peek behind the curtain than being in her blending room."

Charlotte stopped polishing the highball glass in her hand, glass and towel suspended in midair. "She invited you to her house?"

Lauren frowned. "Is that bad?"

"No." Charlotte looked, if anything, confused.

"What, then?"

She resumed the methodical wiping, removing any trace of a water spot from the glass. "It's just that Cam doesn't invite a lot of people to her place. She's not antisocial or anything. Private, I'd say. An introvert. Has a pretty close circle."

Lauren's brain raced ahead, reading all sorts of meaning into Cam's invitation. Maybe they were finally friends. Or maybe Cam was attracted to her after all.

"I swear it's not a bad thing. I think it's quite good, honestly," Charlotte said.

Lauren laughed. She and Charlotte hadn't been friends for all that long, but they'd gotten pretty close. Lauren trusted her, and her take on Cam. "I'm just trying to figure out if it's a thing at all."

"Oh." Charlotte let the word drag out, leaving Lauren embarrassed by where her thoughts had gone.

"I shouldn't even be going there, should I?"

"I think you should one hundred percent go there."

Lauren closed her eyes for a second and let her imagination run with what going there might look like. Cam's gorgeous, strong hands on her. Cam's breath hot against her skin. Cam's mouth on her.

"Lauren?"

"Sorry." Lauren blushed.

Charlotte snickered. "I didn't mean to go there right now."

Lauren's face warmed further. "I know."

Charlotte laughed. "Oh, my God. You were having a sex fantasy about Cam."

She didn't normally have any shame around having sex fantasies. This was Cam, though, who'd only just come around to tolerating her. And Charlotte, who was not only Cam's best friend, but who also had her own romantic past with Cam. "Um."

Charlotte smacked her arm in a way that was clearly friendly, but still managed to pack a punch. "Girl, don't hold back on me. I think it's awesome. And the two of you have been zinging off each other since the day you arrived."

"Zinging?"

"Sparks flying. Chemistry. You two have it in spades. I think everyone will feel better if the two of you just slept together already."

Heat rose in Lauren's cheeks. Even if she enjoyed where this conversation was going, the idea that people beyond Charlotte were speculating about her and Cam was horrifying. Especially if Cam didn't reciprocate the feelings. "Everyone?"

"I exaggerate."

She couldn't tell if Charlotte meant that or if she was attempting damage control. Lauren didn't get the chance to ask. The pub door swung open, and a man walked in with a clipboard and a tape measure. Even without the accessories, the resemblance told her he was Cam's father.

He tipped the flat cap he wore. "Good morning to you, ladies."

"Good morning, Mr. Crawley," Charlotte said.

Lauren crossed the room to shake his hand. "Yes, good morning. I'm Lauren. Thank you so much for agreeing to meet with me."

"Of course. I'm happy to see how I can help you spruce the place up. Poor Albert didn't have much energy for her these last few years."

The way he referred to the inn as a her made Lauren smile. "Fortunately, I've not found too many major issues. There are some minor repairs, though, and some electric upgrades I'd like to do. Cam said if it was just installing new sockets, you might be able to handle it."

He nodded. "We'll have to sort out your panel first. That's above my skill level, but if you have the capacity, it should be all right."

The family resemblance truly was striking, and Lauren thought she might be seeing a hint of what Cam would look like in thirty years. His demeanor was easier, though. It made her wonder if Cam's coolness came from her mother, or perhaps more likely, was unique to their dynamic. She shook off the question, focusing her attention on Mr. Crawley. "Should we start in the cellar, then, instead of upstairs?"

"Let's do that. No point in making a list of things if I can't do them without an electrician coming in first."

Mention of an electrician made Lauren steel herself. She tried not to worry about what that might entail. Just like she couldn't worry about what her evening at Cam's might turn into. It would be what it would be and she'd sort it out when the time came.

Even though she was expecting it, the knock at the door gave Cam a jolt. She shook her head before opening it. Relax.

"Hello." Lauren stood on the other side in a flowy skirt and a snug tee with a deeply scooped neck that Cam instantly wanted to trace with her finger, and maybe her tongue.

She cleared her throat and hoped her face didn't give away where her mind had gone. Maybe inviting Lauren over was a terrible idea after all. "Hi."

Lauren beamed. "I'm so excited for this."

Cam tried for a casual smile. Terrible idea or no, here they were. "Come on in."

Lauren stepped over the threshold and handed Cam a brown paper bag. "Mrs. Lucas has been experimenting with recipes. I thought I'd bring some samples to try with the cocktails."

"Oh, that's a great idea. Better than the crackers and cheese I had planned to soak up some of the alcohol." Even if sharing a meal made this whole thing feel like more of a date.

"The curry pies are literally the best thing I've ever put in my mouth. I've already eaten two today, which maybe I shouldn't have told you since I plan to eat at least one or two more."

Cam chuckled. This was fine. Friendly. Just because Lauren had this flirty energy and a come-hither smile didn't mean anything needed to happen. "Your secret is safe with me."

Cam led the way to her kitchen, where she'd turned her tiny island into a makeshift bar. She set the bag on an open stretch of counter. Lauren took in the space, nodding slowly. "Your place is really cute."

"Uh, thanks." Why was this feeling more like a date with every passing second? "Do you want to eat now or start with drinks?"

"How about we start with a drink and work our way into food?"

"Sounds good." Grateful to have something to do with her hands, Cam pulled the rum punch she'd made earlier from the fridge and poured two small glasses. "Let's start with this and then I'll talk you through everything."

Lauren took the glass Cam offered and lifted it. "Cheers."

Lauren said a bunch of nice things and Cam listed out the ingredients. The punch was the token sweet and fruity thing on the menu. She didn't have much use for it personally, but in her experience, every bar needed to have one. Especially if that bar planned to cater to tourists. Before moving on to the next, she handed Lauren the notebook where she'd jotted down the ten cocktails she'd come up with. "I haven't named them. That seems like your forte. But the descriptions are meant to convey the essence of each without reciting a whole recipe."

Lauren skimmed the list, making hums and other noises of approval. At least Cam hoped they were noises of approval. When she looked up, she was smiling. "Wow."

The genuineness in her voice sent a wave of relief through Cam. Since she'd not owned being nervous, it was a bit of an odd sensation. "You don't have to put them all on, of course, but I think I gave you a good balance of classic and new, and covered all the major spirits."

"I want to try them all."

Her enthusiasm was infectious. "That can certainly be arranged." Lauren clapped her hands and rubbed them together. "I might end up smashed before we're through, but I don't even care. I put myself in your hands."

Cam pulled out a stool for her and got to work. She made her way through the menu, shaking up her take on an American old-fashioned, a serrano chili margarita, and a pink peppercorn infused martini. They broke into the food, a crayfish salad and a curried chicken pasty. The food was good, interesting while keeping with the spirit of traditional pub fair.

She thought back to their first conversation about the menu, how much she'd pushed back and how quickly Lauren had deferred to her opinion. She'd been unfairly harsh and still felt like a bit of a prat about it. But since bringing it up would only draw attention to the fact that she'd been a git, she moved on to the next round of drinks.

Lauren laughed and told stories about bars she'd been to in New York. She seemed so completely at ease, Cam couldn't help but relax. Even if she found herself staring at Lauren's lips. Or wondering if the skin below her ear was as soft as it looked.

Cam had what she considered a healthy tolerance for alcohol, but by the sixth or seventh, she started to feel a bit fuzzy. Not that she was making full drinks every time, but they were adding up. Lauren was holding her own, but her cheeks had gone pink and her laugh had gotten just a bit louder and freer.

By the time she served up the grand finale—a gin drink featuring Carriage House—Cam had a solid buzz going. Lauren appeared to be in the same boat. And Cam was having a hard time not thinking about what it might be like to kiss her.

"Oh, I like this one a lot." Lauren licked her lips, then took another sip. "What's in it again?"

Cam fought to clear the image of Lauren's tongue from her mind. "Lavender and honey."

"Mmm-hmm. This is definitely my favorite. Which isn't to say they aren't all amazing." Lauren punctuated the last statement by putting her hand on Cam's arm.

Cam looked at Lauren's hand and swallowed. "You don't have to shower me with compliments, you know. My ego is pretty healthy, at least when it comes to mixing drinks."

"Only then?" Lauren blinked and Cam would have sworn she was giving some very intentional bedroom eyes.

"Not only, but especially then."

"Ah." Lauren didn't break eye contact. "You strike me as someone quite confident in all things."

"Not all."

Lauren bit her bottom lip, then smiled. "But most."

Was Lauren teasing her or calling her an arrogant ass? "Sure. Most."

"Women?" Lauren's tone was definitely teasing.

"Excuse me?" Why was it so bloody hard to concentrate when Lauren looked at her like that?

"I asked if you were confident when it came to women."

This had to be a test. There was no possible answer that wouldn't get her into trouble. "Uh."

"I'm thinking you are. You have to like them, though. I've been certain up until now that you didn't like me very much."

If her brain had contained actual warning bells and red flags, they'd be going full steam. As it was, the word danger flashed over and over in her mind. "I don't dislike you."

"Grudgingly, I'd say." Before Cam could respond, she lifted a hand. "It's okay. I get it. I breezed in, representing everything you think is wrong with the world."

Shit. Had she really given such a bad impression? "I'm sorry I was so gruff."

"It's fine, really." Lauren laughed. It shouldn't have been such a sensuous sound, especially given the current conversation, but damn it all to hell if it didn't make Cam want to grab her and kiss her and drag her to bed.

"I feel like a proper ass right about now." Even at her most contrary, she'd not meant to be an ass. A pang of guilt lodged in her stomach.

"Please don't." Lauren's expression grew serious.

"Be an ass?"

She shook her head. "Apologize. Or feel like an ass. Especially if..."

Lauren trailed off, and for the life of her, Cam couldn't fathom where she was going. "If what?"

Lauren's eyes narrowed, and she studied Cam long enough to make her fidget. Cam wanted to look away, needed to, but she was transfixed. She remained that way as Lauren set down her glass, as she took Cam's and did the same. Cam stood frozen, equal parts dread and desire coursing through her, as she realized what Lauren intended.

Lauren leaned in, paused. Cam could have said something, could have pulled back. Even a few inches would have sent a message, likely stopped Lauren in her tracks. But Cam didn't speak, didn't move. She held Lauren's gaze, and in doing so, invited her in.

Lauren's lips were warm, soft but not yielding. She tasted like gin and lavender and honey, like summer and promise and warm nights under clear skies. And in that moment, brief as it was, Cam saw stars.

It ended far too quickly. The absence of Lauren's lips was jarring and left her feeling exposed, like having the blankets yanked off on a cold morning. She opened her eyes and found Lauren regarding her with questioning eyes. She looked so vulnerable, like she had no idea if her advances were welcome and wasn't sure she wanted the answer.

The juxtaposition of Lauren's usual confidence with the hesitation undid her. Cam buried her hands in Lauren's hair and gave in to the wanting that had haunted her for weeks, pulling their mouths together once more. She wanted to honor and reassure, protect and devour, all at once. Lauren leaned in, and it was all Cam could do not to take everything she wanted.

Realizing just how close she was to doing just that, she released Lauren and took a step back. "I'm sorry."

Lauren was breathing hard and the skin of her chest was flushed. "Sorry you kissed me or sorry you stopped?"

Fuck. "I'm not sure."

"Can we go with the latter? Because I'm really sorry you stopped."

Not the time to be speechless. Even if she had no idea how to respond or where to go from here. "You are?"

Lauren smiled and there was nothing hesitant or vulnerable about it. "If you recall, I'm the one who started it."

Right. "So, you want this." Cam couldn't decide if it was a statement or a question. "It's not just the alcohol talking?"

"Cam?"

"Yeah?"

"Did you enjoy kissing me?"

Cam merely nodded.

"Did you want to stop?"

She shook her head.

"Do you want to take me to bed?"

Cam swallowed. She couldn't bring herself to lie. "I do."

Lauren extended her hand. "Lead the way, then. Please."

CHAPTER FIFTEEN

Cam took her hand, but they remained standing in the kitchen. She appeared, not nervous, but hesitant. "Are we really doing this?"

"Are you having second thoughts?" Lauren closed her eyes for a second. Please don't let her be having second thoughts.

"No. It still seems a bit bonkers is all. I—"

Lauren didn't let her finish. "Cam, I've wanted to get in your pants from the moment I saw you sitting at the bar the day I arrived. If it weren't for this business of disagreeing about pretty much everything, I think we'd have tumbled into bed long before now."

Cam's shoulders dropped. "Exactly. We disagree about everything."

Lauren closed the distance between them. When was the last time she'd wanted to sleep with someone she spent so much time arguing with? She trailed a finger down the front of Cam's shirt, stopping right above her belt. "Not everything."

"I'm being serious."

She looked up at Cam through her lashes, pulling out all the stops. "I am, too. We both want the Rose & Crown to be successful. We've even managed to compromise on some of the ways to make that happen."

Cam nodded slowly. "That's true."

"And I'm pretty sure the attraction is mutual." Cam might have thrown her off her game, but she knew desire when she saw it. She wasn't that rusty.

"That's true, too."

"I won't bite." She smirked. "Unless you want me to."

Cam returned the smirk, which Lauren took as a good sign. "It isn't that I don't want to."

"I know it feels like there's a lot at stake, but it doesn't have to be anything more than you and me and the moment."

Cam's thumb traced lazy circles on the inside of Lauren's wrist. Hardly anything, but everything. "Is it really that simple?"

Lauren took a deep breath. A little part of her brain said Cam was right. They'd finally managed a détente, and sleeping together could screw it all up. Still. If she and Cam didn't just fuck already, she might literally burst into flames. "It can be. We can make sure it is." She stuck out her free hand, essentially wedging it between them. "We can even shake on it."

Cam looked at Lauren's hand, then right into her eyes. "Are you making fun of me?"

She shook her head without breaking the stare. God, she loved the way Cam stared at her. "No."

"Okay."

Was that a yes or a no? "Okay?"

"Yes." Cam smiled, the reticence gone from her eyes.

Lauren put her hand on Cam's arm, stroked down to her wrist and back up. She was prepared to take the lead, but she didn't want to come across as too eager. Cam lifted both hands, slid them into Lauren's hair. She paused for just a second, her gaze shifting, like she was taking in every detail of Lauren's face. The attention made her feel like something to be appreciated, treasured. It made her heart beat erratically and sent an unfamiliar flutter of butterflies to her stomach.

"Kiss me." She hadn't meant it to come out as a command, but the intensity of her reaction was making her uncomfortable. She was just really turned on. That had to be it.

Instead of obliging, Cam pulled back. Only a couple of inches, but it felt like a mile. She looked right into Lauren's eyes. "You're used to running the show, aren't you?"

"Maybe." Not that it was a matter of always wanting to, but she played to her strengths. She tipped her head slightly. "It's because I'm good at it."

"We'll see about that."

Lauren opened her mouth to retort but didn't get the chance. Cam's mouth covered hers with a kiss far more demanding than their first. The hands in her hair tightened, and Cam used the grip to angle her head. Cam took the kiss deeper, a skilled exploration with her lips and tongue. Lauren had always rolled her eyes when people said a kiss made them weak in the knees. Now she understood.

She moved her hands from Cam's arms to her sides, gripping her shirt and pulling her closer. She wanted her hands on Cam's skin. She started tugging at the fabric, untucking and hitching it up. At the first touch of Cam's skin, warm and smooth under her fingers, she sighed. She'd been waiting for this for so long.

Before she could get to work on the buttons, Cam grasped the hem of Lauren's shirt and eased it up. Lauren lifted her arms and Cam slipped it over her head. One of Cam's hands returned to her hair and the other caressed her back, tracing her shoulder blade and then kneading the muscles at the base of her neck.

She moaned before she could stop herself.

Without a word, Cam's arms wound around her, lifting her off the ground. Lauren wrapped her legs around Cam's waist, and Cam carried her through the kitchen to a bedroom at the back of the house. The journey didn't take all that long, but Cam never stopped kissing her.

In the room, Lauren reluctantly released her grip and returned her feet to the ground. She focused her attention on getting Cam out of her clothes. In a matter of seconds, they both wore nothing but underwear. Cam yanked back the quilt and nudged Lauren onto her back. Assertive. Unexpected.

Even more unexpected was how much she liked it.

She propped herself on her elbows and waited for Cam to join her. Cam took her time, her gaze traveling down Lauren's body and back up. Lauren licked her lips in anticipation. "Come here."

"Patience." Cam smiled at her, clearly taking pleasure in drawing it out, making her wait.

She bent over, wrapped her fingers around Lauren's ankle. Shoes. She was still wearing shoes. Cam took each strappy sandal off slowly, letting them drop to the floor with a light thud. She trailed fingers along Lauren's calf, still smiling.

Lauren was on the verge of asking again, of saying please, when Cam set a knee on the mattress. Finally.

Cam crawled up the bed and pulled Lauren into another kiss. Lauren matched her this time, a dance of tongue and teeth that sent her libido into orbit. She roamed her hands over Cam's back, down to her ass and over the plaid boxers she wore. She slipped a hand into the waistband, scratched her nails lightly over Cam's skin.

Cam shifted, taking her mouth with her. Before she could protest, Cam's lips were sucking her collarbone. In a move more practiced than she expected, Cam reached around and flicked open the clasp of her bra. Her mouth moved to Lauren's breast, sucking and biting at one nipple, then the other. Lauren arched, pleasure bordering on pain in the most perfect balance. She put her hand on the back of Cam's head, not wanting her to stop.

Only Cam did stop. It was all Lauren could do not to whimper. Cam got up on her knees, and for a split second, Lauren thought she was putting the brakes on. But no. The look in her eyes said she had no intention of stopping.

After an excruciatingly long minute, Cam hooked a finger into either side of Lauren's panties and slid them down her legs. Lauren sat up enough to grasp at Cam's boxers and off they went as well. The anticipation of full-body contact made Lauren smile. But Cam remained on her knees. "You're so beautiful. I'm looking forward to watching you come."

Oh. She didn't know what exactly she expected from Cam, but it wasn't this. The surprise of it turned her on almost as much as the directness.

Cam's right hand returned to Lauren's breast, pinching the nipple gently and rolling it between her fingers. Her left slipped between Lauren's thighs.

"Wait. Are you left-handed?"

Cam gave her a quizzical look. "Did you not know that?"

Lauren chuckled. "I hadn't noticed before."

"I mean, I'm sort of ambidextrous." Cam gave her a playful look. "But my left is more dominant."

The comment, silly and not relevant, turned Lauren to mush. "Well. Sure."

Instead of making another joke, Cam slid her fingers over Lauren. Lauren knew she was aroused, but even she was surprised by just how wet she was already. She looked into Cam's eyes and smiled. "I've been wanting you for a while."

Cam nodded, but didn't speak. She eased one and then a second finger into Lauren. Lauren arched her hips, wanting as much of Cam as she could get. The skin on Cam's hands was rough, the calluses creating the most delicious friction.

Lauren thought they might start slow, but Cam increased the pace and the force almost immediately, brushing her thumb up the length of Lauren's clit with each stroke. It didn't take long to establish a rhythm, Lauren rising to meet Cam, adding to the intensity of each thrust. She gripped the sheets beneath her, already feeling the pressure build low in her abdomen.

She made noises. Not the kind of encouraging sounds meant to convey yes, more, right there. No, these were the raw, uninhibited moans of being fucked really well. She didn't hold them back. Nor did she hold back the orgasm that crashed over her, stealing her breath and leaving her weak.

She'd barely started to recover, to think about how it was even better than her fantasies, when Cam said, "On your stomach."

It was a command, not a question. Lauren's body responded, betraying any argument she might have made over being told what to do. She did as Cam instructed. Without waiting for her to get settled or think about what was coming, Cam once again plunged inside her. Lauren came up onto her knees slightly, spreading her legs wider in silent invitation.

"That's a good girl."

Cam's words, smooth as a sixty-year-old Scotch, addled her brain. But they made perfect sense to her body. She pushed back against Cam's hand. She couldn't bring herself to beg for more, but she didn't have to. Cam pressed a finger to her ass, used her free hand to stroke Lauren's clit. The orgasm ripped through her, a quaking of muscles and a tide of pleasure that made her cry out. The sound was so primal, she wasn't sure at first it had come from her.

She collapsed onto the bed, rolled onto her back. "Fucking A."

Cam came up and lay beside her, propping herself on one elbow. "That's good, right? In American?"

Lauren let out a ragged chuckle. Her heart continued to thud against her ribs. "Yes. Very good. Lots of verys."

"Just making sure." Cam caressed the underside of her breast, then slid her hand down between Lauren's legs.

"I don't think I can." The words came out staccato, breathless.

"You can and you will." Cam grazed her free hand over Lauren's stomach. "Just relax and trust me."

Such a simple command, yet laced with so much meaning. Lauren swallowed the bubble of panic. Sex. They were only talking about sex. And on that score, Cam had proved herself more than deserving of trust. She took a steadying breath, looked into Cam's eyes, and nodded.

Cam's fingers moved gently, more caress than anything that would make her come. They eased in and out of her slowly, soothing almost. Her thumb traced wide circles, avoiding Lauren's oversensitive center. It was like a sensual massage, coaxing her back to arousal.

"Fuck, that feels good."

"Just let go. I've got you."

It wasn't exactly power play. She'd dabbled in that, with mixed results. No, this was something different, new. Some heady mix of confidence and skill, all bound up in an almost overwhelming focus on her, her pleasure. It was probably for the best that her brain was barely operating, because if she could really think it through, it would freak her the fuck out.

But just as the pseudo-thought threatened to take root, Cam tightened the circles with her thumb and timed them with the lazy thrust of her fingers. What would have been too much a minute before was now exquisitely perfect. Cam wound her up slowly, and Lauren's body followed her lead.

"Come for me, Lauren."

At the sound of Cam speaking her name, she came unglued. But it wasn't an earthquake that rocked her, or even a tidal wave. Pleasure rippled over her like the warm water of a shallow beach in summer, sensual and easy and enveloping her whole body. She said Cam's name, whispered it like a promise, as Cam held her there, suspended in a spell she never wanted to break.

When her pulse slowed and her breathing returned to normal, Lauren opened her eyes and rolled toward Cam. "That was not fair."

Cam raised a brow. "What do you mean, not fair?"

Lauren walked her fingers up Cam's arm. "I mean it isn't fair for you to put me in a coma before I get to have you at all."

"I'm sorry, did you want to file a complaint?"

She lifted a shoulder. "Not a complaint, technically."

"I could give you the number of the bureau. There's a bureau for that, you know. We're England. We have a government bureau for everything."

Lauren snorted before she could stop herself. "I think I'd rather rectify the situation myself."

Cam nodded and her expression remained serious. "I respect that about you. You're not afraid to tackle projects head-on."

"And here I thought you hated that about me."

"Not hate. I never said hate. And for the record," Cam pointed, "I took issue with your ideas, not your methods."

"I see. Well, let's see how you feel about these methods." Lauren rolled over and slinked down the bed.

Cam sat up partway. "I don't want you to feel like you need to reciprocate. I mean, I'm not opposed or anything, but—"

Lauren silenced her with a kiss. "Shut up, Cam."

She poked a finger into Cam's chest and gently pushed her back. Cam didn't fight her or offer any words of protest. Lauren took that as a good sign. She continued down the bed, nudging Cam's legs apart with her body. Cam lifted her head. "You really don't—"

"Cam?"

"What?"

"I'd like to go down on you right now. If you're not cool with that, please just say the word. I'm all about consent."

"Uh."

"Would you like me to go down on you?"

Cam nodded.

"Excellent. Now, to quote this really hot person I just had sex with, let go. I've got you."

Without waiting for a reply, Lauren plunged her tongue into her. Cam was hot and hard and her taste was almost enough to turn Lauren on all over again. Almost.

She started with long strokes, pressing the flat of her tongue into Cam's wetness and sliding up over her clit. Cam groaned and grabbed a fistful of her hair. God, did she love a woman who wasn't afraid to pull her hair.

Despite her intentions to draw it out, she couldn't resist the urge to suck Cam's hard center. She wrapped her lips around it, tugging it gently toward her throat. Cam arched toward her, mumbled her name.

Lauren continued to work her, feeling powerful and sexy. She wrapped her arms around Cam's thighs, not so much to hold her in place, but so they could move together. She could feel the muscles in Cam's legs tighten and quiver. Her breathing grew rapid and her sounds pitched higher.

Lauren forced herself to slow down, savor what was happening. She hoped it was the first of many times together, but still. She knew she'd look back on tonight for years to come and she wanted to make it last.

"Fuck. Lauren. What are you doing to me?"

The question, punctuated with panting, made her smile. She didn't want to let go long enough to say anything but she hummed her pleasure and quickened her pace. Cam really started to tremble then, her body bearing down in search of release. Lauren followed, pushing her higher and willing her to climax.

Cam tumbled over the edge with a gush of liquid heat. It was so over-the-top sexy, Lauren groaned. Cam bucked and Lauren stayed with her.

When Cam's grip on her hair eased, Lauren slowly pulled away. She rested her forehead on Cam's thigh. "Fuck."

Cam blew out a breath. "I think that's my line."

Lauren chuckled. "Let's just agree the feeling is mutual."

"Deal. Come up here."

Lauren obliged, curling into the crook of Cam's shoulder. She kissed the side of Cam's breast. "You know, by rights, I get to do that two more times."

"Is your goal to kill me? Because I'm pretty sure that's what would happen."

Lauren lifted her head and shot Cam a look of mock indignation. "I wasn't given an opt out clause."

Cam, who'd been running her fingers through Lauren's hair in the most delicious way, gave it a little tug. "One, that's the most corporate phrase I think I've ever heard. Two, are you saying you'd like to rescind one of your orgasms?"

Lauren liked this playfulness in Cam. She'd seen glimpses of it as they'd spent more time together, but this felt like an all-around easier, more genuine version of Cam. "One, I come by it naturally. You can't hold that against me. Two, hell no. I'm a very satisfied customer. My sole desire at this moment is to give you more orgasms so we're even."

Another tug on her hair, this one a bit harder. "It's not a competition."

Lauren lifted her head, looked into Cam's eyes, and raised a brow. "It's not?"

"No."

She'd been kidding, but the ferocity of Cam's reply told her this, at least, was not something to kid about. Which was fine, really. As competitive as she was in just about every aspect of her life, being competitive about sex seemed rather skeevy. "Okay. I concede the point."

"You concede? I didn't know you knew the word."

"Stop." She was pretty sure Cam was kidding, but she didn't want to risk blowing her post-coital glow on a dumb argument. "In this case, yes. You win."

Cam planted a kiss on her temple. "Banner day."

The gesture did as much to reassure Lauren as Cam's comment. Not that she needed reassurance. "I'll just have to make up for it next time."

"Since it's not a competition, I have no problem with that."

Lauren smiled, drowsiness and contentment starting to envelop her in a soft haze. "Look at us, in complete agreement."

"Like I said, banner day."

Cam reached over and shut off the lamp. Lauren cozied back into Cam's embrace. Banner day indeed.

CHAPTER SIXTEEN

Cam stirred at her usual six and found Lauren sprawled on her stomach, one arm slung across Cam's middle. She'd half expected Lauren to be up before sunrise, a tornado of tackle-the-day energy. The fact that Lauren had an off switch proved oddly reassuring. Or maybe it was something about seeing her so at peace. Either way, Cam liked being able to study her without fear of being caught staring.

Unable to resist, she ran her fingers through Lauren's hair. It might be cliché, but she was such a sucker for filling her hands with long, thick hair. It was the kind of gesture that could be tender or demanding, gentle or possessive. Lauren liking the latter had been a surprise. A damn pleasant one at that.

Cam continued stroking. Lauren didn't open her eyes, but she turned her head and let out a contented hum. Cam kissed the top of her head. "Good morning."

Lauren smiled, eyes still closed. "Good morning."

"I don't want to chase you out of here, but I need to get ready for work. You're welcome to stay as late as you want."

That seemed to push her wide-awake and alert button. She opened her eyes and looked around. "What time is it?"

Cam chuckled. "Early still. Barely six. I need to be at work early today."

Lauren rolled to her side. "Wow. I hardly ever sleep that late."

"And the truth comes out." Cam hadn't meant to say that out loud, but apparently her guard was down.

Lauren propped herself on an elbow and gave Cam a curious look. "What does that mean?"

Hopefully, Lauren would take it as a compliment. "You always seem to be bursting with energy. I think I was surprised to wake up before you."

Lauren trained a finger down her arm. "Well, someone did a pretty bang-up job of tiring me out last night."

Or that. That was good, too. "I see. So multiple orgasms is the way to get you to relax?"

Lauren considered for a moment, making Cam wonder if she'd overstepped. But then, with a perfectly serious expression on her face, she nodded. "Yes."

"Good to know." Cam kissed her again, this time on the mouth. "I'm rather sorry now that I have to get up."

"Don't be. I do, too." She sat up and the sleepy, sexy Lauren disappeared. All-business Lauren was back in full force.

"Would you like to take a shower here? You're welcome to."

She was already out of bed and pulling on clothes. "Thanks for the offer, but I'm good. Since I didn't bring clothes, it'll be easier at my place."

Cam didn't have time for a shared shower that might lead to more, but it didn't prevent a small pang of disappointment. "Of course."

Now fully dressed, with the exception of the shirt she'd taken off in the kitchen, Lauren came and stood at the edge of the bed. She leaned down, kissing Cam just long enough to make her departure seem unhurried. "I had a really great time last night."

Understatement of the century. "Same."

"Does that mean we get to do it again?"

As much as she'd bristled at Lauren's directness at first, Cam had to acknowledge it came with some perks. "I think that's a fine idea."

"I'll see you this afternoon, though, right? To go over the mock-ups for your campaign."

Cam had to fight the urge to pull her back into bed. Not good, given that she was the one who'd declared she needed to get up. "Yes. I'll be there around one."

"Perfect."

And with that, she was gone. Cam sat in bed for a moment, uneasy, but unsure why. She shook it off and got up, heading right to the shower. Where she didn't wonder what it would be like to have Lauren wet and soapy and in her arms. She got dressed and headed to work. Where she didn't think about seeing Lauren in a few hours.

When noon finally rolled around, Cam decided to have lunch at the pub. She hadn't seen Charlotte in a few days and wanted to catch up. She'd not yet decided whether to tell Charlotte about sleeping with Lauren, but she could sort that out later. The walk was drizzly, but she didn't mind. The temperatures had been holding steady, and it still managed to feel like early summer. Early summer in England, at least.

She took her usual stool at the bar, ordered a sandwich and a pint. A small flurry of customers came in shortly after, and it wasn't until she'd finished eating that Charlotte was free enough to exchange more than pleasantries. It didn't bother Cam. They'd been friends long enough that simply sharing space counted for something. When she finally made her way over, she looked Cam up and down and narrowed her eyes.

"What?" Cam asked.

"You slept with her, didn't you?" Charlotte didn't seem bothered or even surprised by the idea, but it did come out as more of a statement than a question.

"What makes you say that?" She wasn't being coy, but she wanted to know if this was one of those cases of Charlotte's crazy intuition or if Lauren had told her. She hoped it was the former. Not that she wanted to keep it a secret, but she didn't need everyone in town knowing her business, especially if she'd started mixing business with pleasure.

"You have this look about you."

To hide her relief, Cam folded her arms and gave Charlotte an exasperated look. "What does that even mean?"

Charlotte mimicked the gesture. "It means I know you. Some days I think I know you better than you know yourself. And there's something different about you. A little softer around the edges maybe."

Cam suppressed a chuckle. Soft would not be a word she'd use to describe what she and Lauren had been up to last night. Except, perhaps, to describe the skin of Lauren's inner thigh, or what it felt like to slip inside her. Cam cleared her throat. "Softer?"

Charlotte's face went from exasperated to smug in two seconds flat. "You did. I wasn't a hundred percent sure, but now it's beyond obvious. Subtle you are not, my friend."

Cam frowned. "I can be subtle."

"I bet you weren't subtle with Lauren. She's a firecracker, isn't she?"

At that exact moment, Mrs. Lucas emerged from the kitchen with a plate of scones for the guests of the inn around for afternoon tea. She offered Cam a greeting and bustled off in the direction of the library.

"Jesus, Charlotte. Could you be any crasser?"

Charlotte must have thought that was the funniest thing she'd heard in weeks. She laughed and laughed, the kind of laughing that sent tears running down her cheeks. Lauren chose that moment to come into the bar from her office, because that's the kind of day Cam was having.

"What's so funny?"

Before Cam could formulate an answer—perhaps one with a trace of subtlety—Charlotte wiped her eyes and said, "The two of you having sex."

Lauren blanched and it was all Cam could do not to reach across the bar and throttle Charlotte.

"Not that the two of you sleeping together is funny," Charlotte added quickly. "I was mostly poking fun at Cam for wearing her thoughts on her chest like a badge. I knew the second she walked in what you two had been up to last night."

Lauren bit her lip and Cam thought she might literally melt into the floor. Or perhaps that was merely wishful thinking on her part. But then Lauren smiled. "I'm glad it was you who gave it up instead of me."

That sent Charlotte into another fit of laughter and left Cam— what? She couldn't decide whether to be relieved or mortified, and the whole thing left her unsettled. Not that being unsettled was anything new when it came to Lauren.

"Poor Cam. I don't mean to tease." Charlotte looked at her with what appeared to be genuine sympathy.

Cam pinched the bridge of her nose. She didn't like being teased. Something about having four sisters. But that wasn't the point. What was the point again? She had a hard time holding a clear thought in her brain with Lauren only a few feet away.

"No more teasing." Lauren crossed the room to where she stood. In heels, she was almost exactly the same height as Cam. "Could we talk for a minute? Maybe in my office?"

Cam nodded and followed her. Charlotte made a show of being very attentive to something behind the bar. Once they were in her office, Lauren closed the door. Cam took a deep breath. "Sorry about that."

Lauren angled her head slightly. "Sorry for what, exactly?"

"For having no poker face, apparently. For inadvertently telling Charlotte what happened between us. For making it seem like something to laugh about."

"Do you think it's something to laugh about?"

Cam shook her head. "Of course not."

"Do you regret going to bed with me?"

It might have been the dumbest decision she ever made, but Cam couldn't bring herself to regret it. "No."

"Then I think we're okay." Lauren smiled. It wasn't amused or sympathetic. Encouraging, maybe. And definitely sexy.

"Good."

Given the conversation, she shouldn't have this overwhelming desire to kiss Lauren. But there it was. Apparently, she couldn't be within arm's reach of Lauren and not want to kiss her. It was going to prove very problematic if they continued working together, which they'd agreed to do. She was just going to have to find a way to keep herself in check and not act like some horny teenager.

Without a word, Lauren took Cam's face in her hands and brought their lips together. The first kiss felt like a statement, a brief declaration that everything between them was okay. The second was more meandering, hot but unhurried. Nothing funny or subtle about it.

Once the surprise of being kissed by Lauren in her office subsided, desire quickly took over. The play of Lauren's mouth over hers conjured every erotic detail of the night before. The planes of Lauren's body, the sounds she made when she came.

When Lauren pulled away, Cam realized how close she was to setting Lauren on the desk and having her way with her. The intensity of it left her shaky. Unsettled might turn out to be a colossal understatement.

"We shouldn't fuck on my desk, should we?" Lauren bit her lip. "At least not in the middle of the afternoon."

That Lauren's question so closely mirrored her own thoughts made Cam laugh. "Probably not."

"It's tempting, though, right? It's not just me?"

Lauren's lipstick had vanished and her hair was slightly mussed from where Cam had run her fingers through it. In that moment, it was hard to imagine a sight more alluring. "Not just you."

"Good. That's good." Lauren tucked her hair behind her ears and nodded. "So, work. Shall we get to work?"

"Yes, work." Something, anything, to put her mind on besides how badly she wanted to kiss Lauren again.

Lauren took another step back, then went behind her desk. She pulled out the large portfolio she'd brought to their first meeting. "Okay. Based on our last conversation, I've created mock-ups for a new website, social media ads, and a couple of print pieces. I know you were still on the fence about those because of cost, but I think we might be able to get a few creative placements that will be worth the investment."

She handed Cam several pieces of paper, each laid out with sketches, images, and blocks of text. Lauren had printed stock photos to give the feel of what she was going for. Cam had no trouble imagining the finished product and she liked it. She liked it a lot. Bold and fresh, but nothing too loud or over the top. It felt distinct from Barrister's branding, but not wholly unrelated. "This is perfect."

"You don't have to say that just because we had sex last night. I can take constructive criticism, and I can keep our personal relationship separate from our professional."

The firm tone made Cam smile. She appreciated the sentiment, even if it wasn't called for in this situation. "I'm not trying to get— or is it stay?—on your good side. I really mean it."

Lauren squared her shoulders and beamed. Cam imagined it was the look she gave anytime she nailed a presentation. And damn it all to hell if it wasn't as sexy as the looks she gave in bed. When had she started to find ambitious types so attractive?

"Excellent. Because I have another idea I want to pitch you."

"Should I ask what it is or how much it's going to cost me?"

"If we play our cards right, it won't cost you a penny."

"I like the sound of that."

"I thought you might." Lauren gestured to one of the chairs opposite the desk. Cam sat and Lauren took the other instead of sitting at her computer. "I know a guy who writes for *Traveler*. It's a trade journal for the hospitality industry. I told him about what I was doing here, pitched him the idea of a story about the pub, but also the distillery."

It didn't surprise her, necessarily, that Lauren had those sorts of connections, but it hadn't occurred to her she might benefit from association. "And he's going to do it?"

"He is. He does a column called 'Hidden Destinations.' It's about places off the beaten path and how places without a high profile attract visitors and keep local businesses thriving."

"Wow."

"It's not as good as something in a Condé Nast or an airline mag, but it's got an impressive distribution, including some travel agents and bloggers."

Cam shook her head. She'd tried to keep her expectations low—for Lauren, for the work she was doing, for everything really. She wasn't quite ready to think of Lauren as the savior, but the cards were stacking up in her favor. Even if she didn't long for waves of strangers in town, she couldn't argue the financial boon that would accompany them. "It sounds pretty perfect for us."

"Right? I've convinced him to come to the grand reopening of the inn and I'm going to give him pick of the images from the photo shoot Anja is doing." Lauren straightened like she'd just remembered something important. "I told you about scheduling the photo shoot, didn't I?"

"You did not. I mean, I know we agreed to take photos at some point, but we'd not gotten that far."

Lauren smiled. "Right. Well, now's as good a time as any. My friend Anja is a photographer. She did a lot of the shoots for the campaigns I did back in New York. She's brilliant. I was able to get on her calendar."

Of course she would also be friends with a photographer. "When is she coming?"

"The week before the relaunch. Oh, we also need to talk about that."

Cam could keep up with the conversation, but she wasn't sure how Lauren could keep up with all the balls she had in the air. "When is that?"

Lauren picked up the planner from her desk. "I've penciled in August twelfth. It's ambitious, but I should be able to get the work here done in time. And it would leave a few weeks of summer to squeeze in some reservations. I'm really hoping to bring in some revenue before winter."

She couldn't fault the logic or the ambition of the plan. But she'd seen how much there was still to be done in the rooms. Between that and the work she knew went into planning any sort of event, it was enough to make Cam's head spin. To say nothing of the two marketing campaigns Lauren now had in the works. "You're going to be busy."

Lauren smirked. "It's my favorite way to be."

Now that she'd given in to the attraction, it was easier to let herself like Lauren. But perhaps more surprising was the idea of respecting her as a person and a professional. She had good ideas, but even more, she wasn't afraid to work hard. And she seemed to have integrity. That earned a lot of points in Cam's book. Not that she was keeping score. "What do you need from me?"

The smirk turned into a coy smile. Cam couldn't know if it was meant to have a calculated effect on her, but it sure as hell did. "I need you to agree to be the face of Carriage House."

The words registered. The meaning did, too, at least technically. But Cam didn't follow. "Excuse me?"

"We're branding a handcrafted product. That plays better if there's a craftsman as part of the story."

Cam frowned. "Can't you accomplish that with the words or something?"

Lauren folded her arms. "Are you reluctant or a hard no?"

For some reason, the choice of words had Cam thinking about limits in the bedroom. She shook off the images her brain conjured. She'd come back to that later. Maybe. "Somewhere in between."

Still with the coy smile. "I can work with that."

"I—"

She was spared having to come up with a coherent thought by a knock at the door. Mrs. Lucas poked her head in. "Phone call for you, ma'am. It's an Alejandro."

Lauren's eyes lit up. "That's the writer. I gave him the main number. I need to take this."

Cam pounced on the opportunity to escape. "I should get back to work anyway."

"You can put it through," Lauren said to Mrs. Lucas. Then, to Cam, "Think about what I said, at least for the article. I'm not saying we have to put your face on the side of a bus."

Cam nodded and offered a wave good-bye. Charlotte wasn't behind the bar, so she didn't linger in the pub. On the walk back to the distillery, she couldn't help but think about seeing her face blown up tenfold and plastered to a bus or a building or any other large, public surface. That was the thing with Lauren. It was impossible sometimes to know if her comments were hyperbolic or if she meant them literally. Cam didn't like the uncertainty of that, especially since Lauren seemed undaunted to try just about anything.

CHAPTER SEVENTEEN

They moved the dresser into position. Lauren stepped back to assess its location, and Cam took in the whole of the room. The bed was original, but with a new mattress. One of the chairs she'd helped Lauren refinish sat at the table turned writing desk, replacing an armchair that had remained well past its prime. The whole space had come together quite nicely.

"I think a couple inches to the right, so it's square under the mirror." Lauren angled her head in that direction.

"You got it." She picked up her end and shifted accordingly.

Lauren stepped back again and nodded. Then she stepped forward, pulled out her tape measure and checked that it was centered. Cam found the precision of it endearing. She nodded a second time. "Perfect."

"Great. What's next? I'm at your disposal for another hour." She could stretch that if needed, but she didn't want to admit—to Lauren or to herself—how readily she'd blow off work to spend the afternoon together.

Lauren crossed her arms and gave Cam a questioning look. "Are you helping me as a thank you for managing your photo shoot, or to try to get me to change my mind about putting you in it?"

Cam frowned. "Neither."

"So, you're just trying to get me into bed again."

Lauren winked, but Cam didn't like where the conversation was going. "Why do I have to have an ulterior motive?"

"I'm teasing you, not accusing you of something." Lauren adjusted the pencil behind her ear and clipped her tape measure to the front pocket of her very tight jeans, a gesture that managed to be both sexy and distracting.

"Oh." How was it that Lauren reduced her to single syllable answers?

Lauren crossed the room and slid her hands around Cam's waist. Cam reciprocated, resting her hands just above the swell of Lauren's bum. "You're adorable. You know that?"

Cam felt her lip curl. "Not adorable. That's the kiss of death."

Lauren leaned back but didn't let go. "What does that mean?"

"Adorable. It's like the least sexy compliment ever." God. Did she really just say that?

"I think it's plenty sexy."

Cam shook her head. "No. Puppies are adorable."

"Would you feel better if I called you smokin' hot?"

Cam didn't let go, but she closed her eyes and moved one hand to pinch the bridge of her nose. "No. I mean, yes. But no. Can we finish hanging pictures, please?"

Lauren laughed. Like, threw her head back and really laughed. Her grip on Cam tightened. "Do you not want to get me back into bed, then?"

It had been only a few days since they'd slept together, but Cam hadn't been able to stop thinking about the possibility of doing it again. She couldn't know if it was the press of Lauren's body or the suggestive comment, but her own body responded with no trace of ambiguity. And though it wasn't really her nature to banter in that way, something about Lauren made her bold. "Oh, I didn't say that at all. It's just not why I offered to move furniture and hang pictures."

Lauren did step away then, but she gave Cam's bum a quick squeeze first. "So why did you offer?"

"I'm a nice person and you needed help."

Lauren raised a brow that was pure incredulity. "Really? Hero complex?"

The comment struck a nerve, although not in an altogether bad way. Still, she didn't need to own it. "I wasn't trying to get in your bed when I came and pulled you out of that ditch."

Lauren poked a finger right into Cam's chest. "Exactly. You were playing hero."

She'd walked right into that one. "But that was a favor to Charlotte."

Lauren gave her a bland look.

"Maybe I do enjoy helping out now and again. It makes me feel good." Why did she suddenly feel self-conscious about it?

"I won't say that's adorable, but it is very sweet." Lauren leaned in and kissed her. "And I appreciate you helping me hang pictures."

They spent the next hour doing exactly that. Well, first they had a brief argument about the absurdity of some of the paintings Lauren had selected—woodland creatures in tweed blazers and reading glasses. "They're trendy," Cam said with a scowl.

"But by a local artist," Lauren countered.

"They're kitschy."

"They cost two hundred quid each. And I'm going to keep the artist's contact info for anyone who wants to visit her gallery."

Cam couldn't bring herself to counter that argument. And they were cute. Just so bloody trendy.

They finished sorting the furniture—the old, the new, the pieces they'd refinished together. At least in the rooms that were otherwise done. The floors of the previously carpeted rooms still needed a few days of drying and a final coat of varnish.

Even without the bedding or the little odds and ends that would make the rooms homey, Cam was impressed with the results. The changes weren't dramatic, but every room felt fresher and lighter, updated without being modern or jarring. Hipster animals notwithstanding. "You've done a really nice job, you know. With everything."

Lauren planted her hands on her hips and narrowed her eyes. "Camden Crawley, are you complimenting me?"

They'd moved past the initial animosity. Or, perhaps more accurately, Cam's animosity. And her suspicion. But this teasing felt new, different. "I am and it's well deserved. Especially after I gave you such a hard time."

Lauren offered her a seductive smile. "Okay, now I know you're just trying to get me back into bed."

This kind of playful back and forth wasn't typically her style, but something about Lauren brought it out in her. It didn't feel entirely natural, but it was rather nice. "Can't it be both? I think you've done a bang-up job and I want to get you in the sack?"

"It can most definitely be both."

Cam bit the inside of her cheek. Why the hell not? "When can we schedule that? The getting back in the sack part."

Lauren seemed to consider it for a long moment. "Well, there's tonight. And tomorrow night. And the night after that."

Since she was on a roll, Cam pressed on. "Are we talking an either/or situation here?"

Lauren angled her head slightly. "I wouldn't be opposed to a both/and. Maybe even all three."

Even though they'd only slept together the once, Cam had the nagging feeling that getting enough of Lauren would be an elusive goal. That should probably worry her. It did, actually. But not enough to eclipse how badly she wanted her hands on Lauren again. How badly she wanted the feeling of Lauren over her, under her, wrapped completely around her. "That could be arranged. Want to come to my house for dinner? I'll cook for you this time, not just get you drunk."

"I wasn't drunk." Lauren poked a finger at her. "Tipsy, maybe, but I was fully in control of my faculties."

Cam had a flashback to the way Lauren's body responded to her touch, the way Lauren drove her absolutely crazy. "Yes, I'd say you were."

"But I'm not going to turn down dinner. What can I bring?"

"Not a thing." Cam looked around the room. "Are we done here, at least for the time being?"

Lauren's gaze followed and she nodded. "I think so. I really can't thank you enough for all your help."

"I'm not doing all that much. I mean, the carpet, yes. And reining in some of your crazier ideas. It's been fun, though, and I'm convinced I'm getting more out of this arrangement than you are."

"It's a mutually beneficial arrangement."

Cam smiled. That was one way of describing it. "The very best kind."

After Cam left, Lauren spent a couple of hours in her office, then embarked on a lazy pampering and grooming regimen. Given the amount of manual labor she'd been up to, it felt more like a necessity than an indulgence. She took her time getting dressed, then checked her reflection in the mirror and tucked a loose bit of hair behind her ear. She was going for casual but sexy. If that was even a thing. She left the bathroom and went to her dresser, picking up her favorite perfume and spritzing a little behind each ear and between her breasts.

Why was she nervous?

She'd been to Cam's already. They'd had sex already. All the pressure should be off. Only this time it was a given they'd sleep together. It wouldn't be some impulsive thing, giving in to a moment under the soft haze of a few drinks. No, this was intentional, deliberate.

She couldn't stop that from translating into having meaning. Or the possibility of meaning. Were they dating? Did she want to be dating? She'd never been obsessed with labels and had certainly had her share of hookups and friends with benefits through the years. This felt different, though. And she definitely got the sense Cam didn't operate that way.

Lauren slipped on a pair of flats and shook off the unease. She didn't feel the need to define it and, if Cam did, then it was on her to figure it out or start a conversation. Right? Right.

She grabbed her phone and the keys to Albert's car, mentally reminding herself that it was her car now. She'd just started to chuckle at herself when the phone rang. She smiled. Anja.

"Hey, girl."

"How would you feel if I descended on you a week early?"

"Uh." She'd love to see Anja sooner rather than later, but she wasn't ready for the photo shoots yet. "Does that mean you have to leave a week early, too?"

"No, I'd crash with you for a full three weeks, unless that's too much."

Lauren did a little happy dance at the answer. "There's no such thing as too much. I just wanted to make sure you're not in a hurry to take pictures. I'm still a work in progress over here."

"I'll help," Anja said quickly.

Anja was always ready to lend a hand, but something in her tone seemed off. "You okay?"

Anja groaned. "Yes. No, but yes. I was going to stay in Nice a couple of weeks, but I'm not feeling it anymore."

Lauren put two and two together. "Did things head south with Collette?"

Another groan. "She asked me to move in with her."

She fought the urge to laugh. "Horror of all horrors."

"Don't make fun. I think she was thinking about the M word."

"I'm sorry. I really am. Especially since you were only dating for like a month."

"Right? Even if I was the marrying sort, I'd be like, slow the fuck down. Christ."

Lauren did laugh then. For a woman so adamant about never settling down with a single person, Anja had the terrible luck of having women fall in love with her at the drop of a hat. "I would love to have you here for as long as you can stand to be in one place."

"Aw. Even if you're just saying that for free labor, it's sweet."

She thought about the look of concentration on Cam's face as she measured and banged in nails, the reluctant amusement at some of her quirkier artwork selections. "I'll never turn down the help, but things are in better shape than I thought."

"Did you cave and hire out more of it? I don't blame you."

"Sort of. I enlisted Cam's help in exchange for a photo shoot and a website." Although she had a sneaking suspicion Cam would have helped her regardless.

"Oh, so you just hired me out. Genius, you."

She appreciated the irony, even if she didn't agree with the sentiment. "I'm paying you for all the photo shoots."

"No, you're not. You're letting me stay for free in exchange for labor."

Lauren rolled her eyes. "We can argue about it when you arrive."

"Deal. So, what are you up to tonight?"

At the thought of her plans, Lauren's stomach did a flip. "Cam's making me dinner and then taking me to bed."

The statement was met with silence.

"Anja? You there?" Surely Anja wasn't scandalized. Lauren had told her about hooking up with Cam after their cocktail tasting.

"Huh? Oh, yeah. Just processing that."

"What's there to process? We've already slept together."

"Yeah, but sleeping together and making plans to sleep together are two different things." Of course Anja would go and have the same thought she'd just managed to shove out of her brain.

"Not really, though." More silence. Like a good twenty seconds. Damn it. "I mean, yes, it's intentional this time. But it doesn't have to mean anything."

"It does not."

Anja's agreement did more to get under her skin than flat-out denial. She had a unique talent to turn a mirror back on a situation and make Lauren see all the things she was trying to ignore. "But it might."

"Yes, it might."

Lauren closed her eyes. "I won't know either way if I'm late and blow my chance."

Anja laughed. She had a great laugh. Lauren was pretty sure women fell halfway in love with her for that alone. "Go. Get laid. Be merry."

"Thank you. When will I see you?"

"I'm going to change my flight and I'll send you the details. I can't wait to see this place. Oh, and this woman you've bedded."

Lauren laughed in spite of herself. "I'm excited to see you."

"You, too, lady."

Lauren ended the call and headed out the back door that led to the garage. She wouldn't be late, but she was cutting it close. She got into the car and hurried on her way, happy to focus her attention on the road instead of what her night with Cam might or might not mean.

CHAPTER EIGHTEEN

L auren pulled into the tiny drive adjacent to Cam's house. She sat for a minute, pulling herself back from the swirl of her thoughts and into the moment. The moment mattered, not the rest of it. She'd come to England to live in the moment, to seize it. She didn't need to know what the future held, at least not right now.

She'd just started up the walk when the front door opened and Cam appeared. She looked freshly showered and relaxed in a pair of jeans and a short-sleeved shirt. "Hello again."

This gorgeous woman was happy to see her, spend the night with her. This was a moment she could get behind. Lauren smiled and let the rest of her worries melt away. "Hi."

Cam took her hand and pulled her into the house. "I'm just roasting a chicken. I hope that's okay."

Lauren considered her meager attempts at cooking. She'd managed a roasted chicken once or twice, but considered it an impressive feat. Maybe now wasn't the time to own that. "Sounds and smells delicious."

"I thought we could eat outside. There aren't that many evenings around these parts good for it."

She followed Cam through the small living room to the kitchen. "I'd love that. I've actually been thinking about adding some outdoor seating at the pub. Do you think I'd need a permit? Just a few tables where the sidewalk is wide."

Cam angled her head. "I don't know, but I bet Jane would."

Not that she had a few thousand extra dollars in her budget, but more seating meant she could accommodate more paying customers. Assuming, of course, she might get to the point of having capacity issues. "I'll ask her."

"Something to drink? I have wine, if you'd like."

Lauren spied a half-empty pint glass on the counter. She'd surprised herself with how much of a beer drinker she'd become in a few short weeks. "Beer is fine."

Cam opened the fridge. "I've got Guinness and Landlord Pale Ale."

She'd yet to get on board with stouts. "I'll take a pale ale."

Cam poured the beer into a glass and handed it to her. "Cheers."

While Cam carved the chicken and served up plates, Lauren told her about Anja's accelerated arrival. Although still hesitant about being the subject of a photo shoot, Cam seemed genuine when she said she looked forward to meeting her. Which made sense, really. She'd learned a lot about Cam from getting to know Charlotte and, to a lesser extent, Cam's family. Cam didn't have that context for her.

She imagined sitting at the bar with Cam and Anja, Charlotte chiming in from the other side while she pulled pints. It was so vivid, so damned cozy, it made her breath catch.

"Are you okay?" Cam looked at her with concern.

Lauren shook off the sensation—mentally and physically. "Totally. Just a chill."

"I can get you a sweater or something."

So chivalrous. Did Cam even do it intentionally or was it ingrained? "I'm good. Promise. Let's eat."

They sat outside in what might have been the most charming garden Lauren had ever seen. Climbing vines dripping with flowers, herbs whose aromas wafted every time the breeze stirred. It was almost enough to make Lauren forget about what was to come. Almost. "This is magical."

"My mum has a green thumb. I'm a novice compared to her, but I like getting my hands in the dirt. Growing things."

"You're full of surprises, you know that?"

Cam blushed. "I've plans to grow vegetables, but I haven't managed to carve out enough time."

Much like the mental image of cozy time at the pub, Lauren's mind took off. She could see Cam on her knees, hands in the dirt. And she was right there with her, in garden gloves and a big floppy hat. What had gotten into her? "That sounds nice, but this is very pretty."

Cam smirked. "This isn't entirely impractical. I bring the herbs to work and use them."

"Of course you do." It shouldn't be so charming, but it was. Cam, like the garden, was turning out to be the manifestation of a fantasy Lauren didn't even know she had.

"You're making fun of me, aren't you?"

Lauren shook her head. She couldn't admit just how far she was from making fun. "Not at all."

"I'm going to take you to bed now. You'll have to take me seriously there."

The playfulness proved even more seductive than Cam at her most serious. Rather than assuring Cam she took her plenty seriously, Lauren lifted a shoulder in a casual shrug. "I guess you'll just have to show me."

They paused only long enough to bring the dishes inside. Cam waved off her offer to help wash. "Bed."

Lauren tucked her hand into Cam's and followed her to the back of the house. It was such a casually intimate gesture, at once foreign and familiar. Lauren couldn't take her eyes off of Cam's fingers, couldn't stop herself from imagining them on her skin, in her hair. Her breath caught for the second time that night. Only this time didn't come laden with meaning. No, this was one hundred percent desire.

In the bedroom, Cam flicked on a single lamp. She turned to face Lauren and rested her hands on the swell of Lauren's hips. Anticipation pulsed through her, without the worry of what might happen after. "I'll confess I've been thinking about getting you back here since the moment you left."

Lauren's smile was slow and sexy. "Then I'll confess I've been thinking about being here. You leave quite the impression on a girl."

Cam thought back to the first time, the way Lauren's body responded to hers. Part of her wanted simply to re-create that night, to strip Lauren of her clothes and lay her on the bed and do everything she'd been thinking about and craving for days. She resisted, saying instead, "You can be the boss this time, if that's what you want."

She had the pleasure of watching Lauren's eyes go wide. "I—"

"I'm teasing. Well, sort of. I know I pushed back last time, but it was more on principle than always needing to be on top."

The surprise in Lauren's eyes vanished. In its place, desire. It reinforced Cam's own desire to drag her to the bed and do all sorts of wicked things to her. The only thing that stopped her was having just told Lauren she didn't need to be in charge. And maybe a hint of curiosity about what it would be like to have Lauren running the show. Now that she'd made peace with her doing it in other arenas.

"Cam Crawley, are you ceding control?"

"Not sure I'm fond of the word ceding in this scenario, but—"

Lauren cut her off with a kiss. A long, slow kiss that turned her on but didn't give any indication of whether Lauren was going to take her up on the offer. When Lauren finally broke away and leaned back, her eyes were full of mischief. "It's not a competition, you know."

Cam had a reputation for being overly serious. She could trace it all the way back to elementary school, when she lost her temper with her friends' propensity for changing the rules halfway through a game. As an adult, it served her better, professionally if not personally. Now, with that teasing look in Lauren's eyes and the very phrase she'd used turned back on her, she longed to let go. And maybe, this once, she could. "I know."

"That said, I'm totally taking you up on it."

The playfulness caught Cam off guard. It shouldn't at this point, but it did. She wasn't sure what to do with it. She knew one thing not to do, and that was to analyze the shit out of it. "Right."

Lauren kissed her again. Still slow, but more demand than promise. She grabbed the front of Cam's shirt in her fists and pulled their bodies closer. Cam moved to wind her arms around Lauren's waist, but Lauren stepped back. "Nope. Not yet."

Her tone remained playful, but Cam could tell she was far from joking. Instead of saying anything, Cam placed her hands behind her back and laced her fingers together.

Lauren smiled. "Better."

Lauren closed the separation she'd created and started undoing the buttons of Cam's shirt. She nudged it from Cam's shoulders and Cam released her hands so it could fall to the floor. Lauren started on her jeans next, her manicured fingers nimble. She worked the jeans down Cam's legs, leaving her in a pair of trunks and a bra.

It felt strange to be wearing so little when Lauren remained fully clothed. "Is this a fully hands-off situation or do I get to touch you?"

Lauren stood and looked right into Cam's eyes. She was just a touch shorter, a fact Cam tended to forget because Lauren wore heels so often. "You can touch, but you can't take over. How's that?"

Hearing her say it made Cam want nothing more than to take over, but she wasn't going to take back the offer. And she had a feeling she'd have her way by the end of the night. "May I undress you?"

Lauren took a step back and offered a coy smile. "No, but you can watch."

There was no music, but that didn't stop Lauren from starting a slow, sensuous performance. Even in jeans and a tank top, she had the look of a legitimate erotic dancer. Not that Cam would know, technically speaking. But the way her hips dipped and swayed made Cam think this wasn't her first time doing a striptease.

Without stopping her movements, Lauren grasped the hem of her shirt and pulled it over her head. She tossed it at Cam. "Why don't you have a seat?"

It was as much a command as an invitation. Cam obliged, perching herself on the edge of the bed. Lauren's jeans came next. She took her time working them down her legs and somehow managed to step out of them gracefully. That left her in a candy apple red bra and matching lace thong.

She danced around a bit more, doing turns and pulling the clip that held her hair in place. The sandy waves fell around her shoulders, and Cam's fingers itched to touch. "How long are you planning to torture me?"

Lauren turned innocent eyes on Cam. "Are you not having a good time? I'd hate for you to feel tortured."

Cam laughed at the fluttery eyelashes and near pout on Lauren's full lips. "You know exactly what you're doing to me."

Lauren didn't stop moving, but she unclasped her bra and tossed it aside, slid the panties down and kicked them away. She pointed a finger at Cam and flicked it a couple of times. "Up."

She wasn't a fan of being bossed around in general, but this, this was different. She stood and made to take off her underwear, but Lauren shook her head. Cam cocked her head slightly. "I'm not going to dance for you, if that's what you're after."

That got a laugh out of Lauren. The low, sexy sound tested Cam's patience. She closed the distance between them and, without speaking, stripped Cam of her remaining clothing. Then she poked Cam in the chest, nudging her back onto the bed. Again with nothing more than a flick of her finger, Lauren got Cam to slide back and lie down.

Lauren took an eternity crawling up Cam's body, letting her nipples graze Cam's stomach, her chest. Then Lauren straddled her thighs. The heat of her body, the wetness, practically sent Cam over the edge. Then Lauren leaned in, placing a hand on either side of Cam's head. Her hair fell forward, creating a golden curtain around their faces. It was the sexiest thing she'd ever seen.

Of course, the view had nothing on the sensations Lauren was creating with her movements—a slow, deliberate grinding that drove Cam absolutely insane. Or the things Lauren whispered in between kissing and biting her neck and shoulders—things she wanted Cam to do to her, and just how hard and fast she wanted Cam to do them. But not yet. Each erotic suggestion came with a "soon" or a "not yet." Cam dug her fingers into Lauren's hips, unsure how much longer she could take it.

She was on the verge of saying as much, or of turning the tables and taking exactly what she wanted, when Lauren sat up. She put her hands in her hair and arched her back, writhing against Cam with even more intensity. She'd been wrong earlier. This, this exact moment, was the sexiest thing she'd ever seen.

Cam slid her hand across the front of Lauren's hip and pressed her thumb against Lauren's clit. She gasped. Cam fully expected to have her hand swatted away. At the very least, she anticipated Lauren telling her to wait, that she'd get her chance later. Instead, Lauren lifted herself slightly, giving Cam even more access.

It was an invitation she couldn't pass up. She slipped two fingers into Lauren. She expected her to be hot and wet and ready, but the way Lauren clamped around her, pulled her in, was exquisite. She let out an oath, let the fingers of her other hand sink just a bit deeper into Lauren's hip. She'd probably leave bruises, but Lauren didn't seem to mind.

If anything, Lauren wanted more. She rocked against Cam's hand. Her earlier statements about wanting things hard and fast returned, but there was nothing teasing about them this time. No, this was all command. Even as Cam fucked her, Lauren made it clear who was in charge. Rather than making Cam feel powerless, it spurred her on. Like only she could give Lauren exactly what she wanted.

When Lauren tightened around her, said her name in a hoarse whisper, Cam stayed with her. Lauren's whole body trembled, but she remained on her knees. It was a stunning thing to behold. She was glad Lauren's eyes were closed, because she didn't need Lauren knowing just how in awe the whole thing left her.

They stayed like that—Lauren's hands braced on Cam's shoulders and Cam's fingers buried inside her—for a long moment. Lauren's breathing evened out and she seemed to come back into herself. Her eyes fluttered open, and she looked at Cam with a smirk. "That wasn't fair."

Cam moved her fingers gently, but didn't pull them away. "I don't know what you're talking about."

"I was supposed to drive you crazy."

"Oh, but you did."

"Even if that's true, I'm going to have to take my revenge."

"Revenge? That sounds ominous." It didn't, at least in this context, but she was more than happy to play along.

Lauren eased herself away from Cam's hand and sat back, resting lightly on Cam's thighs. Cam would have been more than happy to keep doing that all night, but it was clear from the look on Lauren's face she had something else in mind. Cam smiled up at her, not worrying that she probably looked arrogant as hell.

Lauren scraped her nails lightly up Cam's side and across her rib cage. Up her breastbone and down her arms. Hovering somewhere between a scratch and a tickle, it drove Cam nuts. Lauren's gaze followed her hands and left Cam feeling exposed. She expected it to bother her, but it didn't.

After what felt like an eternity, Lauren paused and looked right into Cam's eyes. "I'd really like to put my mouth on you again, but if you like or want something else, I want you to tell me."

The directness would have been hot by itself. Paired with what Lauren said she wanted to do, it sent Cam's body into overdrive. "No. Nothing else."

"Are you sure? Because I aim to please."

The memory of Lauren's tongue, her lips wrapped around her, was permanently seared into Cam's brain. That Lauren wanted to do it again, that it might be her preference—it was enough to nudge her dangerously close to the edge.

"No? You're not sure?"

Cam realized that she'd been shaking her head. "No, sorry. I'm sure. So completely sure."

Lauren's smile conveyed a mixture of amusement and desire. It was a good look on her and made her, if it was even possible, more beautiful. "Good."

With that apparently settled, Lauren leaned forward and kissed her. A tease of tongue and teeth, it foreshadowed what Cam knew would follow. She worked her way down Cam's body, kissing and licking and nipping Cam's collarbones, her breasts, her stomach.

Lauren pressed her tongue to Cam's throbbing clit. Cam arched, the pleasure almost bordering on pain. Slower than the first time, teasing but still deliberate, Lauren made circles with her tongue. Cam settled into it, rocking slightly and letting the sensations radiate through her.

It would be so easy to come like this. Cam lifted her head and looked down. Yes, the swirl of Lauren's tongue and the image of her—eyes closed in concentration—would be enough to do it. But as though reading Cam's thoughts, Lauren chose that moment to open her eyes and look up at her. Those gorgeous hazel eyes conveyed just how much Lauren was enjoying herself. It made what she was doing all the more alluring.

Cam slid her fingers into Lauren's hair. She felt Lauren smile against her, heard her hum of pleasure.

Lauren shifted her mouth, wrapping her lips around Cam and beginning to suck gently. The extra sensation sent lightning bolts through her body, crackling through every muscle and organ. Cam tightened her grip on Lauren's hair, needing that contact, something to ground her and keep her from losing her thin hold on reality.

Lauren sucked harder, making the most incredible noises as she pulled Cam deeper into her mouth. Cam gave herself over to it, the orgasm crashing over her in waves. She rode it, powerless to do anything else.

She had no idea how much time passed between the end of her orgasm and when she had the wherewithal to open her eyes. It had gone fully dark outside, but Lauren remained between her legs, head resting on her thigh. Cam's mouth was dry and her limbs weak. "Oh, my God."

Lauren lifted her head and offered her a self-satisfied smile. "I know."

Cam shook her head, willing her mind to clear enough to formulate a coherent thought. "You're incredible. Do you know that?"

Lauren worked her way up the bed, once again straddling Cam's thighs. Cam didn't have quite enough circulation going to be aroused again, but the thought crossed her mind. "I really love doing that," Lauren said.

Cam swallowed the comment about it being the best sex of her life and settled on, "I love that you love it."

Lauren kissed her and then settled herself against Cam's side, draping one thigh over Cam's and an arm over her middle. Despite being only their second night together, it felt comfortable, familiar. Like they'd done it a thousand times before. Cam cleared her throat.

Lauren lifted her head and raised a brow. "Is that your way of getting my attention? Are you ready for round two?"

Cam wasn't one for spanking, but she took a swat at Lauren's bum. "Settle down, now."

Lauren turned her head and nipped Cam's shoulder. "You settle down."

The command ended in a yawn, answering any questions Cam had about Lauren wanting another go. She gave Lauren's shoulders a squeeze and kissed the top of her head. "Thanks for coming for dinner."

Lauren cozied into the crook of Cam's arm. "Thanks for having me."

Cam turned off the light and Lauren settled back in. In under a minute, Lauren's breathing grew even. Cam couldn't blame her. They'd put in a long day's work. She sighed and tried not to think about the mountain of work that would be waiting for her at the office after taking the day off.

It worked, but instead of drifting off, her mind turned to just how perfect Lauren felt in her arms. Those weren't thoughts she could afford to have. Even if—or maybe especially if—she'd already had a few unguarded moments of imagining what it would be like if Lauren stayed.

CHAPTER NINETEEN

Two nights at Cam's led to a third, then a fourth a few days later. Lauren might want nothing more than to spend every waking—and sleeping—moment in Cam's bed, but the clock was ticking and she had things to do. The floors of the final two rooms were done, and they had to be put back together. The furniture for the outdoor seating area had been approved and ordered and was scheduled to be delivered. She had one final run-through of the new menu with Mrs. Lucas and the cook she'd hired. And that said nothing of the new furniture for the pub itself, which she'd timed to come closer to the grand opening so it could be a big reveal.

She also had to get ready for Anja's arrival. Anja had refused a ride from the airport and Lauren hadn't argued, given a drive to London and back would take the better part of a day. But she wanted Anja's room to be perfect and everything to be comfortable and nice. She'd been casual about wanting to get out of Nice, but Lauren had a feeling she harbored some angst, if not a broken heart.

Even as she worked harder than on any campaign she'd ever run, she managed a handful of dinners and a half dozen nights more with Cam. They had intense conversations that reminded Lauren of the kind of all-consuming connections she'd experienced her first couple of years of college. They had pretend fights over some of the more whimsical artwork—beyond her animal portraits—and whether or not fish and chips needed to be an everyday thing on the menu.

And the sex. Good God, the sex. Lauren wouldn't have expected it to fizzle already, but she couldn't believe that it somehow managed to get better. Every night they spent together, and perhaps a couple of mornings, were consistently the best sex she'd ever had. It was like the better they got to know each other, and each other's bodies, the more pleasure there was to be had. It was bordering on absurd, to be honest.

Lauren shook off the daydream that threatened to take over her mind and looked around. She had the sketch of the new pub layout in her hands, and she was trying to decide if she could manage one more high-top table with stools. She shook her head. It was close, but probably better to order it now than risk not being able to get another in the same style. She could always tuck it away if it messed with the flow.

She pulled a pencil from behind her ear and made a note on the schematic. She'd call the company today and see if she could add on to the order. At this point, what was another thousand dollars?

"Ma'am?"

Lauren turned to find a burly redhead giving her an inquisitive look. She did a quick look past him to see a delivery truck parked in the street. The outdoor furniture. She smiled. "Yes?"

"Are you," he looked down at his clipboard, "Lauren Montgomery?"

"That's me. Please tell me you come bearing picnic tables."

He let out a chuckle and grinned at her. "You're right. I do."

His accent was Irish and his smile charming. Had she swung that way, she would have found him attractive. "Excellent. They're going right out front."

She led him out to the sidewalk and gestured to the area where she wanted them. The four tables had their own bench seating and would be difficult to move or steal. And since each one could hold six people, she could officially accommodate two dozen more patrons. Even if the math of that didn't work out perfectly much of the year, it made the front of the pub look more inviting.

The delivery guy waved his arm and another man climbed down from the truck. "All right?"

His accent matched the redhead's. It made her think about New York City, how you never quite knew who you might encounter or where they might be from. She expected a stab of homesickness, or at least nostalgia, but it didn't come.

"Could you sign here?"

Lauren pulled her attention back to the moment and signed for the delivery. She stood back and watched as the gorgeous wood tables came off the truck. With just a point of her finger, the guys set them where she wanted them and were on their way.

"Hey, those look really good."

The mere sound of Cam's voice sent a ripple of warmth through her. Lauren turned to find Cam and Jane walking up the street from the direction of Jane's office. "They do, don't they?"

Jane gave her a brief hug, then Cam leaned in and gave her a kiss on the cheek. The casual intimacy of it, especially in front of Jane, caught her by surprise. Pleasant surprise, but still. Jane gave her arm a gentle squeeze. "We were coming for lunch. May we be the ones to christen them?"

Lauren smiled. "Nothing would make me happier. Well, almost nothing."

Jane tipped her head to the side and offered her a curious look. "What would make you the happiest?"

To stay here and live happily ever after with Cam. The thought popped into her brain unbidden. Fortunately, it didn't pop out of her mouth. "Um," she struggled to formulate the response she'd initially intended. "For it to be the day after the opening and for everything to have gone perfectly."

"But then you would have missed the party," Jane said.

Lauren braved a glance at Cam. She looked relaxed and maybe amused. Nothing indicated she had any clue where Lauren's mind had gone. Phew. "The real party will be with all of you once all the work is done. This is like pitching to a client—a massive amount of work that you hope will impress, but you really have no idea how it will be received until it's done."

Lauren shrugged and Cam nodded, surprised by how much Lauren's assessment of the situation resonated. She'd have imagined

Lauren to be all about the big show, being the center of attention. Which maybe she did some, but she also acknowledged it as work. Just one more little surprise along the way. "I know what you mean."

Lauren took a deep breath and rolled her shoulders a few times. "I'm not panicking. It's all going to be fine."

The mini pep talk was downright adorable. But before she could say as much, Sophie came strolling toward them. Cam offered her a nod of greeting. "Decide to come after all?"

"The pull of lunch is strong."

"Would you like to join us?" Jane asked Lauren.

Just a couple of weeks ago, the prospect of sharing a meal with her sisters and Lauren would have filled Cam with, if not dread, apprehension. Now? It sounded quite nice, actually. "You should. I'd wager money you haven't eaten."

"I'll have you know I ate a full breakfast this morning." Lauren grinned. "Mrs. Lucas made me."

Cam chuckled. "It doesn't preclude you from lunch."

"No, but my to-do list does. My best friend arrives today and I need to be ready for her."

"The photographer." Cam resisted the urge to cringe.

"Yes, the photographer. Stop acting like it's going to be torture."

"Cam is going to be photographed?" Sophie didn't even try to hide her amusement.

Lauren nodded enthusiastically. "She doesn't want to be the official face of the campaign, but I've convinced her that a few shots of her with the still and in the tasting room would enhance the editorial spreads we're doing."

Sophie's gaze went from Cam to Lauren and back to Cam. "You have to let me watch."

Cam shook her head. "Absolutely not."

Sophie turned an imploring look to Lauren. "Please."

"I'm getting the feeling your intent is to make Cam squirm. Since I need her to be relaxed, I'm going to have to side with her." Lauren's tone was equal parts apologetic and playful. She might not have siblings, but she was getting the hang of how they worked.

"Thank you." Cam shot Sophie the same look she used when one of their parents took her side. Some habits, it seemed, died hard.

Sophie huffed, but with no malice. "Fine. I'll laugh at you from afar."

Cam rolled her eyes. "You always do."

Lauren cleared her throat. "As much fun as this is, I need to get back to work. Enjoy your lunch and the new seating."

"It really does look nice," Jane said.

"Thank you." Lauren waved a hand in the direction of the tables. "And you all sitting here will be like free advertising."

Sophie made a point of sitting on one of the benches and posing. "Happy to help."

Lauren went back inside, leaving Cam on the sidewalk with her sisters. "Shall we go order?"

"Shall we first talk about how you're all loved up?" Sophie stared pointedly after Lauren.

Cam shook her head. "No. We shall not."

Sophie gave her a most exasperated look. "Come on. I've barely given you a hard time and you were practically drooling over her."

Jane pinched her arm. "Don't be mean, Sophie."

"Yes, Sophie. Don't be mean." She didn't really mind Sophie's teasing, but if she didn't push back, Sophie would be completely out of control.

Sophie scowled dramatically. "I'm not mean. I'm telling the truth. A truth Jane was in perfect agreement with a bit ago."

Cam turned to Jane. "*Et tu?*"

Jane shrugged, looking sheepish and innocent in that way she always could. "I only agreed that you seemed happier than I've seen you in a long time."

It was hard to argue that point. Feelings for Lauren aside, she was happy. Even with all the battles over the pub, she felt good about the outcome. And she had a renewed energy about Carriage House, fueled by Lauren's enthusiasm and a real optimism about the new marketing strategy.

"See." Sophie pointed at her. "You're not even denying it."

"Happiness is a lot more than being head over heels for someone." Not that she was ready to use that phrase about Lauren anyway.

Jane gave her a pat on the shoulder. "Exactly. You have plenty to be happy about."

Although Jane didn't have a patronizing bone in her body, Cam cringed at the gesture. If Jane felt compelled to reassure her, it meant she saw something, too. Which meant Lauren might very well be picking up on it, whatever it was. She lowered her voice so that only her sisters could hear. "I like Lauren. Things with us are good. But let's not turn it into more than it is."

Sophie nodded slowly. "You're not sure if she loves you back."

As much as Sophie could be a thorn in her side, she was insightful. It made her a great ally and also a giant pain. "We like each other fine, but no one is using the L word or talking about the future."

Jane offered a sympathetic look. "It's okay. You don't owe us any explanation. Unless you want to talk about it, of course. Then we're happy to listen. Right, Sophie?"

Sophie sighed but nodded. "Right. We want you to be happy and stuff."

Cam chuckled at the reluctant affection. When push came to shove, she'd lucked out in the family department. It was something she tried not to take for granted, especially when she thought about people like Lauren, who didn't seem close to her family at all.

She shook off the doldrums that threatened to creep in at the thought of Lauren being estranged from her family. Lauren didn't seem too bothered by it or, at least, like she managed it just fine. She had—what did she call it?—her family of choice. And from what she'd gathered, Anja sat pretty close to the top of that list.

It made Cam all the more interested in meeting her. First, to see the kind of person Lauren chose to associate with. But perhaps even more importantly, to see Lauren in that dynamic. She'd meant what she said to Sophie and Jane. She wasn't in love with Lauren, but it had started to feel like more than a passing thing. That meant she wanted to get to know her on a deeper level. And in her book, meeting the family was one of the best ways to do it.

CHAPTER TWENTY

A nja turned in a slow circle. "Damn, girl."
Lauren smiled, more pleased with the declaration than any elaborate compliment. "Thanks."

"It looks like a movie. For real."

She thought back to the day she arrived, exhausted and overwhelmed. She'd envisioned a complete makeover, had fought Cam tooth and nail on some of the original details that felt just a little too tired, a little too tacky for even a quirky design. They'd compromised on so many things. A wave of giddiness bubbled up in her chest.

"You're not even thinking about the inn right now, are you?"

"What? Of course I am. The grand opening is in two weeks. What else would I be thinking about?"

"A certain distiller you've promised to introduce me to."

Lauren smiled in spite of herself. "You'll meet her soon enough."

"You're in love with her, aren't you?"

They'd not used that word, at least not out loud. But she'd thought it a few times. It still felt too soon. She'd not added it up, but it seemed like Cam had disliked her for longer than she hadn't. Even though they couldn't seem to get enough of each other now. Even though the sex was, without a doubt, the best she'd ever had. Even though the prospect of selling the inn and going back to New York held less and less appeal with each passing day.

"You don't have to say anything. Your face tells me all I need to know."

Lauren lifted a hand. "I'm not sure about capital L love, but it's more than I bargained for. That much I'll give you."

Anja laughed—not a titter or a chuckle, but long and loud, the kind of laugh that told Lauren she had her number. "I can't wait to meet the woman who's put you in this state of more than you bargained for."

"How about I show you to your room first? I'm sure you'd like to settle in."

Anja nodded affably. "Whatever you say, boss."

Lauren hefted one of Anja's bags and led her through to the inn. Upstairs, she opened the door to the room she'd reserved for Anja. Not the biggest room, but her favorite. It held the most personal touches—bits of her and bits of Cam.

"Okay, this is even better than I imagined." Anja dropped her bag and turned another slow circle. "How much of this is you?"

"New paint, new art, new linens." She smiled at the portrait of the hare in a blazer, then pointed to the table turned writing desk. "Oh, and that. Cam helped me refinish it."

Anja crossed the room and trailed her fingers over its glossy surface. "You did this?"

Lauren shrugged. "With help. Cam is handy."

"Handy, a craft gin maker, and amazing in the sack. Why aren't you marrying her, again?"

"It's not that simple." Lauren closed her eyes and let out a sigh. When she opened them, she found Anja looking at her expectantly. "She really didn't like me at first."

"She didn't think she liked you. The second she gave you a chance, she was a goner." Anja tipped her head from side to side. "Which is not surprising, by the way."

How could she explain? Even after coming to a detente, even after hopping into bed together, she couldn't help but think Cam was holding part of herself back. "She's come around, for sure. But I don't think she thinks of me as marriage material."

"What is that supposed to mean? I'd marry you in a second."

Lauren fisted her hands on her hips, but smiled. "Are you proposing?"

"No, but only because you'd want me to settle down."

Lauren laughed. "I know better than to think you'd be so inclined."

"If I were to settle down, and if I didn't already know I'd drive you crazy, you'd be at the top of my list." Anja crossed the room and gave Lauren a noisy kiss on the cheek.

"I love you, too." Lauren glanced at her watch. "It's early still. Do you want to take a nap?"

Anja shook her head. "Just a shower. And then I want the full tour and to meet all your people."

"Charlotte will be here any minute. Cam will stop by at some point. She wants to meet you, too. Why don't you meet me back downstairs when you're ready?"

"Can there be food in my future?"

Lauren smiled. Anja was always hungry. "Of course. Do you need a snack to tide you over?"

Anja seemed to consider, then sighed dramatically. "No. I ate a sandwich on the ride."

She shook her head. "All right. Lunch service will be starting in about an hour. You can have your pick."

"Excellent. I can't wait to try your new menu."

Mention of the menu made her think, once again, of Cam. "You will be well fed, I promise."

"You know just what to say to a girl." Anja hefted one bag onto the bed and unzipped it.

"Towels and such are in the bathroom. And I'd love your thoughts on the new line of toiletries I picked."

"Ooh." Anja's eyes lit up. "I bet they're amazing."

Lauren backed toward the door. "Take your time and message me if you need something. Or, even better, call the front desk. We could use the practice."

"Do you want me to pretend I forgot my toothbrush?"

Lauren chuckled. She'd stocked a cabinet of emergency supplies for just such a thing. "No. But really, if you need anything, just holler."

"Yes, ma'am."

"Enjoy your shower. Or bath."

"There's a tub?"

She forgot how many hotels, even on the high end, had done away with tubs. "Claw foot. Original."

"Sweet lesbian goddess. I may be a while. Don't wait up."

"It's ten thirty in the morning."

Anja quirked a brow. "And your point is?"

Lauren laughed again. God, she'd missed her. "Like I said, take your time."

She left Anja to her own devices and headed downstairs. She'd check on Mrs. Lucas, then head back to the pub to do some ordering with Charlotte. Because as much as Anja joked, Lauren figured it would be at least an hour until she emerged, and Lauren didn't have an hour to waste.

An hour and a half later, Lauren sat at the bar, oddly nervous. It made no sense for her to be nervous. It's not like Anja was her father, impossible to please and even harder to impress, or her mother, kind but still at a loss over what to do with a daughter who was ambitious and attracted to women. This was a friendly blending of her worlds—her favorites from each coming together in celebration. She had nothing to prove to any of them.

"You okay?" Charlotte studied her from across the bar, a look of concern on her face.

"Absolutely." Lauren smiled and hoped it didn't look forced. "I'm excited to meet Anja. It feels like getting a little glimpse into New York Lauren."

She'd not meant anything by it, but the phrasing struck a nerve. That's what had her anxious. Not that Anja wouldn't like Charlotte and Cam, or vice versa. She was afraid of starting a chain reaction, one where her old self took over and steamrolled everything her new self had built and, in the process, sent Cam running for the hills. She shook her head. That wouldn't happen, for more reasons than she could count. At the top of the list was the fact that Anja was about as easygoing and un-New York as it got. Well, maybe not un-New York. More Greenwich Village than Madison Avenue.

"I can't believe those tubs are original. Absolute gold mine." In usual fashion, Anja didn't bother with a hello. She bounded up to the bar and pulled Lauren into a hug. Like they'd not hugged four times already since her arrival. "I want to stay forever."

Lauren smiled and gestured toward the bar. "Charlotte, this is my friend Anja. Anja, this is my right-hand woman, Charlotte."

Charlotte extended her hand, but Anja was already running around the back of the bar. "I'm so excited to meet you. Lauren has been raving about you since the day she got here."

Charlotte seemed taken aback by the display of affection, but not bothered. In fact, she returned the hug with enthusiasm. Was that a hint of attraction? Impossible to know for sure, but Lauren had known Anja long enough to sense when she was into someone. This definitely felt like one of those times.

Anja stepped back but didn't immediately retreat from behind the bar. She surveyed the setup and nodded. "Nice bar."

Charlotte smiled. Or was it a flirtatious smirk? "Lauren let me make some improvements."

"She's cool like that. You'll let me take pictures, right, of you back here?"

Charlotte glanced at Lauren, then Anja, and raised a brow. "Me?"

"Featuring staff in the photography makes a place feel more cozy," Anja said, and Lauren nodded her agreement. Then she added, "The fact that you're gorgeous is a total bonus."

Lauren feared for a second that it was too much, that Anja's big, flirtatious personality might overwhelm Charlotte's more staid British sensibilities. But as she watched Charlotte give Anja a slow smile, it became clear she worried for naught.

"Good morning, ladies."

Lauren knew it was Cam before she even turned around. As it seemed to do these days, her heart rate ticked up a few notches. She turned around slowly, letting her eyes rake over Cam and letting her brain relive a few moments of the night before. The sex had been fueled by the knowledge they'd probably not have a moment alone until after the opening, which was well over a week away.

But neither that knowledge nor just how sated she'd felt only hours before had any effect on her libido at the moment. No, all she wanted to do was push Cam up against the wall and undo her pants and—

"Lauren?"

How long had she been staring? Lauren looked around. Long enough for both Charlotte and Anja to be watching her with amusement. And Cam. Cam looked amused, too, but also aroused. It helped to know she wasn't alone on that front. "What?"

"You need to make introductions," Anja said, even though it was apparent she already knew exactly who'd come in.

Before Lauren could stitch together a sentence, Cam stepped forward. "You must be Anja. Lauren's been talking about you nonstop."

Anja took Cam's extended hand. "And you must be Cam." She offered Cam a wink. "Same."

She would have expected the attention to make Cam uncomfortable, but it didn't seem to. Cam offered Anja a warm smile and asked about her trip, where she'd been before. So different from their first meeting, when Cam had been cool and aloof. They'd certainly come a long way. "Why do I get the feeling you two will be dishing about me before the day is through?"

"It's best friend, girlfriend prerogative," Anja said without hesitation.

Lauren glanced at Cam, but again, not even a trace of discomfort. A long way indeed.

"Speaking of, don't you have that interview to do?" Anja asked.

She did. The writer from *Traveler* was due to call within the hour. She should go prep for it. Even if the idea of leaving Cam, Anja, and Charlotte alone left her a hair uneasy. "Do any of you need anything from me before I go hole up?"

Anja shook her head blandly. Cam looked amused. Charlotte called over from the bar. "Will you go already so we can talk about you?"

Lauren chuckled. At least they were honest. "You know where to find me."

She escaped to her office and spent a bit of time sorting out the talking points she wanted to work in and a list of photos she already had in mind to send along to accompany the story. When Alejandro called promptly at one, she was in full PR mode.

After a brief exchange of pleasantries, Alejandro dove right in. "Tell me about how you came to take on this project?"

Lauren took advantage of the fact they were doing a phone interview and rolled her eyes. There were some parts of the story that didn't need to be told. "The inn and the attached pub, the Rose & Crown, fell into my lap, quite literally. It was left to me by a relative. I considered a quick sale, but once I arrived, it really spoke to me. I decided to try my hand at this end of the hospitality industry and never looked back."

"You went beyond basic sprucing up, though. You've given this place a whole new identity."

"Well, it wasn't without its charms, but people weren't beating down the door to stay here, if you know what I mean. Netherfield isn't a place that brings in a lot of visitors, so the Rose & Crown had to be a destination unto itself."

Alejandro made noises of agreement. "You've partnered with Barrister's, though, haven't you? They're based nearby?"

"Yes, and I couldn't have asked for a better company to work with. Not only are they a tried-and-true brand in the industry, the launch of Carriage House felt like a perfect match for the new and improved Rose & Crown."

"Sounds like a match made in heaven."

Lauren smiled to herself. No need for him to know that part of the story, either. "Absolutely."

He asked about the new menu in the pub and the rooms, travel from London, and things to do in the area. Lauren appreciated that he'd clearly written dozens of features like this before and knew what he was doing. She talked up Cam and how great it had been to work with her, got in a plug for the wool works. He wrapped up his questions and she promised to send him the photographs and press kit. She closed with an invitation to the grand opening and was pleasantly surprised when he said he'd try to make it since he'd be in Dublin the week before on another assignment.

Lauren hung up the phone almost giddy. Even if she had the money, she couldn't buy the press a write-up in a magazine like *Traveler* would create. She did a little happy dance, then left her office to go share the good news. She found the three of them exactly where she'd left them. Well, not exactly. Anja and Cam had claimed seats at the bar, and Cam and Charlotte were both bent over with laughter. "Do I even want to know?"

At the sound of Lauren's voice, Cam looked up. She found Lauren regarding her—them, really—with a mixture of amusement and suspicion. The same look might have given her pause just a couple of months ago, but now it stirred up a whole different set of feelings. A few that gave her a whole different kind of pause, but that was a worry for another day.

"Probably not." Anja shrugged. "I was telling them about the Lexington pitch."

Lauren groaned. "Of course you did. I'll never live that down."

Cam had found it endearing to hear about one of Lauren's misadventures. It made her all the more real, more relatable. "How did the interview go?"

"Amazing." Lauren paused on each syllable. "He's doing a full feature on the inn and pub and might even make it to the opening."

"He's going to write an article, just like that?" Cam shook her head in disbelief. Lauren had implied that might be the case, but she figured it would be something small. Not inconsequential, just small.

"I mean, it helps that I've worked with him before."

"So, is he doing you a favor?"

Lauren tipped her head back and forth. "Yes and no. More a mutual benefit thing. I pretty much gave him the story wrapped up pretty with a bow on top, saving him a ton of legwork. I also gave him first dibs on the story."

Cam continued to shake her head. It made sense, the way Lauren explained it, but she still couldn't believe it was as simple as that. Either Lauren was more talented in her line of work than Cam had given her credit for or her own efforts on that front had been even clumsier than she cared to admit.

"I think Barrister's and Carriage House will get a nice mention, too. I was able to work in the classes as well as the tastings and tour."

"That's really great." And almost too easy.

"Why do you look so unhappy, then?"

"I'm plenty happy. Surprised, maybe. You make it seem so easy."

Lauren crossed her arms over her chest. "I am pretty good at this, you know."

"You are." Cam nodded. "I'm sorry if I haven't given you enough credit."

"I think I like it when you're conciliatory." Her smirk managed to be both playful and sexy.

Cam knew Charlotte and Anja were watching and likely forming opinions as the conversation played out, but she couldn't resist returning the suggestive look. "Don't get used to it."

Lauren laughed teasingly. "Don't worry. I won't."

Before Cam could respond, Jane walked in. Another round of introductions ensued. It didn't take long for Cam to find herself scheduled for her photo shoot and tasked with securing a long list of props Lauren insisted they needed. She had a quick lunch with Jane and headed back to the distillery. As she had on so many occasions with Lauren, she felt a little bit like she'd been swept up in a whirlwind of tasks, ideas, and energy. The funny thing was, she didn't mind so much anymore. In fact, she was kind of getting used to it.

CHAPTER TWENTY-ONE

When Lauren gave her the list of things she wanted for the photo shoot, Cam almost didn't take her seriously. But then the list was so detailed, with descriptions that bordered on paragraphs, it became clear she wasn't kidding. The bossiness of it should have bristled, but it didn't. Maybe because the intensity of Lauren's attention was focused on her, on something she cared so much about.

It took the better part of the morning to hunt up everything on it, including a trip to the market and to her herb garden. They'd agreed to do the shoot in the tasting room, so she hauled everything there and arranged it on the back bar. Once she had it all set up, and no longer had a task to keep her busy, the nerves kicked in. She'd never been the subject of a photo shoot. To be honest, she had no desire to be. She liked working behind the scenes, letting her product shine instead of herself.

But Lauren had been adamant. And for all that her friend Anja seemed more laid-back, she'd been adamant, too. Cam had managed to convince herself it wouldn't be a big deal, but now that the day had arrived, it was a different story.

She'd just started to work out an excuse to change course when Lauren and Anja arrived. Their energy took up all the space in the room and they talked a mile a minute, not giving her the chance to speak, much less argue. They bustled around, arranging things and setting up lights. In spite of getting more anxious by the minute, she had to admire how efficient and professional they seemed. Like they did this sort of thing for a living.

By the time they were done, she'd talked herself out of throwing a tantrum and refusing to participate. Mostly. "Tell me again why I have to be the face of Carriage House?"

Lauren laced her fingers together and gave her a patient smile. "Because having the distiller be the face is way more authentic than hiring a model and your brand is about authenticity without pretense."

"And you're hot," Anja said without looking up from her camera.

Cam pinched the bridge of her nose. "You don't have to fluff me up with flattery. I've already agreed to this."

"I'm not flattering you, I'm speaking the truth." She pointed at Cam and made little circles with her finger. "You've got a nice face there. The camera is going to love it."

She couldn't tell if they meant what they were saying or if this was the standard spiel to butter up a reluctant subject. Not that it mattered. Either notion made her squirm. "I'm going to stop complaining because the compliments are making me more uncomfortable than the prospect of being photographed."

Lauren grinned. "That's the spirit."

The concept seemed sound enough, but the reality of her face appearing in adverts gave her more panic than she cared to admit. She reminded herself doing it was cheaper than hiring a model—a silly argument, but she clung to it, like she was taking one for the team or something. "All right. Let's get on with it, then."

"I'm going to do a few test shots for lighting." Anja pointed to the bar they'd set up for the shoot. "Stand there, but you don't have to pose or anything."

Cam did as she was told, giving herself a pep talk that included the veto power she'd been promised if she hated how the photos came out. Anja's camera clicked away, giving her the chance to practice tuning it out. Instead, she focused her attention on the setup. Three bottles of Carriage House stood in a little cluster. A cutting board, some lemons and grapefruit, and a vintage cocktail shaker were artfully arranged. She'd thought the sprigs of juniper cheesy, but they provided a nice splash of green to the arrangement.

When exactly had she started using the phrase "splash of green"? She shook her head. She just needed to get through the next hour. Lauren had promised it wouldn't last longer than that. She could do anything for an hour.

"Okay, we're ready."

Cam expected Lauren to take charge, but she didn't. In fact, she stepped out of Cam's line of sight entirely. Anja gave her directions—pouring gin, shaking a cocktail. There was a lot of clicking. A few times, she asked Cam to look her way. Smile, don't smile, look at the cutting board. She also took some shots at close range, capturing the label and nothing more than Cam's hand. Maybe she'd get lucky and they'd use those.

"You're doing great. Just a few more." Anja's voice was encouraging without being patronizing and her directions were clear and confident. It was enough to make her relax, at least in relative terms.

When Anja announced they were done, she was genuinely surprised. "Really?"

Anja grinned at her. "Unless you want to keep going."

Cam chuckled at the statement and the gentle teasing behind it. "No, no, I think I'm good."

Lauren appeared from the background. "You were a natural."

She'd not forgotten Lauren was there. She could never really lose track of Lauren being in the same space as her. But it was the closest she'd come since they'd met. Cam chalked it up to Anja's skill as a photographer that she'd commanded so much focus. "Let's not exaggerate."

Anja shook her head. "No, she's right. I do this a lot. You looked comfortable, completely in your element. These shots are going to be perfect."

"Now what?"

Lauren came up next to her and slid an arm through hers. "You can look at them with us, but I warn you it can be overwhelming. If you want, we'll do the initial round and bring you a couple dozen to consider."

Although Lauren was in a sundress and a cardigan, Cam could imagine her in the power suit, gently steering the client where she wanted. "I'm getting the full treatment right now, aren't I?"

Lauren balked and Anja laughed out loud. She angled her head in Cam's direction. "She's got your number, doesn't she?"

Lauren gave Cam a coy smile. "Something like that."

It would be easy to while away the rest of her day like this, but she had work to do. "Can I make you two a cocktail with all these ingredients we have out? You're welcome to stay here while you work."

Anja actually clapped. "Oh, I was hoping there'd be cocktails."

Cam made them each a drink and escaped to the quiet of her office. Once there, she booted up her computer and pulled up the distilling schedule for the next couple of months. Carriage House was only booked for two of the next ten weeks. She didn't want to cut production of Barrister's, but it would be nice to need more Carriage House. They had the capacity to add some cycles to the calendar if demand increased, but she was hesitant to make the investment without the orders in hand.

She let herself think about what that might be like—demand she could hardly keep up with. It came with its own host of problems, of course, but at this point, they'd be problems she'd be happy to have. Cam shook her head. No point putting the cart before the horse. She chuckled at herself, along with the cheesy analogies she'd resorted to, and got back to work.

"Oh, that's a good one." Anja pointed at the screen. "Cam is so photogenic."

"She is." Lauren swallowed the emotion that swelled in her chest. Arousal, sure, but there was more to it.

Anja continued to scroll through the images. "Seriously, there isn't a bad one here."

"Yeah." She thought of her own photo shoot the day before. They'd come away with quite a few keepers, more than enough to use in the campaign and enough to give Lauren's ego a little boost. But she had nothing on this. Seeing Cam this way—confident, at ease, completely in her element—did things to Lauren's heart. She shook her head. She was being sentimental. It had to be the magnitude of the opening right around the corner. Right?

"Are you still going to try to convince me you're not in love with her?"

Lauren pulled her eyes from the screen and looked at her. The reality of her feelings felt like an elephant on her chest. "No."

Anja beamed. "I'm so happy for you."

"I'm not sure the feelings are mutual." She shook her head. "And even if they are, I don't know what to do with them."

"You always make everything so complicated."

Lauren chuckled at the assumption. "I don't make them that way. They just are."

"Are you happy here?"

God. What a loaded question.

"Don't layer it with all the ifs and buts and bullshit. Simple question, yes or no answer only. Are you happy here?"

"Yes." She didn't need to think about her answer and it absolutely terrified her.

"Well, I'm glad you can admit it. I won't poke at you more, at least for now. We've got too much to do."

So much to do. "Thanks."

"Let's pick the ones we want for your article so I can polish them up and plug them in. Then I'll make a flash drive of all the others for you to use for Carriage House."

Lauren nodded, relieved to have tasks that would demand her time and attention for the next few days. "You're the best."

Anja tipped her head to the side and winked. "I know."

They packed up Anja's equipment and the laptop. Cam hadn't returned, and Lauren felt strange seeking her out while she was working, so they left without saying good-bye. Back at the inn, she helped carry everything into Anja's room and then went to her own office.

Her to-do list for the opening still felt at least a mile long. The rooms, at least, were done, along with the minor refurbishments to the pub and common area. Everything that remained was important, but if people literally showed up today, she'd at least have somewhere to put them.

She started with a couple of phone calls—one to the florist she'd contracted with and one to the musicians she booked. She smiled as she placed a check mark next to each. So satisfying.

Next up, email. She wanted to confirm with Alejandro she'd be sending all the photos they'd discussed for the story in the next couple of days. Lauren pulled up her inbox and frowned. At the top of her unread messages sat one from Chrissy, her admin from KesslerAldridge. It was marked urgent. She clicked on the message and skimmed its contents. The vague foreboding from seeing the header multiplied exponentially. The misgiving took shape, clear and concrete and ugly. With it, the image of Philip filled her mind.

She went back to the beginning and read the email again. Phrases like "sexual harassment" and "hostile work environment" blurred together with "wrongful termination" and "civil suit." Lauren's vision blurred. She closed her eyes for a moment, took a few breaths, and tried again.

On the third read, meaning began to take shape. Philip, it seemed, had made quite a habit of treating women in the company badly and was now the subject of a massive complaint and possible civil lawsuit. She was being asked to give a deposition, and possibly, eventually, testify.

Her palms grew sweaty and a muscle over her left eye started to twitch. A torrent of emotions vied for the top spot in her mind. Renewed anger over what he'd done sparred with grim satisfaction that he might be held accountable. Wanting to be part of taking him down warred with never wanting to see him again. And on top of it all, a blanket of guilt for not reporting him the second he touched her.

The most suffocating part was the guilt, the idea that another woman might have been touched, been undermined, because she didn't act when she could have. It left this hollow ache in her rib cage, but also made it feel like she couldn't breathe.

She couldn't deal with this right now. She didn't have time. After the opening.

Even as she told herself that, she shook her head. No. She wouldn't run this time. She would face Philip and KesslerAldridge head-on, and she'd take them down. Well, at least Philip. She didn't necessarily wish fire and brimstone on the agency. She flashed back to the day she was fired without even the courtesy of being asked for her side of the story. Maybe a little fire and brimstone.

Before she could second-guess herself, she hit reply. Yes, she would give a deposition. Yes, she could be in New York sometime in the next month. Yes, she was interested in learning more about a wrongful termination suit.

She clicked send and then stared at the screen. It would be fine. She did want to deal with this once and for all. And she hadn't been home in almost three months, much longer than she anticipated when she left.

She sighed. Home. She'd not stopped thinking about New York as home, but putting it into words felt off. It must be a time and distance thing. She hadn't been away from the city for so long since, well, ever. And she'd let her life here consume everything. Intentionally, but still.

The full reality of her life and choices came crashing down on her. Not in a devastating or traumatic sort of way. More like an ostrich with its head in the sand. Focusing on the Rose & Crown had been so easy. It demanded her energy and her skills, challenged her to do and try things she never had before. Along the way, it had stopped feeling like a means to an end. That wasn't a bad thing in itself, but it wasn't a viable long-term plan. Nor did she want it to be.

She just needed to remember that and keep perspective. That went for the career and the plans she'd left in New York as much as the heart and soul she'd poured into making over the pub. And whether she liked to admit it or not, it also went for her relationship with Cam.

CHAPTER TWENTY-TWO

With the grand reopening only a day away, Lauren felt like she should be frantic. Really, though, everything was ready. More than ready, actually. Thanks to Cam's help and Anja's last-minute design inspiration, both the pub and the inn were ready to show off. She almost felt bad about closing the pub to the public for a couple of days since she didn't technically need to, but it would build excitement.

She could use all the excitement she could get.

The inn was booked to capacity with invited guests. Everyone in town was buzzing with enthusiasm. That would only carry her so far, though. If the excitement didn't carry over into sustained bookings and more daily customers, she'd be no better off than when she started. Worse, really, since she'd sunk close to a hundred grand of her savings into the place.

She wouldn't think that way. She couldn't. Lauren stood up from her desk and decided to go in search of Charlotte. She could obsess about Cam instead.

Charlotte was at her usual spot behind the bar, arranging bottles. She looked up at Lauren and smiled. "Have I thanked you yet today for my new setup?"

Lauren chuckled. "Not yet today, but I think you've thanked me a hundred times, so we're good."

"It's so perfect, though."

"And a solid management decision on your part. Having a stylish and functional space behind the bar makes for a better experience for those in front of it."

"Right." Charlotte nodded. She'd settled into her additional responsibilities nicely. Whatever Lauren ultimately did with the place, she felt good about how the pub would be managed. And she'd do everything in her power to make sure Charlotte stayed on.

"Are you feeling ready for tomorrow?" Lauren asked.

"Beyond ready. Cam and I were just talking about how far everything has come."

Lauren laughed at the choice of phrase. "And I think she might finally believe it's a good thing."

Charlotte's face softened. "She really does, you know."

"I do." Lauren sighed, uneasy, but unable to put her finger on why.

"Change hasn't always been a good thing in her life, if you know what I mean." The way Charlotte looked down, shrugged slightly, made Lauren want to press.

"I know it's technically none of my business, but," she hesitated for a moment, not sure how much she wanted to know. "You and Cam?"

Charlotte smiled. "You want to know the specifics of our history?"

"I mean, yes, but you're completely within your rights to tell me it's none of my damn concern."

"I'm pretty open, in case you hadn't noticed."

"Oh, I noticed." From talking about herself to the easy way she'd clicked with Anja, Lauren had both admired and envied Charlotte's obvious comfort with feelings and relationships.

"There really isn't that much to tell beyond what I already have. I'm not the one who broke her heart."

Lauren's own heart lurched. Was it wrong to learn details like this from someone other than Cam herself? "Who was?"

"Her name was Amelia. I shouldn't overstate matters. It wasn't some devastating heartbreak for the ages or anything."

"But?"

"But it just reinforced all her instincts that change is a bad thing."

"Oh." That explained a lot.

"They were together for a while. Two years, maybe? I never thought they were right for each other, but I'm pretty sure Cam would have married her."

It was clearly in the past, but the thought of Cam marrying another woman did unpleasant things to her stomach. "Why didn't she?"

"Amelia was a restless sort. Wanted to move to London and live a more fast-paced life. Cam took it really personally that Netherfield wasn't enough for her."

Or that Cam wasn't enough. It made perfect sense that Cam started out resistant to her ideas, to her very presence. "Thank you for sharing that with me."

Charlotte shrugged again. "None of it is secret, really."

No, but it was information she'd not gotten from Cam. Not that Cam was withholding, just that they'd had no conversations about past relationships. Even without knowing what her future with Cam would be—or if it would be—understanding her better mattered.

As if summoned by their conversation, Cam rapped a knuckle on the window of the pub door. Lauren hurried over to unlock it and Cam walked in carrying a large flat parcel wrapped in brown paper. Lauren raised a brow. "What'cha got there?"

Cam offered her a playful smile. "A present."

"For me?" Lauren indicated herself.

"Sort of."

She planted her hands on her hips and feigned exasperation. "What's that supposed to mean?"

Cam shrugged, the playful expression not leaving her face. "It's a little bit for you, but also for the pub."

Art. It had to be a picture or painting of some sort. "You didn't have to do that."

"I wanted to. A housewarming gift of sorts. Or pub warming." She extended the parcel toward Lauren.

Lauren took it from her and could feel the frame through the wrapping. "Do I get to open it now?"

Cam chuckled. "Yes, you do."

Lauren tore into the paper. Her parents had never been big on gifts. Holiday presents were often money or a trip. Small, thoughtful things never factored in, certainly not for no reason. Just the fact that Cam had gone to the trouble meant more than she wanted to admit.

She recognized Albert's face immediately, if from the few photos she'd seen more than from memory. It was a portrait, but nothing stuffy or formal. He was painted in a style similar to her woodland creatures, in a tweed jacket and with a jaunty expression on his face. Not quite cartoon, but definitely whimsical.

"Oh, my God."

"It's the same artist as the one who did your animals. She remembered you and was happy to do something on commission when I told her the story."

They'd argued about those damned paintings. Getting Cam on board with them had been such a battle. A silly, stupid battle, but one of the first places they'd really compromised. Lauren's eyes filled, the tears spilling over.

"You don't have to hang it in the pub. You can put it in your office or tuck it out of the way if you don't like it."

There was a trace of worry in Cam's voice. The last little thread holding Lauren's heart back gave way. She shook her head. "It's perfect."

"You don't have to say that. I know you weren't all that close to Albert."

Lauren sniffed and tried to swipe away the tears without ruining her mascara. "I feel closer to him now than I ever did when he was alive. This place is so him. I love the idea of paying him tribute."

"He'd be happy with the changes you've made. I hope you know that."

She started crying in earnest then—for the man she'd hardly known, for the unexpected turn of events that saved her from the darkest moment in her life, and for the future that felt like a massive question mark.

Cam took the framed canvas from her and set it on a nearby table. She wrapped her arms around Lauren and pulled her close. She didn't mind when women cried, although she wished she had a better sense of what had upset Lauren so. "Shh. It's okay."

"They're happy tears." The words came out staccato, in time with Lauren's choppy breathing.

Her mother did that—cried when she was really happy. It didn't usually come out with quite so much sobbing. Not that she was judging, she just wanted to be sure she'd not struck a bad sort of nerve. She continued stroking Lauren's back, attempting to soothe both of them. "Okay, then."

After a long moment, Lauren pulled away. Her eyes were red and puffy, her makeup a bit of a mess. Rather than being turned off, it made Cam feel tender. Protective, but also proud. Desire, but something deeper.

The reality of it hit her like a kick to the stomach. Somehow, somewhere along the way, she'd brought herself to the precipice of falling in love with Lauren. Cam tried to offer her a smile even as her own breathing hitched. This was not the time or the place to have this conversation, and not only because she had no idea if her feelings were reciprocated.

As if to reinforce her thoughts, the pub door opened and a man came in with a keg of beer on a dolly. Charlotte crossed into Cam's line of vision, reminding her she'd been there the whole time. She waved a hand in their direction and greeted the delivery guy by name.

They were standing in the middle of the pub. And even if the pub wasn't open and bustling with patrons at that very second, they were one day from what might turn out to be the biggest day of both their careers. It was not the time to get sappy.

"Are you sure you're all right?" Cam asked.

"I am. Promise." Lauren offered a smile and nodded. She seemed sincere.

"Okay."

"I love it. Absolutely love it. And I know just where it's going to go." Lauren picked up the painting and carried it to the wall adjacent to the bar. She took down the painting that was there—a traditional hunting scene—and hung the portrait. "What do you think?"

Cam had envisioned the painting in that exact spot. She'd even used it to give the artist an estimate of measurements. "It's perfect."

Lauren stood back and smiled. "It really is. Thank you."

Cam cleared her throat, suddenly anxious to change the subject. "How are you feeling about tomorrow? Do you need help with anything?"

Lauren took a deep breath and squared her shoulders. "I think we're all set."

Paired with the streaky mascara, she looked like she'd come through some sort of epic battle. It was an interesting juxtaposition to the fragile look she'd had just a moment before. Although the former had tapped into something deep inside Cam, the latter suited Lauren better.

"You're feeling good about the staff?" she asked. Lauren had hired some temporary staff to work the event, including a couple of people from the distillery. Cam had helped Charlotte train them on the cocktail menu for the night, including the signature drink, the one featuring Carriage House, that Lauren had decided to name the Gin Flip.

"I really am. I think it's going to go well." She tipped her head to the side. "As long as people show up."

"They will." The idea that people might not come hadn't occurred to her. Even if she wasn't the most optimistic person, she had the sense that Lauren didn't fail at anything she set her mind to.

"They will." Lauren nodded again, more determined than the first time.

"I should let you get back to whatever." Even though the last thing she wanted to do in that moment was leave.

"Yeah. I need to go check in on the kitchen and," she moved a hand back and forth in front of her face, "fix this."

"Text me if you need anything, okay?"

Lauren smiled. "I will."

"Not that you need it, but good luck." It surprised her just how much she meant it.

"Thanks." Lauren leaned in and kissed her lightly. "For everything."

Cam took the long way back to the distillery, soaking up the sunshine and ruminating on just how close she was to falling for Lauren. The shock of that first moment had already faded. In its place, more of a calm certainty. Certainty about her feelings, at least. She might not have wanted to, but she wasn't one to deny reality. Of course, she had no idea what Lauren's feelings were. They'd need to talk after the opening.

Lauren hadn't said much about leaving, but she'd not talked about staying, either. Did she miss her life in New York? Did she miss anyone she'd left there?

Cam shook her head. No point pondering questions she couldn't answer. They'd talk and she'd get her answers. Then she'd know what to do going forward. In the meantime, she needed to get ready herself. It might be the grand reopening of the Rose & Crown, but it was a debut of sorts for Carriage House as well. And since she'd agreed to be the face of it, she'd have a lot of hands to shake and schmoozing to do. If that wasn't enough to distract her from the state of her heart, she didn't know what was.

CHAPTER TWENTY-THREE

Cam wasn't one for fancy parties, but when the day actually arrived, she found herself looking forward to it. Part of it was being involved, not just in the planning of the event, but in the underlying work it was celebrating. Part of it was being so happy with that work. Lauren had taken her opinions to heart and the result was a place that felt fresh but authentic.

It also proved impossible not to be pulled in by Lauren's enthusiasm. It was downright infectious, and she'd included not only Cam, but a good chunk of the town. It hadn't occurred to Cam, but having something to rally around had brought people together. The renewed sense of community made her far less worried about an influx of tourists. And the potential influx of money, well, that would do everyone good.

She did a fairly good job of convincing herself that was the sum of her feelings, but it didn't work entirely. The reality was that the party represented an end of sorts—an end to the project that brought them together, and an end to Lauren's grand plans. Cam had no idea what would come next and, if she thought about it too hard, it terrified her.

For the tenth or so time in the last few hours, she shook it off. Today was too important to borrow trouble. There'd be plenty of time to worry about the future tomorrow.

She finished getting dressed, opting for a tie with the one suit she owned for important business meetings. She'd let Jane help her pick out a new shirt which helped her feel more like a classy dyke out on the town and less like a banker. Hopefully, Lauren would agree, especially since she'd made a thing about Cam being her date and not just another guest. She had no idea what Lauren would be wearing, but no doubt she'd look absolutely gorgeous.

On the walk to the pub, her stomach started doing this weird thing that felt like butterflies. Which was such a soppy phrase, but she couldn't find another one that fit. Was she nervous on Lauren's behalf or her own?

The pub doors were locked, but lights blazed from the inside. Even though it was still light out, the windows emitted a warm and welcoming glow. She could see Charlotte behind the bar, giving directions to the staff. Cam tapped on the glass to get her attention.

Charlotte looked up and smiled, then hurried over to let her in. "Don't you look like a stunner."

"As do you." Cam leaned in and kissed her on the cheek. "I can't remember the last time I saw you in a dress."

Charlotte poked her in the chest. "That's because you only see me behind the bar."

"Fair do's." Cam looked her up and down. The black dress fit her perfectly, showing off curves she often kept hidden, and the smoky eye makeup gave her a sultry look that suited her. "You really do look pretty."

Charlotte stepped back and did a turn. "Thank you. I bought it special."

Cam caught movement out of the corner of her eye and turned, expecting to see Lauren. Instead, she found herself looking at Anja, beyond hip in skinny black pants and a paisley button-down with a loose-fitting tie—a look Cam couldn't even pretend to pull off. Charlotte seemed to be appreciating it on an entirely different level. She'd have to ask her about that the next time they were alone.

"You're here."

Cam turned toward the sound of Lauren's voice. It might be cliché, but she'd have sworn her heart stopped. Lauren wore a shimmery pewter cocktail dress that hit every line of her body just right. The scooped neckline revealed only a hint of cleavage, but knowing what was underneath made her mouth water. Her hair was pinned up in an elaborate twist, and she wore impossibly high heels.

She looked every inch the glamorous New York City powerhouse, and Cam had a moment of disbelief that she'd managed to capture the attention of such a woman.

But then Lauren smiled, the kind of knowing smile that's only shared between people who know one another intimately, and every magical detail roared through her brain. Cam swallowed, not entirely trusting her voice. She cleared her throat and said, "You look amazing."

"So do you." Lauren walked slowly toward her, hips swaying slightly with each step. Her dress caught the light, making her appear almost ethereal.

Cam allowed one hand to graze up Lauren's side. The fabric was silky against her fingers and so thin she could feel the warmth of Lauren's skin. Cam leaned in and kissed her softly, not wanting to ruin her makeup, but she lingered, unable to pull herself away from the feel of Lauren's mouth on hers. The sound of whistles coming from the bar reminded Cam she and Lauren weren't alone. She stepped back reluctantly.

Mrs. Lucas came bustling out of the kitchen with a pair of waiters in tow. And like a switch being flipped, the entire pub came to life. The band arrived to set up, the first wave of food emerged from the kitchen to be arranged artfully on a table in the corner. Everyone seemed to want Lauren's attention at once.

Cam stepped back, a little in awe of how smoothly Lauren gave directions and instilled a mixture of confidence and enthusiasm in each person who had a role to play in the evening. Finally, just a few minutes before the door was slated to open, Lauren turned that attention to her.

"And you? Are you feeling ready?"

Even if she wasn't, Cam would have faked it. She wanted nothing more than to give Lauren just a fraction of what she'd given everyone else. Fortunately, she didn't have to fake it. In that moment, Cam had not a shadow of doubt that everything would go exactly as Lauren wanted it, and that the pub and the inn and the town and her gin would all be better for it. "Utterly."

Lauren gave her hand a squeeze. "Let's do this."

❖

Lauren paused for a second. She took a deep breath and tried to absorb the moment—the pub, packed with close to a hundred people. But more than the people, it was overflowing with energy. Good energy.

She'd taken Cam's advice and not done anything special in terms of lighting or other "special event" paraphernalia. Since the point was to showcase the Rose & Crown for what it was, it had been the right call and made the evening feel more like a party among friends than some glitzy who's who.

It also showed off the changes that had been made. The new furniture was warm and inviting, no longer sagging and worn. The light fixtures she'd added were vintage and looked as though they'd been there all along. And the portrait of Albert couldn't have been more perfect—for her, but also for the space, and for the patrons who'd known him for the better part of fifty years.

She worked the room, smiling and shaking hands. She asked questions and accepted compliments, giving one variation or another of her elevator pitch at least a few dozen times. It had been months since she'd been in full networking mode, but it felt as familiar and natural as breathing.

It helped that everyone seemed genuinely enthusiastic, eager almost. The locals were decked out like it was New Year's Eve, and the twenty or so guests from out of town didn't stand out like a sore thumb. Even Anja, in all her edgy hipness, seemed to fit right in. That's what she loved most of all. Yes, it was about making money, but it was about so much more. Creating a place where people came together—that made it feel like she'd done the right thing.

A couple of travel bloggers had accepted her invitation, along with Alejandro from *Traveler*. Lauren lavished them with extra attention, making sure they sampled Carriage House and met Cam face-to-face. If their enthusiasm was anything to go on, she'd be seeing some really nice write-ups in the coming weeks.

Anja sidled up next to her and slid an arm around her waist. "How are you feeling about things?"

Lauren nodded. "Really good. Everyone seems happy. Like, everyone."

"A far cry from New York, isn't it?"

For all that she loved about the city, Lauren had to concede the point. At least in the circles she moved in, everyone had an agenda and, as a result, drama and backstabbing were par for the course. She didn't have that with her closest friends, obviously, but acquaintances and colleagues were another story.

Like Philip. His leering smile lurched into her mind, and she quickly shoved it aside. She'd booked a flight to New York for the following week, but not yet told Cam. She would, she just didn't want it to put a damper on tonight. She wanted tonight to be perfect.

"Hey, you okay?"

Lauren nodded. "Sorry, just a little overwhelmed I guess."

Anja gave her a squeeze. "Is it because you're, once again, a smashing success? Or, perhaps more likely, it's that gorgeous woman staring at you from across the room with stars in her eyes?"

She followed Anja's gaze, although she already knew who Anja was talking about. Cam stood at the opposite end of the pub, talking with Alejandro. But even as Cam gave him her attention, she stole glances in Lauren's direction. "I don't know about stars, but she seems to want me."

"Seems? Have you lost your mind? She's gone over you. Completely."

"Yeah." She'd been hesitant to believe Cam might reciprocate her feelings, but the last few days—the photo shoot, the stolen moments, the portrait of Albert—all of it had begun to add up. She couldn't quite picture what it meant for their future, but it gave her this warm, safe feeling she could only describe as hope.

"So, let's go with smashing success and thoroughly smitten." Anja rested her head on Lauren's shoulder for a second, then let go of her waist. "You deserve both, you know."

Lauren smiled. "We all deserve it. Or, at least, whatever version of it we want."

"I'll drink to that. Speaking of drinks, I need one. Can I get you one, too?"

"No, thanks." She'd managed to greet everyone as they arrived, but there were still a handful of conversations she wanted to have. It might be a party, but it was work, too, and she wanted every drop of focus to make sure good impressions were made.

Anja stole a glance at the bar, or perhaps more accurately at Charlotte, before giving Lauren a wink. "Go get 'em, tiger."

Lauren chuckled at the phrase and sent Anja off to get her drink and flirt. Then she turned her attention to the travel agent from Dublin. She got the sense he handled corporate clients and not just older folks still leery of the internet. Not that she wouldn't happily welcome both with open arms.

As the crowd began to thin, she allowed herself to make her way over to Cam. She'd been almost as popular as Lauren had, chatting with guests and writers and a couple of the business owners Lauren invited from adjacent towns. She'd held her own, but at the moment, was looking a bit peaked. "How are you holding up?"

Cam nodded. "Good."

"You don't have to pretend to enjoy this, you know. It's work."

She chuckled. "I enjoy it and it's work. It's hard to complain when there are people who want to talk to me about Carriage House."

"You do seem to be in high demand."

"I think my face hurts from smiling. Is that normal?"

Lauren laughed. "Completely normal. And it looks like people are starting to clear out, so the end is in sight."

Cam leaned in, her mouth close to Lauren's ear. "Does that mean I get to take you to bed soon?"

The effect of Cam's words was immediate and intense. The rest of the room faded to a blur, and all she wanted was to drag Cam to her room and rip off all her clothes. Unfortunately, or maybe fortunately, she was a professional. And being turned on did not make her guests or her responsibilities disappear. She turned, bringing her own lips close to Cam's ear, letting them graze Cam's neck for a fraction of a second. "Soon."

CHAPTER TWENTY-FOUR

Cam stood off to the side as Lauren bid the final guests a good night. Despite being on her feet and going nonstop for the last ten hours, Lauren's smile was wide and her enthusiasm unwavering. It left Cam with a strange mix of emotions. Awe and desire for sure, but something more, something deep in her chest that was possessive and protective at the same time.

Lauren flipped the lock on the pub door. She turned and gave her attention to Charlotte, who was overseeing the cleanup. They settled on what could wait for morning, and she encouraged Charlotte to head home. Charlotte didn't argue, making Cam wonder if she'd made plans for after the party.

After what felt like an eternity, Lauren's hazel eyes settled on Cam. The smile remained, but Cam saw the fatigue in her eyes. "You were incredible tonight."

Lauren slowly crossed the room. "You were, too. I couldn't have done it without you."

Cam slid an arm around her waist. God, it felt good to do that. "I find that hard to believe, but thank you."

"It's true." Lauren leaned in and kissed her jaw. "You and your cocktails were half the draw. People couldn't stop talking about them."

Cam shrugged. "I do make a mean cocktail."

"It was more than that, though. You being here, being a part of this, it means so much to me."

"Ms. Montgomery, are you getting sentimental on me?"

She'd said it to keep the conversation light, but Lauren didn't laugh. Instead, she looked at Cam with such intensity, Cam actually felt her knees weaken. "Maybe I am."

Cam swallowed. What was she supposed to say to that?

"What? You think you have a corner on that market?" Lauren asked.

There. The mischief was back. That was a relief. She knew what to do with mischief. Why, then, did it leave her disappointed?

"Oh, no. I've learned never to underestimate you."

"That might be the nicest thing you've ever said to me."

Was that true? She had a stab of regret for how hard she'd been on Lauren when she arrived. "Clearly, I need to start paying you more compliments."

"Be careful. It might go to my head and make me unbearable."

Cam shook her head. "I'm not worried. I've decided I can bear you quite well."

"I do like the sound of that." Lauren looked around the room, as though assessing whether there was anything left to do, then looked back at Cam. "Take me to bed, please."

Cam didn't need to be asked twice. She took Lauren's hand and led her through the door connecting the pub to the inn. Around the office and down the hall to the room she knew now belonged to Lauren. "It feels strange this is the first time I'm staying here."

Lauren stopped at the door. "Wait. With me, or ever?"

"Ever. I live a mile away. What cause would I have had to spend the night?"

Lauren nodded slowly, as though absorbing the logic of that statement. "No, that makes perfect sense. If anything, I'm realizing it's strange you haven't stayed here with me."

She shrugged. "It's okay. My place is a little more," she paused, searching for the right word, "private."

"I'll give you that." Lauren slid the key into the lock and opened the door. "Still, I'm glad you're here now."

"Me, too."

Lauren flipped a switch and a small lamp by the bed came on. She kicked off her shoes and let out a loud sigh. "God, my feet hurt."

Cam turned Lauren around and eased the zipper of her dress down. She took her time with it, enjoying the slow tease of newly exposed skin. She pressed a kiss to each of Lauren's shoulders, taking pleasure in the way Lauren's head dropped to one side. "How about you let me draw you a bath?"

Lauren turned, the motion causing the dress to fall at her feet. "Only if you join me."

It took Cam a second to find words. Despite being with Lauren at least a dozen times, the sight of her—golden skin, matching bra and panties in deep purple—took her breath away. "An invitation I couldn't possibly turn down."

Cam led them both into the bathroom. Thanks to her work hanging new towel bars, she'd at least seen the space before. She pulled back the curtain around the tub and turned the water on. When Lauren reached around her to squirt in a generous dose of bubble bath, she chuckled. "I hope that doesn't smell too girly."

Lauren quirked a brow. "Just vanilla. You'll live."

Cam reached over and gave Lauren's rear end a pinch. Lauren swatted at her, but without any force. She slipped off Lauren's bra and slid the panties down. She pointed at Lauren, then the water. "You, in."

"So bossy."

"That's me." Cam shed her clothes while Lauren situated herself in the tub. As much as she wanted Lauren's body pressed against her, she positioned herself at the opposite end, nestling her feet on either side of Lauren's hips. "Give me a foot."

Lauren obliged, lifting one soapy foot from the water. Cam took hold of it with both hands and started to rub. Lauren's head fell back and she moaned, making the whole thing more sensual than Cam would have expected. Without lifting her head, she said, "If there's something you want me to agree to, now is the time to ask. I'm pretty sure I'd say yes to anything."

Marry me. Stay here forever. The thoughts popped into Cam's mind unbidden. She shook her head. She was just tired and, despite teasing Lauren about it, probably a little sentimental herself. "I won't take advantage of your compromised state." She switched to the other foot, rubbing the arch and pressing her thumbs along the ball. When Lauren seemed completely relaxed, she set that foot down as well. "Come here."

Lauren shifted, settling her back against Cam's front. She slid down, resting her head on one of Cam's shoulders. "Oh, this is nice. I could stay like this all night."

Cam slicked her hands over Lauren's breasts, reveling in the way her nipples hardened on contact. "Well, maybe not all night."

"If you keep touching me like that, I'm not going anywhere."

Cam had plenty of other things in mind, but she wasn't in any hurry. She massaged Lauren's breasts, trying to figure out exactly what combination of motion and pressure caused her to make those perfect little sounds.

After a while, she couldn't contain herself any longer. She slipped her hand down Lauren's torso, into the sudsy water, and between her legs. Lauren gasped. "Cam."

Cam had to swallow her own gasp at how hot and slick and utterly perfect she was. "You are so beautiful."

Lauren lifted her head. "I—"

"Shh. Relax. Let me enjoy you." For all her confidence, Lauren seemed profoundly uncomfortable being the center of her undivided attention. The vulnerability of that, hidden where few if any saw it, stirred the deepest parts of Cam's heart. But instead of fighting them, tonight she just let them be. Just like everything else, her feelings would be waiting for her in the morning.

For her part, Lauren didn't argue. She settled back against Cam and sighed. She draped one of her legs over Cam's, giving Cam better access. Cam didn't say anything more. She slid her fingers over Lauren, easing two inside her. She felt like velvet, soft and hot, but also strong. The way Lauren enveloped her, pulled her in, made her feel whole.

Lauren grabbed one of Cam's thighs. Cam continued to stroke her, using her free hand to trace lazy circles over her nipples. Lauren undulated slowly. Each movement of her backside against Cam sent arrows of lust right to her core. Cam quickened her pace, not wanting to rush, but also thinking if she didn't get Lauren out of the tub and into bed soon, she'd lose her mind.

She abandoned Lauren's breasts, sliding her other hand down. She stroked Lauren's clit in time with her thrusts. Lauren moved with her, her head rolling from side to side, eyes closed. Cam clenched her jaw, trying to ignore the incessant throbbing between her thighs. The bath water sloshed, threatening to spill onto the floor. Cam couldn't bring herself to care.

"Cam." Lauren's voice was as restless as her body—seeking, begging.

Cam quickened her fingers, willing Lauren to come. "That's it. Let go. Come for me."

Lauren stiffened. Her back arched and her hips lifted. Cam stayed with her, pressing into her and holding two fingers against her pulsing clit. Lauren slumped against her, panting. Cam was short of breath, too, almost like she'd had an orgasm of her own.

"Cam." Lauren whispered her name this time, with something resembling reverence.

Cam swallowed the emotion that bubbled up in her chest. "Come on, let me take you to bed."

They got out of the tub. She handed Lauren a towel, wrapped a second one around her waist. "You all right?"

Lauren smiled. There was almost something shy about it. "Do you mind if I wash my face? I'm sure my makeup is a mess."

"You're gorgeous, but I understand. Go ahead." Instead of going to the bedroom, Cam stayed. Something about watching her felt intimate. She stood behind Lauren at the sink, pulling pins from her hair one at a time. "I can't believe you did this yourself."

"Lots of practice."

Cam counted seventeen pins before Lauren's hair tumbled down. She ran her fingers through it. "It looked great, but I have to confess I'm partial to this."

"I'm partial to your hands in it."

"Yeah?" Cam figured it was something she did for her own pleasure more than Lauren's.

"I love the way it feels. I really love when you give it a nice pull."

Cam felt herself flush. Whether it was embarrassment or arousal, she couldn't be sure. "You do?"

Lauren lifted a shoulder. "I don't confess it to many people because they usually take it the wrong way."

Cam swallowed. Just when she thought Lauren had no more surprises up her sleeve, she had to go and say something like that. "You are an infinitely fascinating woman."

"That's much nicer than calling me a bundle of contradictions."

It was hard to tell if she was kidding. "You're complex."

Lauren made eye contact with Cam's reflection in the mirror and raised a brow. "Coming from you, I'm not sure that's a compliment."

"You know, it's grown on me."

She turned, wound her arms around Cam's neck. "I'll take it."

"Good." Cam slid her arms around Lauren's waist, pulled her close, and kissed her.

Without breaking the kiss, Cam walked them into the bedroom. Lauren's tongue teased Cam's bottom lip. Cam pulled it into her mouth. A little voice in the back of her brain told her she'd never get tired of this, that it would never get old.

Cam ignored the voice but gave Lauren's towel a tug, sending it to the floor. She loosened her own and they tumbled into bed, a tangle of still-damp limbs on the cool sheets. Cam propped herself on her elbow and stopped kissing Lauren long enough to look down at her. "You really are gorgeous."

Lauren smirked, and before Cam realized what was happening, she wiggled free and rolled away. And then Cam was on her back and Lauren on top, straddling her thighs and looking like a Valkyrie poised for battle. If Cam wanted to protest the abrupt shift, the sentiment—not to mention the words—were lost in how fucking sexy it was.

Lauren leaned in and kissed her. "I think, by rights, it's my turn."

Cam opened her mouth, but still, she had no words. Taking her silence as all the agreement she needed, Lauren kissed her again. She made a trail of kisses along Cam's ear, bit gently on the lobe. Cam let out a moan.

Lauren's teeth scraped lightly along her neck. The juxtaposition of teeth and tongue sent Cam into overdrive. She dug fingers into

Lauren's hips. Lauren worked her way down Cam's torso, continuing the delicious torment. When Lauren nipped her inner thigh, Cam arched off the bed.

"Shh. Relax. Let me enjoy you."

Having her words flipped back on her was perfection. She dropped back to the mattress, made an effort to ease the parts of her tense with anticipation.

"Better."

Lauren pressed featherlight kisses all around where Cam wanted her, avoiding her center. Despite her efforts to relax, Cam's body tightened again. "Please."

Lauren's tongue slid over her, into her. Whether it had to do with just how badly she wanted it or the emotions swirling around inside her, she didn't know. But the orgasm tore through her like a dam giving way. Immediate and intense, it left her battered and soaked.

"Lauren." Cam practically panted her name.

Lauren looked up at her and smiled. "Oh, no. You're not getting off that easy."

She wasn't sure she could handle another, but Lauren started slowly. Lazy circles, a gentle massage. Lauren eased into her, the strokes soothed as much as they wound her up. The pleasure was different, but no less exquisite. Lauren's touch felt both new and familiar. Cam's body knew exactly what to do with it, even if her brain was busy tripping over itself.

As if sensing she'd started thinking about it, Lauren shifted gears. The thrust of her fingers picked up force, more command now than invitation. Again, Cam's body stayed a step ahead of her thoughts, keeping up with wherever Lauren wanted to lead.

Cam lifted her head and found Lauren watching her. Her eyes were intense, no longer playful. There was a challenge there, not to yield, but to match. Cam accepted, pushing herself harder, higher, closer to the release she was suddenly desperate to find.

There was nothing quick or sneaky about the orgasm this time. It built, gathering magnitude like an avalanche hurtling down a mountain. It swept up everything in its path, carrying her with its sheer force into the unknown.

When the roaring in her ears finally stopped, when her limbs felt like rubber and each breath no longer felt like fire in her lungs, Cam lay sprawled on the bed, sweaty and spent. She blinked up at the ceiling, like a skier who'd just survived a near-death tumble might stare at the sky, and realized exactly what she'd been hurtling toward. Release, yes, but something much bigger and far more dangerous. She'd barreled herself past feelings and right into love. All the way in love. The kind that could lead to happily ever after. Or heartbreak.

"You okay?"

Lauren smiled down at her. Cam hadn't noticed her crawl up the bed to join her. Cam nodded, not trusting herself to form words.

"Just checking. You look a little shell-shocked." Lauren kissed her, then curled against her side, draping an arm over Cam's ribs.

"I'm good." Cam wrapped an arm around her shoulders and pulled her in a little closer. Terrified, maybe, but good.

Lauren reached over and shut off the lamp then settled right back in. "Good. God, I'm exhausted."

"Get some rest. You've earned it."

Lauren mumbled agreement and then grew silent. Her breathing slowed and Cam thought she'd drifted off to sleep already. Cam stroked her hair and stared into the darkness, trying to acclimate to the shift—or, perhaps more accurately, the revelation of the shift—in her feelings. What she was supposed to do about them. And whether Lauren felt anything close to the same.

"I'm glad I came here." Lauren's words were muffled, a combination of near-sleep and being nuzzled into Cam's shoulder.

Cam took a deep breath, let it out slowly. She pulled Lauren a little closer, placed a kiss on the top of her head. "I'm glad you came here, too."

CHAPTER TWENTY-FIVE

Thanks to Lauren's relationship with Alejandro, along with her ability to deliver the photos ahead of time, the issue of *Traveler* featuring the Rose & Crown came out only a week after the grand opening. The copies had come express, and she'd had them delivered around town to everyone who'd had a hand in the relaunch.

She fingered the magazine page—glossy and beautiful and better than any press she could have paid for. Anja's photos of the rooms and the pub, of her, and of Cam at the distillery complemented the story perfectly. The write-up was smart, charming, and highly flattering.

At this point, it didn't even feel like revenge. It just felt right.

Paired with the buzz from the grand reopening, the Rose & Crown would have more business than she knew what to do with. And not just the Rose. The inn was booked to capacity. Cam's distillery and the shops in town—all of them would see a huge boost in traffic and, in all likelihood, revenue. Not like the village was on the brink of collapse, but the infusion would go a long way to helping its businesses stay afloat.

She'd done that. Her ideas, her hard work, her sheer force of will to make it happen had done that. Alone, and to herself, she could admit how much more satisfying it was than any advertising campaign she'd ever launched. Lauren shook her head. It didn't hurt to admit it. It didn't mean she was going to put herself in the business of rehabbing old hotels and pubs. It meant she had a better handle on the kinds of clients she wanted when she opened her own agency. And it proved she could take a vision from its earliest stages and see it through execution, launch, and promotion.

She practically floated from her office into the pub, where Charlotte stood behind the bar with a copy of the magazine in her hands. "What do you think?" Lauren asked.

Charlotte turned to her and beamed. "I can't believe they used a picture of me. I'm in a magazine."

"I might be the face of the business, but you're the face customers see when they come in for a meal or a pint. And it's an incredibly lovely face."

Despite the compliment, Charlotte's smile faded. "Are you planning to stay the face of the Rose & Crown?"

Lauren sighed. Alejandro had played up her plan to sell the place and move on to her next adventure more than she'd expected. She'd let him ply her with questions about it, though. It was the sort of angle that would up her professional brand, not to mention put a bug in the ear of potential buyers. Yes, the thought of selling at this point felt less appealing than when she arrived, but it still needed to be on the table. She didn't want to spend the rest of her life running an inn and she couldn't start a business with the alarmingly low amount of money she had on hand.

"I'm not jumping on the next train out of here, if that's what you're asking."

"But a future train? If someone comes along and the price is right?"

Now that she was being pressed, Lauren hesitated to own that part of her plan. Not because Charlotte was guilting her about it, but because the thought of walking away left her with a knot in her stomach and a tightness in her chest that reminded her way too much of the day she got fired from KesslerAldridge. "Selling is an option. I think for me professionally, it has to be. That doesn't mean I'm going to unload the place on the first offer that walks in the door. Or even the highest offer."

"All right." Charlotte nodded. She seemed reassured, if not entirely convinced.

"Just putting it out there is good for business. We'll get some developers, people who fancy themselves real estate flippers. If they want to book a room and buy a pint, I'm not going to turn them down." Even as she said it, it sounded a bit like rationalization. Lauren shook it off. She wasn't going to let anything bring her down today.

"Does Cam know that?"

"What do you mean?"

"Does Cam know that you're considering selling, or that the article was going to focus on that?"

Lauren frowned. "I wouldn't say focus."

Charlotte merely raised a brow.

"I didn't know exactly how it was going to be written, so no. Do you think she's going to be mad?" In asking, she already knew the answer. "Let me rephrase. How mad is she going to be?"

Charlotte raised both hands defensively. "It's not my place to get involved one way or the other."

"That bad?" Why hadn't she thought of that when she was doing the interview? Would it have made a difference?

"I just think it's going to be a shock. It was to me."

All the elation of the last hour evaporated. Lauren set the magazine down on the bar and looked Charlotte right in the eyes. "I'm sorry you felt blindsided."

She took a deep breath and squared her shoulders. "We all thought that might happen before you got here, but then you did and, I don't know, you seemed so invested."

"I am invested. I just—" What? "I just have this whole other life, all these other plans and goals, you know?"

"I do. I get that it's not all about us." Charlotte's smile returned. This time it was encouraging. As much as Lauren appreciated it, the fact that she needed an encouraging smile didn't sit well.

"But it is about you as much as about me. I'm not heartless."

"You aren't. I've not thought that once about you."

Great. Now she was getting a pep talk. The day had taken a turn real quick. "I suppose I should go track down Cam."

"I didn't mean to get you upset."

"No, I appreciate the warning. Hopefully, she'll understand what I was going for." She shrugged. "And maybe be glad for the free publicity. That was the whole point." Surely Cam would get it. She had her own brand, her own business, to think of.

Charlotte nodded, but didn't say anything more. Lauren picked up the magazine and brought it back to her office. She used the moment alone to steel herself for whatever was to come and tried not to be annoyed that she needed to steel herself in the first place.

❖

Cam set the magazine down. The betrayal wasn't personal, but it sure as hell felt like it. Lauren's face smiled back at her from the page, radiant and perfect. The accidental innkeeper, the beautiful entrepreneur. The woman who'd swept into her life like a tornado and turned everything upside down. Who'd made everything seem possible, but who had her eye on the exit the whole time.

"The phone's been ringing off the hook all morning. Do you know what's going on?" Sophie stood in the doorway, looking more amused than perturbed by the situation.

Cam picked up the magazine and strode toward her. She slapped it into Sophie's hand and said, "I need to get out of here."

"Kind of the opposite of what I was going for there."

"Page thirty-six."

Without offering anything else by way of explanation, she left her office. She had to walk past the tasting room on her way out. The fact that it looked to be near capacity gave her no satisfaction. Like winning after cheating. The victory was hollow and left a bad taste in her mouth.

She avoided eye contact with anyone and didn't risk looking up until she was well clear of the building and the parking lot. She cut across the field that led toward her house, but made a wide circle around it, picking up the road that led south toward Nottingham. Even the short walk through the grass had her feet soaked. She should have changed into boots before storming out.

Feeling like she'd successfully dodged having to talk to anyone, she slowed her pace, shoving her hands in her pockets and looking up at the pale gray sky. What a colossal idiot she'd been.

That was the worst of it—not that Lauren had ulterior motives. Cam had suspected as much from the very beginning. No, the worst part was that she'd let herself forget all those suspicions. She'd fallen for a pretty face and a gorgeous body and an infectious laugh, like some hormone-crazed teenager. It was a mistake she'd managed to avoid for the last fifteen years and, in the matter of a couple of months, it was like she'd never learned her lesson at all.

Cam stopped walking. Her desire to escape evaporated. It its place, a burning desire to tell Lauren exactly what she thought of her photo spread and her fancy marketing ideas and her willingness to sell to the highest bidder. She turned on her heel and headed straight for the pub.

Instead of diffusing her anger, the walk only intensified it. Each step was a tiny "I told you so" echoing in her mind. She never should have trusted Lauren. She never should have taken her to bed. And, she realized with a sinking feeling deep in her stomach, she never ever should have fallen in love with her.

When she got to the pub, a good two dozen people were there. Copies of the magazine seemed to be in every pair of hands. Even if it felt like all eyes turned toward her, she told herself it wasn't true. No one else had the personal stake she did. No one else had foolishly given their heart to the woman who saw everything as one more deal to close.

Cam searched the sea of faces for Lauren's but didn't find it.

"You've seen it, haven't you?" Charlotte had appeared at her side and was now studying her with concern.

"Where is she?"

"She didn't know it was going to be written that way. She's not looking to sell to the first person who walks in the door."

The fact that Charlotte was defending Lauren, trying to smooth things over, only made matters worse. "Is she here? Or off meeting with some broker?"

Charlotte sighed. "She's in her office."

Cam nodded once and headed that way. She didn't mean to be an ass to Charlotte, but she didn't trust herself to speak without exploding. And if she was going to explode on someone, she didn't want it to be Charlotte.

Lauren's door was closed. Cam took a deep breath and knocked. Maybe she'd manage not to explode at all.

"Come in."

Cam entered and found Lauren standing behind her desk. She at least had the decency to look worried. Cam made a point of closing the door behind her and taking a breath. Yelling wouldn't get her point across any better. "I think we need to talk."

Lauren nodded. "Charlotte said you might be upset."

It added insult to injury that she needed to cite Charlotte. "Do you understand why?"

Lauren let out a sigh of what seemed like exasperation. "Because the article talks about me flipping the pub, selling it."

"Or maybe because you are flipping the pub and selling it. Because that's been your intention all along."

"I let Alejandro angle the story that way. It's a good marketing strategy. It builds buzz."

The muscles in her jaw tightened. "That's what it comes back to for you, isn't it? Everything is one big marketing strategy."

"You say that like it's a bad thing." Lauren's eyes darkened. Cam had never seen her angry and had a flash of thinking how beautiful the ferocity made her.

"It is when it's my life." How could she not see the difference?

"Don't get self-righteous with me. Your work is just as much a part of your life as mine." The anger in Lauren's eyes gave way to defiance, daring Cam to push back.

"I do my work with integrity. I don't pretend to be one thing and then do the opposite when I think no one is looking."

"You know, I had half a mind to apologize." Lauren shook her head.

"Save your breath. I wouldn't believe you anyway."

She thought Lauren might yell, or maybe throw her out. Instead, she took a deep breath and closed her eyes. "What, exactly, are you angry about?"

A half dozen answers leapt forward. That you came here and changed everything and now I kind of like it. That you made me fall in love with you. That you'll sell the inn and leave and I'll never see you again. Cam opened her mouth, then closed it. Of course she couldn't say any of those things out loud. "You pretended to care. You said whatever you had to say to get me, to get the whole damn village, on board with your plans and it was all a lie."

"That isn't fair and it isn't true."

"Are you honestly going to stand there and tell me you have no intention of selling?"

"I haven't decided. It's complicated, Cam. The reasons I came here are complicated. I had a—"

"Stop." Cam lifted a hand. "It's one thing to leave out parts of the truth that suit your purposes. I won't have you stand there and lie to my face."

Without waiting for a reply, Cam walked out. Lauren didn't call after her, or chase her out the door. She didn't utter a single word. As far as Cam was concerned, Lauren's silence was the most damning thing of all.

CHAPTER TWENTY-SIX

Lauren told herself for the hundredth time she wasn't running away. But as the plane taxied to the runway and sped toward takeoff, that was the feeling she couldn't shake. Even though she only had a few days of avoiding Cam before leaving. Even though she'd booked a return flight not two weeks out. Even though she was going to New York for the specific purpose of giving a deposition about Philip and her firing.

It was the look on Cam's face when she said everything between them had been a lie. That look, and Cam's words, haunted her. The resulting tension sat in her stomach like lead. It was chicken shit to leave without telling Cam, but she didn't think she could take one more second of the disdain or, worse, the betrayal she saw in Cam's eyes. Did it count as running away if the person in question didn't care if you stayed or left?

Half an hour into the flight, she caved and took a sleeping pill. She'd regret it when the plane landed and she felt like she'd been hit by a bus, but that seemed preferable at this point to spending seven hours stewing over the mess she'd left, or the one waiting for her.

Why did Cam have to be so fucking stubborn? It was like she'd spent the whole time they were together just waiting for some reason to blow it all to hell. As evidenced by the fact she had absolutely zero interest in Lauren's explanation, an explanation that made perfect sense for what she was trying to accomplish for the Rose & Crown, and for Carriage House. It was like she didn't want either of those things to succeed. She sighed. Maybe the more accurate statement was that Cam was set on their relationship not succeeding.

That's what hurt the worst. Even as anger danced a tango through her brain, the thing that threatened to suffocate her was the crushing disappointment. And even more crushing than the disappointment was the tiny voice in her head telling her she should have expected it all along. That she wasn't for better or worse, in sickness and in health material. At least not in Cam's eyes.

Even with the sleeping pill, she slept like shit. Her dreams were a jumble of memories—the night Philip groped her, the fight with Cam—and the worst parts of her imagination. In one snippet, she was in a wedding dress, ostensibly to marry Cam. But instead of Cam at the altar, it was Eric, waiting to fire her. Based on the way the woman in the next seat looked at her while they waited to deplane, she'd not been still or quiet.

She ordered a car to take her to her apartment and spent the better part of the ride trying not to throw up. She hoped it was the medication and the stress and not some new intolerance for being in a car. Or, worse, some kind of bug or food poisoning. At her building, there was no sign of Nevin. Not that he always worked the same shift, but the guy who greeted her didn't even look familiar.

Once inside, she dropped her bag on the floor and the stack of accumulated mail on the kitchen island. She looked around the space and had that odd sensation of it feeling at once familiar and foreign. The combination made her anxious and the queasiness from the car only intensified. Again, the sleeping pills were probably not the best idea.

Lauren was just resolving to chuck the rest of the bottle when her stomach took another lurch. She bolted in the direction of the bathroom, barely making it to the toilet before losing the meager contents of her stomach. She flushed them away and rested her cheek on the glass of the shower enclosure. God, she hated throwing up.

She sat there for a few minutes, taking slow breaths and willing the churning to subside. When she was semi-confident the worst had passed, she washed her face and brushed her teeth. In the kitchen, she rooted around in the liquor cabinet and found a single, blessed can of ginger ale. She poured it over ice and took it with her into the bedroom. It gave her that same unsettled feeling as the rest of the house, but her stomach didn't revolt. She stripped off her clothes, pulled on an ancient NYU T-shirt, and crawled into bed.

Whether it was the exhaustion of the last few days, the jet lag, or the remnants of sedative in her system, she slept. Fitful and filled with strange dreams, but she slept. She woke up to the sound of her intercom buzzing and for a moment, had no idea where she was or where the noise was coming from. Although tempted to ignore it, she stumbled out of bed and toward the door.

"Yes?"

"Oh, my God. If you don't stop ignoring my texts I'm going to microchip you." Anja's voice radiated exasperation.

"I'm sorry. I didn't mean to. Come on up." She hit the button to clear Anja into the building and used the minute it would take her to get upstairs to pull on a pair of yoga pants. She opened the door before Anja had the chance to knock.

"Seriously. You have got to stop scaring me like this. You were supposed to text me when you got in."

Lauren apologized again and described the hours since she'd landed—the freaking out, the puking, and the weird sleep.

Anja shook her head and gave her a pitying look. "You look terrible."

"Really? That's the angle you're going to work right now?"

"No, I mean, you really look terrible. Should you be going to the doctor?"

Lauren waved a hand back and forth. "Don't be dramatic. I'm fine."

Anja frowned but didn't argue. "When did you eat last?"

Lauren winced. "You don't want to know."

"Okay, here's what we're going to do. We're going to order up some food. I'll even let you pick. And then we're going to watch cheesy movies and not think about the world for twenty-four hours. The deposition is day after tomorrow, right?"

"Yeah." She'd given herself a couple days' cushion so she could meet with the attorney she'd retained to represent her at the deposition and in any future proceedings.

"Perfect."

And just like that, a huge portion of the weight on her chest lifted. Not all, obviously. She remained connected to reality, and Anja wasn't an actual miracle worker, but her presence—calm, sure, and brimming with Anja's secret blend of no-nonsense affection—did wonders. "I love you, you know."

"Right back at you, lady." Anja gave her another hug and then planted her fists on her hips. "So, what are we eating?"

Suddenly, Lauren was ravenous. Ravenous, but not stupid. So they ordered matzo ball soup from the deli around the corner. Anja added on some kugel, insisting it was pretty bland, too, and that bad days deserved desserts.

They ate, they watched *Dirty Dancing*, and then they climbed into bed and cuddled. It was the kind of friendship she'd craved as a child and not really ever had. Or what she'd dreamed about when she thought about having a sister. Half her life might be a giant mess, but she still had a few things going for her. She'd hold on to that as she fumbled through the next few days.

❖

"What do you mean, gone?" Cam swallowed the panic that welled up and threatened to take over her body. Surely, she'd misheard. Even through her anger, the thought of never seeing Lauren again threatened to suffocate her.

"Not gone, gone. Not permanently."

Oh. The panic subsided enough for her to focus on the conversation at hand. She'd have to sort out the whys of it later, but that could wait for a stiff drink and solitude. In the meantime, her anger swooped back in.

"So, where is she? Off in search of her next rundown village to save?" She flinched at the vitriol in her voice but didn't try to take it back.

"I'm not sure it's my place to tell."

"Seriously, Charlotte? How long have we been friends? Are you really going to tell me your loyalty is to her now? Especially now?"

"It's not about that."

"No? Then why don't you tell me what it's about so I can try to be a little less pissed off at you?" She clung to the notion this was about Charlotte's confidences and not about needing to know where Lauren had run off to.

"Lauren was assaulted by an old work colleague."

"What?" Like the initial panic of learning Lauren had left, Cam's reaction was instant and visceral. "Like, just now? Here?"

"No, no, nothing like that. It happened before she came here."

"Oh."

"I guess he came on to her at a work party and she pushed him off and he got aggressive."

"Wait. Do you mean sexually assaulted?" Just the thought made her sick to her stomach.

"I mean, yes. Not rape, but groping. She kneed him in the groin."

Was it wrong to take grim satisfaction in Lauren defending herself in a moment like that? On the heels of that thought came wondering why Lauren hadn't told her. "Okay. What does this have to do with her leaving town?"

"I guess he's a class-A prick and Lauren isn't the only one he went after. A bunch of other women she used to work with are suing the company for a culture of harassment." Charlotte shook her head in that way so many women did when talking about that sort of thing—disgusted, but not surprised. "Oh, and wrongful termination. I think that's what she called it. Getting fired for crap reasons."

"She was fired? When?" Cam's head swam with a thousand questions. At the top of the list: how Lauren had gone through all that and not confided in anyone. But she had the answer to that one. Lauren had confided in Charlotte, not her.

"Right before she came here. That's why she decided to stay and make a go of it."

"She told you all of this?" Cam tried to keep the accusation out of her voice.

"Only a little. I got most of it from Anja."

"Anja, Lauren's friend? The photographer?" It made her feel marginally better that Lauren hadn't considered Charlotte more of a confidante than her.

"Yeah. We've been talking." Charlotte gave her a sheepish look.

"Talking?"

"More than talking."

"Did you sleep with her? Are you still?" Lauren gone, dealing with God knows what, and her best friend and Lauren's best friend hooking up. Seriously, could her life get any more complicated?

Charlotte shrugged. "Yes and yes?"

Not that she wanted to change the subject, but her affection for Charlotte ran deep, and she hated how often Charlotte had her hopes dashed by people who wouldn't even entertain an open relationship. "Does she know you don't do monogamy?"

Charlotte smiled. "She's poly, too."

"Wow. Okay, that's awesome. I want to hear all about it, truly, but—"

"But you're in love with Lauren and you're freaking out."

The comment stopped Cam in her tracks. When it came down to it, that was exactly it. She'd been so wrapped up in herself and her anger, she'd managed to kick Lauren while she was down. And she had no idea how, or even if, she was going to make it right.

"You fucked up, didn't you?"

Did she ever. "Yeah."

"What are you going to do?"

"I think I have to go to New York." Only after she said the words did the reality of it hit her. She had a passport but had never been farther than Germany. And now she was prepared to fly overseas on a moment's notice to try to win back the woman she was in love with. "Is that a terrible idea?"

Charlotte shook her head. "No."

"No, I shouldn't go or no, it's not a terrible idea."

"You should go. You should absolutely, definitely go."

Cam pressed fingers to her temples. "She shouldn't be going through this alone."

"Agreed. It's always better to have the woman you love by your side."

She did love Lauren, and she wanted to be by her side. "What if I'm too late?"

"You're not too late."

"You don't actually know this. You just hope it's the case." At this point, she was asking about the future of their relationship as much as the deposition.

Charlotte mulled that over for a moment. "I mean, I don't know for certain, but I have a good feeling. I mean, she's got plans to come back. That has to count for something."

It did count for something. Cam just wasn't sure it counted where she needed it to. Yes, Lauren had an attachment to this place, but at this point, did Lauren have any attachment to her? She'd been such an ass. "I have to try, right?"

Charlotte nodded. "It's very romantic."

"It's only romantic if it works."

"I'm pretty sure she's in love with you."

A couple of weeks ago, the idea wouldn't have seem far-fetched. Hell, a week ago, she was pretty damn close to being in love with Lauren herself. No, not damn close. She was all the way in love with Lauren. But she hadn't said so. She'd convinced herself it was too soon, that the timing wasn't right. And then the rug had been pulled out from under her, and love was the absolute last thing on her mind.

She tried to conjure Lauren's exact words from their fight, but couldn't. She'd been so overwhelmed by her hurt and her anger, so convinced Lauren had lied about her intentions all along. Cam hadn't paid much attention to her explanations, hadn't wanted to hear the marketing guru put a spin on her just like she'd put a spin on everything else.

But she hadn't known the whole story. Would that have changed things? Even in her current state of self-loathing, she had to think she'd have been more understanding, more compassionate. Not that it mattered now. She'd said what she'd said and now Lauren was gone, off to face something Cam didn't even want to imagine. Alone.

CHAPTER TWENTY-SEVEN

L auren sat in the small waiting area, hands folded in her lap. The lawyer she'd hired, a woman who specialized in this sort of thing, sat beside her. She studied the cream walls and gray patterned carpet that screamed generic office space and willed herself not to fidget. It was funny. She'd imagined sitting on a wooden bench in the hallway of an ornate courthouse, called in to sit on a witness stand and give her testimony to a dozen of her peers. She knew that's not how depositions worked, but she'd watched perhaps one too many *Law & Order* reruns.

She picked up her phone and realized she'd missed a text from Anja. *Give 'em hell.*

She smiled and sent back an *A Few Good Men* GIF. That got her some smileys in return. She promised to call when it was all over.

Lauren set the phone in her purse, then picked it up. She pulled up her last exchange with Cam. It had been a week ago, the day before the magazine feature came out. It was silly flirting, plans to have dinner the next night.

Did Cam even know she'd come back to New York. And if so, did she care?

In hindsight, she could see why Cam didn't take the feature well. Lauren hadn't been dishonest, but she had also let Alejandro frame the story the way he wanted, the way that would make the Rose & Crown seem like this up-and-coming hipster mecca, rescued by Lauren from antiquated oblivion. Fixed up and ready for the right developer to add it to their portfolio. Sure, the tone was a little smarmy, but that came with the territory.

She knew that, expected it. But even if Cam didn't, it didn't warrant blowing up like she did.

The problem was that Cam had to go and be so damn unreasonable. She'd not even given Lauren the chance to explain. By rights, she was the one who should be livid. To be so quickly dismissed, to have Cam immediately assume the worst. Like the time they'd spent together meant nothing. Like they were back at square one, or worse.

"Ms. Montgomery? Ms. Ortiz?"

She looked up to find a woman in a boxy suit looking at her expectantly. Lauren squared her shoulders and nodded at her attorney. Camila offered her a reassuring smile before saying, "Yes."

"We're ready for you now."

She followed the woman into the room, sat in the vacant chair the woman indicated. Camila took the seat next to her. Four other people sat around the conference table, all in drab suits and with boring haircuts. Was it some kind of corporate lawyer code to look bland and uninteresting? Or maybe it was something about the subject matter. Perhaps sexual harassment cases brought out the frumpy in everyone.

In any case, she didn't recognize any of them. That was a relief, really. She'd been told Philip wouldn't be present, which she was grateful for, but even the attorneys for KesslerAldridge didn't look familiar. They'd probably been brought in from the outside. Neater that way.

"Ms. Montgomery, we appreciate you taking the time to come in and speak with us," brown suit lawyer said.

"Of course."

Gray suit lawyer nodded. "Yes, especially since you're currently residing in England."

"I'm there on a project. I'm still based primarily in New York." She had no idea why she said that—why it mattered to these people or whether or not it was really true—but it was out of her mouth before she'd thought it through. And taking it back wouldn't earn her points for credibility.

Boxy suit gave her an encouraging smile. "Have you done a deposition before?"

"I have not."

"Okay, we'll take a minute to go through how it works, including the fact that you'll be under oath and how your testimony might be used."

Lauren nodded. She'd done some research on her own. She didn't believe in going into any situation blind, and she and Camila had done a dry run the day before. But she listened, relieved that everything they told her lined up with what she'd read, what Camila had told her to expect.

"If you're ready, then, we'll get started. If at any time you need to take a break, please don't hesitate to say so."

"Sounds good." At this point, she just wanted to get it over with already.

"Would you please state your full name for the record?"

Lauren answered. And so it went. The length of her employment, her professional relationship with Philip. Camila interjected here and there, keeping things from straying from the issue at hand. When they asked her about the night at the bar, Lauren froze, just like when she and Camila had gone over it in her office. She'd worked so hard to push it from her mind, she feared it would be gone, that she'd not be able to conjure the specifics. But of course that wasn't the case. It was all there, permanently etched into her mind.

She'd stepped onto the small balcony of the Century Club and breathed in the chilly night air. The space was dim, not yet set up for the crowds that would spill out of the bar looking to bask in the arrival of spring. The sound of celebration faded, partners and creatives congratulating each other on landing the hottest up-and-coming hotel chain as a client.

"You were amazing today, Montgomery."

She'd turned and found Philip Burke standing behind her. They'd been hired at the same time and she'd been worried they'd be in constant competition with one another. Instead, they'd spurred each other on, rising through the ranks of KesslerAldridge and teaming up on some of the agency's biggest clients. She'd smiled at him. "You, too."

The pitch had gone even better than she could have dreamed, and she fully expected it to put her on the short list for partner. And the sooner she became partner, the sooner she'd have the experience and name recognition to strike out on her own. "We make a good team."

"You know, I've been thinking the same thing." He closed the distance between them, standing so close she could smell whiskey on his breath. He put a hand on her arm. "You're an incredible woman, Lauren."

Despite the prickle of discomfort along her skin and the flash of warning bells in her brain, she'd maintained the smile. It was Philip. She trusted him. "You're not so bad yourself."

"Beautiful, too."

It was then she'd known something was wrong, that he wasn't going to keep it professional. But even then, she'd not wanted to make things awkward. She shifted away from him and folded her arms but kept her tone light. "That kind of flattery will get you nowhere and you know it."

"I know, I know. You're a lesbian. You've told me. It just seems like a waste."

The night of the biggest professional win of her career and she was going to have to fend off the advances of a guy she actually kind of liked. "Trust me, it's not a waste in my book."

"You know what I mean." The hand slid up her arm to her neck.

Remembering that touch made her shiver.

"Philip, I think you've had one too many. Let's not do something we're going to regret in the morning."

Even in the low light, his eyes looked glassy. "You know what they say about regret."

She'd been more annoyed than afraid at that point. Less than fifty feet separated them from literally dozens of their colleagues. Still. Things had already gone far enough that there'd be awkwardness in the morning. "I'm partial to 'don't do anything you'll regret.'"

"No, no." He shook his head. "Everyone says you'll regret the things you didn't do more than the things you did."

She lifted her arm to brush his hand away. "I don't think that's a good strategy for—"

His mouth crushed against hers, his beard scratching her chin. The hand on her neck gripped tighter. His other hand groped her breast. Annoyance vanished, along with anger. Genuine fear licked her belly. He was so much stronger than she was and she felt momentarily helpless.

She tried to shove against him, but he only held her more tightly. Panic started to set in, making it difficult to breathe or focus. She had a flashback to the self-defense class she'd taken several years ago, but only one option came to mind. With as much force as she could muster, she plowed her knee right into his crotch.

He let go and stumbled back. He didn't fall, but he doubled over. His hands clutched at his balls like the guys in all those ridiculous YouTube videos. He mumbled expletives. She made out "fucking" and "bitch," but not much else. Maybe "frigid."

She'd wanted to be indignant, give him a verbal lashing to match the knee to the balls, but there were no words. No indignation either, really. All she wanted to do was get as far away from him as possible. Escape. Because even if it had only been for a moment, he really had scared her.

She walked to the door that led back into the bar. The lights were jarringly bright, the sound of conversations a cacophony. The combination made her dizzy. She focused on the exit. She put one foot in front of the other, looking down to avoid any chance of eye contact. She heard her name but ignored it. Just like she ignored the coat check. She didn't stop walking and she didn't look up until she was in the elevator.

She rode down forty floors with a few strangers, holding it together, refusing to draw attention to herself or show weakness. She kept it together in the cab ride to her apartment in Soho, managed a friendly hello to Nevin.

It had felt like an eternity before she was in her apartment, alone, with the door locked behind her. She'd expected to burst into tears, or maybe have the urge to throw something. But all she felt was exhausted, hollow.

She'd leaned against the door, allowed herself to slide to the floor. She pulled off her shoes and dropped them to the side, then hugged her knees to her chest. She was okay. She'd repeated the phrase to herself over and over. Everything was okay. She'd not been hurt. Or probably in any real danger. Philip had let himself get stupid drunk.

Lauren could have stopped then, but she kept going. They needed to know it all, including her decision not to say anything. Camila had said as much during their briefing. And maybe more importantly, she needed to tell it, to have it on the record regardless of the outcome.

She explained how she realized what she was doing—rationalizing, minimizing, and all the other crap women did to let men off the hook. It had hit her like a blow to the chest. Another reality immediately followed. If she reported him, she might get him fired. Or she might draw a whole lot of the wrong kind of attention to herself when she was on the cusp of having it all. She'd banged her head against the door that night, trapped in what felt like an impossible choice. But then the choice hadn't felt so impossible after all.

Being named partner would open the door to striking out on her own. Between that, landing Starbridge, and the money she'd socked away, she figured she was no more than five years from opening her own agency. No way in hell was she going to let Philip, or any other self-entitled prick, get in the way of that.

But of course, it hadn't ended with that. Only weeks later, she'd arrived at work to find her desk packed and security guards waiting. To this day, she didn't know if Philip had been setting her up all along, or if he'd moved quickly, seeking revenge for that night. She realized, finally, how little it mattered.

She walked through the specifics of her firing, the scant evidence and her decision to regroup before fighting back. It felt a little cowardly to own it, to admit how easy it had been to get wrapped up in the pub and the inn and the village. And Cam. But as she explained it, a sense of calm settled over her. She'd done what she needed to do. There was no point wallowing in regret.

Two of the lawyers asked clarifying questions, but neither of them offered anything by way of encouragement or judgment. The whole thing felt sterile, which proved oddly reassuring. By the time it ended, she felt lighter. It shouldn't be a surprise, really. She'd been carrying the trauma with her—along with the indecision over what to do—for months. Of course getting it out in the open, knowing it was part of legal proceedings Philip couldn't ignore, would be a huge relief.

What did surprise her was how little she cared about the outcome. Yes, she'd like to see Philip get what was coming to him, but in terms of her own vindication, it didn't really matter. Her career, her life, were no longer tied up in KesslerAldridge. Her happiness, her future plans, no longer hinged on whether or not she made partner. In her attempt to recover and regroup, she'd managed to build a whole new life.

As she stood on the sidewalk of the 31st Street office, the full truth of that hit her. Her life was in England. Her heart was, too. Lauren took a slow deep breath, letting the realization settle. Cam might not realize it was in her possession, and she might not want it either way, but there it was.

Suddenly, Lauren wanted nothing more than to get on a plane and fly home. Home. A bubble of laughter escaped before she could stop it. She'd go home and she'd fight for Cam and, somehow, everything would work out. In her heart of hearts, she believed it. She'd upended her life for a lot less.

She walked to Sixth Avenue and hailed a cab, thinking of the last time she'd done so after a meeting with a lawyer. Fewer than six months had passed, but everything in her life had changed. She'd taken a risk then and it had paid off. And she was about to press her luck again.

She waited until she was back in her apartment to call Anja. Anja picked up after only one ring, and Lauren proceeded to give her the blow-by-blow. When she got to the end, she kept going, relaying the plan she'd baked up on the ride home. The one where she listed her apartment and began the process of seeking permanent residence in the UK, the one where she threw herself at Cam's feet and hoped for a miracle. To her credit, Anja didn't balk at a single detail. Lauren should have expected nothing less, really. This kind of thing was right up her alley.

"I see only one real problem," Anja said.

Only one? Lauren could rattle off a good two dozen without even trying. Still. "What's that?"

"Cam's on her way here."

"Wait. What?" Surely, she'd misheard.

"Cam. She found out why you'd come back to New York and she's on her way."

"On her way here?" She honestly couldn't imagine Cam in Manhattan, much less what her coming might mean.

"I didn't tell you because she couldn't get a flight that would get her here before your deposition, and I figured it would just distract you. Please don't be mad."

A thousand questions swirled in her mind. She struggled to put her finger on which one to ask first. "How do you know this?"

Anja sighed. "I told Charlotte and she told Cam. I'm sorry for that. I thought you'd told her already. And then Charlotte put Cam in touch with me so she could find you once she arrived."

Lauren did everything she could to tamp down the swell of emotion. And failed. "When?"

"Tonight. I think her flight lands around nine."

She looked at her watch. It was nearly four now. "Tonight. In, like, five hours."

"Don't freak out."

"I'm pretty sure I can't think of a scenario that warrants freaking out more than this one."

"I can. Would you like me to run through them?" Anja's tone was perky and positive.

"No, thank you." Lauren pressed a thumb to her forehead and laughed in spite of herself. "You can, however, tell me everything. Like, what Cam told you, why she's coming."

"How about I do that in person?"

"Yeah, sure. Where do you want me to—"

"I'm here." As she said it, there was a knock on her apartment door.

Lauren shook her head and ended the call. She opened the door and Anja literally flung herself into Lauren's arms. When Anja finally let go, Lauren said, "I'm glad."

Anja walked in, dropped her bag, and spread her arms wide. "I want to tell you everything. But I also get that you might need to process the deposition. Or the Cam situation. Whatever you need, and in whatever order, I'm your girl."

The flitting nature of Anja's commentary matched Lauren's thoughts. So much to sort through. "Tell me about Cam." Anja started to talk and Lauren lifted a finger. "And don't leave out when you got so chummy with Charlotte."

Anja looked at her with feigned surprise. "Right, that. So," and then she launched in. Much like Lauren's stream of consciousness from earlier, Anja laid it all out. The fact that she and Charlotte had stayed in pretty constant contact since she left England. Anja accidentally telling Charlotte why Lauren left. Charlotte telling Cam. Cam deciding Lauren shouldn't be facing that sort of thing alone, but also feeling like an ass and wanting to make it right. All the travel plans.

When Anja finally stopped talking, she looked to Lauren for a response. Lauren merely shook her head. "I don't understand."

"Uh, she's flying across the ocean to be with you. What is there not to understand?"

"I don't know if she's coming here because she wants to be with me or because she's got some hero thing going on."

"Hmm."

"Exactly. What if," the thought dawned on her and she was immediately horrified, "what if she just feels sorry for me?"

Anja looked at Lauren with exasperation. "Do you really think she'd come all the way here because she pities you?"

Sure, it was unlikely. But at this point, it seemed no more far-fetched than the idea that Cam was in love with her and was going to show up on her doorstep to declare it. "No, but—"

"No buts. This is the grand gesture, Lauren. Like a romantic movie. She's coming here so you don't have to wonder if what you have is worth fighting for. She's telling you it is."

Lauren took a deep breath, closed her eyes, and for a second, allowed herself to believe that might be true. As good as she was at imagining best-case scenarios, she almost couldn't picture it. "If it was really a movie, I'd be on a plane to London right now and we'd miss each other."

"That would be a terrible movie."

"No, no. It would be funny. We'd meet up eventually, probably at the airport, and kiss." That, for some reason, she could imagine. "And everyone would clap."

Anja looked at her like she was crazy. "Is that what you want?"

"No." It wasn't. "I'm just saying that would make a better movie."

"Lauren?"

"What?"

"Cam's going to show up on your doorstep in a few hours."

"Right." Right. She needed a plan.

"What are you going to do and how can I help?"

She was so good at winging it. She'd cooked up an entirely new pitch in twenty minutes after an offhanded comment by the client blew up the one she'd spent weeks developing. She'd moved to England on a week's notice. But this? Telling Cam how she felt and trying to salvage their relationship? She was at a total loss. "I don't know."

"Okay." Anja nodded decisively. "First, you're going to text her. She probably won't get it until she lands, but still. She's nervous about coming here and telling her that you know, that you want her here, will make a huge difference."

"Good idea."

"And then you're going to shower and get pretty while I tidy up and change your sheets."

Lauren raised a brow.

"Because I'm pretty sure this is going to culminate in you getting lucky, and I know how you feel about things being just so."

She let out a snort. "I'm glad your brain has gotten there. Mine is still stuck on not breaking down into uncontrollable crying and making a fool of myself."

Anja crossed the room and put her hand on Lauren's cheek. "There's nothing wrong with a little crying. It shows you have all the feels."

Lauren chuckled. Such a departure from her childhood, where crying was seen as little more than a sign of weakness. Knowing she didn't want to be that person anymore, she decided not to argue the point. "It does."

"What's in your fridge? You should have wine and light snacks. You know what? Never mind. You text Cam and I'll take care of it."

Anja turned away, but Lauren grabbed her hand and pulled her back. "I think I like it when you're bossy."

Anja quirked a brow. "I get that a lot."

CHAPTER TWENTY-EIGHT

Cam settled into her seat and tried not to look as nervous as she felt. It wasn't like she'd never flown, but it had been a while. And she'd only gone to Europe, never across the Atlantic. It would be fine. Even if being sandwiched in the middle of a row of four seats made her feel like a sardine. Even if she had no idea how she was going to pass the next seven hours of not knowing how Lauren would react. Not knowing if Lauren would accept her apology. Not knowing if Lauren would take her back.

For about the tenth time in the last twenty-four hours, her heart rate ratcheted up. She closed her eyes and took a deep breath, willing herself to calm down. How did people with chronic anxiety do it?

She realized the guy next to her was giving her a funny look, so she redoubled her efforts to play it cool. She closed her eyes again and conjured Lauren's image. This time, she didn't think of the mess she'd made or the horrible things she'd said. She didn't think about whether Lauren really did want to sell the pub, leave, and never look back. She thought about the way Lauren smiled when she tasted one of Cam's cocktails for the first time. The way Lauren looked at her the night of the grand opening. The way Lauren felt under her the last time they'd made love.

The anxiety didn't dissolve completely, but her feelings felt like an anchor of certainty. She held on to that anchor during taxi and takeoff, during two ridiculous rom-coms and a documentary that provided moderate distraction. She held on to Charlotte's words of encouragement, her belief that Lauren was in love with her, too.

When the plane touched down, Cam's nerves clicked into high gear. The calm she'd managed to hold on to evaporated, leaving her antsy and a little sick to her stomach. The massive line at customs didn't help, nor did the jumble of noises and smells in the terminal. She weaved her way through the throngs of people to the queue for taxis, offering a small prayer of gratitude that only a handful of people waited in front of her. She gave the driver Lauren's address and settled back for the ride into Manhattan.

Crap. She was supposed to text Charlotte when she landed. She pulled out her phone and disabled airplane mode. She waited while it searched for a signal, then agreed to the daily international roaming fee. A string of beeps and chirps announced the messages she'd missed in the interim. One was from Charlotte, no surprise. Another was from Sophie, wishing her luck. Cam smiled. Sophie played the part of pragmatist well, but she was a romantic at heart. And then she saw the text from Lauren.

Anja told me you were coming. Wanted you to know I'm glad. Let me know when you land.

Cam ran a hand through her hair. Lauren knew. That in itself was a relief. Cam read the message again. *I'm glad.* Not the most effusive response, but far better than she had any right to expect. And if Lauren really was glad, it might mean all was not lost. She'd started this insane trip clinging to that belief, but had held hope at bay so it would hurt less if Lauren wanted nothing to do with her.

In a taxi. On my way to your place. She hit send, then added, *If that's okay.*

She glanced out the window and tried to take in the sights, absorb the sheer magnitude of the Manhattan skyline, but her eyes and her attention kept returning to the screen. Fortunately, she didn't have to wait long for a response. *The doorman is expecting you. Come on up.*

Cam's leg bounced up and down. The combination of nerves and sitting for so many hours had overwhelmed any hope she had of remaining still. What did Lauren mean? Would they have a magical reunion and fall into one another's arms? Or was Lauren waiting to throw a drink in her face and slam the door? Even as her imagination spun out one horrible scenario after another, she talked herself down. If Lauren wanted to throw a drink at her, she'd probably have done so already. Even if they didn't get to live happily ever after, it wouldn't devolve into that.

When the car came to a stop outside of Lauren's building, Cam's stomach lodged itself somewhere near her tonsils. It didn't help that the building was taller, the entrance grander, than she anticipated. Oh, and there was a doorman. At least he wasn't in one of those uniforms like she'd seen in the movies. Just a black shirt and pants with a pewter colored tie. Standing out front like he was waiting for her. He wasn't waiting for her, was he?

She paid the taxi and got out, slung her bag over her shoulder, and took a moment to center herself. When she turned her attention to the door, the doorman looked her way. "Ms. Crawley?"

"Um, yes. That's me."

"Ms. Montgomery told me you'd be arriving." He opened the door for her. "She's in 1242, twelfth floor. You can go on up."

"Thank you." To her relief, he didn't follow her into the elevator and press the button.

A muted bell sound announced her arrival and the doors opened. Cam placed one foot in front of the other until she found herself in front of Lauren's door. Deep breath. Gentle knock.

The door opened immediately, as though Lauren had been waiting on the other side. Perhaps the doorman had called to say she was on her way. Was that standard doorman protocol?

Lauren offered a hesitant smile. "Hi."

She looked about as nervous as Cam felt, which should have made her feel better. But Cam was so caught up in how beautiful she was, the only feeling coming through loud and clear was longing. "Hi."

Lauren took her hand and pulled her into the apartment. The touch was at once soothing and electric. It reassured just as it sent a jolt through her that reminded her of a literal electric shock. Lauren let go and closed the door. "I can't believe you flew all the way here."

"I can't believe you didn't tell me why you left." Lauren flinched and Cam wanted to slap herself. Instead she pressed on. "Not as in I'm angry with you. Only that I wish I'd known, that you shouldn't have to face something like this by yourself."

Lauren nodded. "I understand what you mean. It was something I needed to do, though, and by myself seemed like the best option."

The thought of Lauren giving some sort of testimony, having to relate such a personal, traumatic event to a bunch of strangers, made Cam's insides twist uncomfortably. "How are you? It was today, right? Did it go off all right?"

Lauren took a deep breath and squared her shoulders, like she was steeling herself for something. But when she looked at Cam, her eyes were clear and bright. "It went as well as that sort of thing could go. I'm glad I did it and I think it will make a difference." She glanced away. "I'm only sorry I didn't say anything sooner."

Before she could stop herself, Cam put a finger under Lauren's chin, gently nudging until Lauren resumed eye contact. "You were brave then and you're brave today. You can't doubt either of those things for a second."

Lauren's eyes, clear only a second before, gleamed with tears. "You don't have to say that."

Cam fought to keep her own emotions in check. This was not the time to fall apart. "I know I don't, but it's true. It's also the least I can do after saying such horrible things to you."

"I get why you did." Lauren sniffed and the tears spilled over.

She'd prepared a speech. Even if she chucked that out the window, they needed to talk about what happened. But in that moment, words vanished. Along with the need for them. Cam pulled Lauren into her arms and held her.

It was as though a floodgate had opened. Lauren sobbed, her shoulders shaking with it. She clung to Cam's shirt.

Cam tightened the embrace and told herself not to panic. This catharsis was bigger than her and the fact that she'd fucked up so royally. It was the culmination of several emotional roller coaster rides and, she was guessing, Lauren not letting her feelings get the better of her for a long time. Guilt over being the cause of some of that warred with gratitude for being there when Lauren finally let it all go.

After a while, Lauren shifted. Cam loosened her grip and was met with a tear-streaked face and a sheepish smile. "Sorry."

Cam shook her head. "Don't apologize. I should be the one apologizing."

Lauren let out a shaky chuckle. "Well, that's true."

Cam laughed in spite of herself. "I was a total ass. I'm sorry."

"I'm sorry, too. I should have been honest about the specifics of the article so you weren't blindsided."

Cam fisted her hands at her sides and forced herself to say what she needed to say, even if it tore at her. "What you do with the Rose & Crown is up to you. You don't owe me anything."

Lauren regarded her with a look Cam couldn't read. Suspicion? Confusion? "What do you mean?"

Cam swallowed. She could make this about the Rose & Crown and the fact that she'd finally accepted it wasn't hers to control. Or she could be honest. She didn't fly across the ocean to hold back. "I'm in love with you, Lauren. And it has nothing to do with what you decide to do or not do with the pub."

Lauren blinked a few times, her expression giving nothing away. Seconds ticked by interminably. Great. It couldn't be a good sign to have her confession of love met with silence. She wouldn't backpedal, though, or try to take it back.

Lauren's face remained passive. Her eyes swirled with emotion, but for the life of her, Cam couldn't decipher what those emotions were. And then, without saying anything, Lauren placed a hand on either side of her face and drew their mouths together.

The kiss was slow, achingly slow. It was promise and longing and surrender and reassurance, all rolled into one. At least, it felt that way to Cam. She could only hope Lauren felt something similar.

When Lauren pulled back, her eyes shined with tears. She was smiling, though, and Cam got the impression it was an entirely different kind of crying. "I can't believe you came all this way to tell me you love me."

Cam ventured a smile in return. "And to apologize."

"But you hate traveling."

She shrugged. "Aren't you the one who told me desperate times call for desperate measures?"

Lauren laughed and one more tear spilled over. Cam couldn't resist wiping it away with her thumb. "I may have said that once."

She hadn't said I love you back, and Cam was trying not to panic over it. She didn't need immediate and emphatic reciprocation. Receptive was a big step in the right direction. It meant there was hope. At this point, she should be thrilled with that. Even if she ached to hear those words in return, she had no right to expect them.

"I love you, too."

Had she heard it or just imagined it? She kicked herself for not being one hundred percent sure. "I'm sorry. Could you repeat that?"

Lauren's head angled and she gave Cam a look of exasperation. "Are you serious right now?"

It seemed more playful than angry. She hoped it was playful and not angry. "I mean, I think I heard you. But I was busy freaking out about whether or not you loved me back, so I can't be sure."

Lauren looked her right in the eyes. "I love you, too, you dolt. And not just because of the romantic movie hero gesture."

Cam threaded her arms around Lauren's waist and pulled her close. "You better get used to repeating yourself."

Lauren took a deep breath. She moved her hands from Cam's face to around her neck. Her heart was beating wildly in her chest, a mix of adrenaline and emotion. "Are you already planning not to pay attention when I'm speaking to you?"

Cam shook her head. "No, just the love part. I'm going to want to hear you say it again and again and again."

A bubble of laughter escaped, a tiny release of the tension trapped inside her for the last week. Cam was in love with her. What a magical, miraculous turn of events. "I'll say it as often as you'd like as long as you return the favor."

"Hey, Lauren?"

"Yes?"

"I love you."

Yeah, she was pretty certain she'd never get tired of hearing that. "I love you, too."

"Hey, Lauren?"

"Yes?"

"I love you."

This time, she kissed Cam first, then said, "I love you, too."

"I'm very glad of that."

Lauren took another breath, trying to capture enough oxygen for her racing heart. Paired with the giddiness in her chest, her expanded lungs barely seemed to fit in the confines of her rib cage. Such a lovely contrast to the small, constricted feeling that had taken hold when she left England. "How exhausted are you?"

Cam considered for a moment. "I should be, but I think I'm a little amped up."

Lauren grinned. "Perfect."

She took Cam's hand and pulled her in the direction of her bedroom. As they passed the kitchen, she paused. "Hungry?"

Cam seemed to have picked up on what Lauren had in mind. She glanced at the kitchen, then at the doorway to the bedroom. "Nope."

"Good." She led Cam the rest of the way into the bedroom and watched as Cam took in the space. "What?"

Cam frowned. "It's so modern."

"Well, you don't need to look so worried about it. You'll never have to see it again."

"It's not that. I just," another frown, "do you like what we did at the inn at all?"

Oh, she was worried about that. "I love it. I think it's the perfect marriage of old and new. And I love that we came up with it together."

"Are you sure?"

She started working on the buttons of Cam's shirt, hoping that would distract her from the decor. "It's a modern building. This design goes. It's not that I prefer it." She kissed a patch of exposed skin. "I prefer the Rose & Crown." Another button, another kiss. "I prefer you."

Without another word, Cam's arms came around her, lifting her off the floor. She carried Lauren the short distance to the bed, set her down on it. "I prefer you, too."

And just like that, Cam was in charge. She grabbed at the hem of Lauren's shirt, and slipped it over her head, unclasped her bra, and tossed it aside. After nudging her onto her back, Cam slid off her shoes, unfastened her jeans. Cam worked both the jeans and her underwear down her legs and tossed them aside.

Lauren opened her mouth to protest Cam's state of dress, but Cam covered her mouth with a kiss that turned her insides molten. Demanding, hot. But also tender. The feeling behind it stirred something deep in Lauren, in a place she hadn't even known existed.

Cam broke the kiss, brought her mouth to Lauren's ear. "God, I've missed you."

Even more than the kiss, Cam's words affected her. They made her feel powerful and left her breathless at the same time. She grabbed Cam's shoulders, really dug her fingers into the solidness of them. "Missed you more."

"We'll see about that." Cam nipped her earlobe. "Let me show you."

And show her she did. Cam overwhelmed her senses. With teeth and tongue, roaming fingers and the press of her body, Cam worshiped her, played her, possessed her. She took Lauren to the precipice of release, then over. But instead of falling, she floated—weightless, wanted, perfect.

"Shh. There now. Please don't cry."

Lauren shook her head, wanting to dispel the worry in Cam's eyes, but not having any words. Instead, she pulled Cam into a kiss. And then she turned the tables, removing Cam's clothes and embarking on a long and lazy mission to touch and taste every inch of her.

It reminded her of the night of the opening, when everything seemed possible and she let her heart imagine forever. Before everything went so very wrong. Only this night was better, because

THE INN AT NETHERFIELD GREEN

everything had gone so wrong, but Cam loved her enough to want to make it right. She wanted to make it right, too. Even without knowing how it all would turn out, Lauren knew one thing for certain. She loved Cam and had no intention of letting her go.

Hours later, Lauren crawled out of bed long enough to get them each a glass of water and to flip off the lights. She had a fleeting thought of texting Anja, but decided it could wait. No news would surely be read as good news. She rejoined Cam and pulled the duvet up and over them and, for the first time since arriving back in New York, she fell sound asleep.

CHAPTER TWENTY-NINE

In the light of morning, the reality of the situation sat heavy in Cam's chest. Sitting in Lauren's bedroom in her beautifully appointed apartment didn't help. It was so obviously her space, her home, Cam couldn't imagine her wanting to give it up. And, of course, the apartment was merely a proxy for her life here. Now that Cam had a glimpse of it, she couldn't pretend it didn't exist. Should she bring it up? Wait for Lauren to?

When Lauren walked in wearing a short little excuse of a robe and bearing two steaming mugs, she pushed those worries from her mind. There'd be plenty of time for worrying—today, tomorrow, and for the foreseeable future. In this moment, however, she merely wanted to bask in Lauren and in the fact she'd not fucked things up so royally they didn't even have the chance to worry about those things.

"Good morning." Lauren sashayed over to the bed and handed her one of the cups.

"Good morning." Cam glanced down at the contents, then back at Lauren. "Is this tea?"

Lauren offered her a playful smirk. "It is. I've been drinking it the last few days. Craving the familiarity, perhaps."

If Lauren was craving things from England, that had to be a good sign. Especially something that warranted a departure from her coffee addiction. Cam took a sip. English breakfast, brewed nice and strong. Definitely a good sign. "It's just right."

"So," Lauren began, but just as quickly trailed off.

Maybe she wasn't going to get to bask after all. "So."

"What shall we do today? You've never been to New York, right?"

Oh. Cam couldn't decide whether to be relieved or disappointed that Lauren's thoughts seemed nowhere near the vicinity of their future. "I have not."

"I don't want to drag you around against your will, but it would be a shame to come all this way and not see any of the city."

Cam nodded but found herself at a loss for words.

"How long are you staying? I probably should have led with that."

"Um." Not being able to read Lauren had always gotten under her skin. Now, it drove her absolutely mad. "Four days."

Lauren's eyes lit up. "That's perfect."

Perfect for what? For finishing out their fling and ending on a high note? For deciding whether or not they had a future?

"I booked my return ticket for next week, but maybe I can get on the same flight back as you, or at least the same day."

It was no use. Cam raised her hand. "Not to put the cart before the horse, but could we perhaps talk about what comes next?"

Lauren closed her eyes for a moment. When she opened them, she looked at the ceiling. "Right."

Right. Cam searched for the words, the questions, that would bring clarity without making her seem like a controlling ass.

"I should have said as much last night. I'm moving to England permanently."

"You are?"

"I like it there. More importantly, I like who I am when I'm there. So much more, I've realized, than when I'm here."

Surprise, relief, and a hint of elation danced at the edges of her brain. Still, it felt like Lauren might be holding something back. If there was a however looming, she wanted to know. "Is there more?"

She took a deep breath and Cam braced herself. "I don't want you to think I'm abandoning my life on the hope we end up together. I mean, I hope we end up together, but my decision is bigger than that."

A tiny part of her wanted Lauren to want her, want a future with her, badly enough to upend her life to make it happen. The rational, sane, rest of her knew that was a terrible idea. "That's probably for the best." She smiled, then her brain backtracked to the magnitude of Lauren's declaration. "Are you sure that's what you want?"

"I've never been more sure of anything in my life."

The calm certainty of the statement did more to reassure her than the words themselves. "I'm glad."

Lauren set her mug on the table by the bed, then took Cam's and did the same with it. She crawled into bed and straddled Cam's thighs, causing the robe to separate and ride even higher. Cam couldn't resist sliding her hands up Lauren's legs and over her ass. Lauren raised a brow but didn't try to stop her. "So, you'll let me play tour guide and then you'll help me pack up this place?"

Cam stilled her hands. "Packing? You didn't say anything about packing."

To her credit, Lauren didn't even blink. "Really? You're not going to help me pack?"

It still seemed unreal that everything that was wrong in her life just a day ago was now right, that Lauren not only loved her but wanted to make a home in England. "I think I'm prepared to do anything you ask."

Lauren quirked a brow. "Anything?"

"Well, almost anything. I still don't think I'm willing to eat gazpacho."

Lauren's head fell back and she laughed, long and hard. "It's good to know your hard limits."

The gleam in Lauren's eyes proved too much. Cam tightened her grip and flipped their bodies so Lauren was beneath her. "And what are your hard limits, Ms. Montgomery?"

Lauren looked up into her eyes. Arousal, yes, but something more. Love. It took Cam's breath away. But then a gleam of mischief came in and she said, "I think I'm prepared to do anything you ask."

Having her words turned back on her, with such overt sexual connotation, did wicked things to Cam's insides. "I'm going to remember that."

"You know, we don't have to see the city. I could just keep you here for the next three days."

The idea of spending three days in bed with Lauren had its merits. Cam leaned in and kissed her long and slow. "I know I was very resistant at first, but I have to say I like the way you think."

Lauren grinned. "It's about damn time."

They ventured out eventually. Lauren dragged Cam to her favorite restaurants, to the Met, and past the building where she used to work. They met up with Anja for drinks and had bagels from the deli down the block. She showed off the parts of the city she loved, but even as she did so, Lauren realized how much her heart was no longer there.

Despite her initial protest, Cam helped her pack. She even took charge of getting the donate piles to Goodwill while Lauren met with a Realtor. Lauren was pleasantly surprised with the outcome. Even though she'd only been in her apartment about five years, it had appreciated nicely and she stood to make a nice profit on it.

Cam asked whether she wanted to see her parents, but Lauren deflected. She'd have to introduce them eventually, but there was no rush. They'd judge her decisions as rash anyway. Maybe she could invite her mother over for a visit. Albert had been her uncle after all, even if they'd not been close.

By the time she and Cam boarded the plane at JFK, Lauren had this almost overwhelming feeling of wanting to be back. It was, she realized, a longing for something she'd not had before, not really. It was a longing for home.

Cam, still marveling at their upgraded seats in business class, squeezed her hand. "You okay?"

Lauren took a deep breath. "I am."

"It's okay if you're having some cold feet, or regret, or whatever. I won't take it personally."

"It's not that, I promise."

"What, then?" Cam looked genuinely worried.

"I'm," she struggled for the word. "Overwhelmed. But in a good way."

"You really don't need to sugarcoat things for me. I don't want you to change your mind, obviously, but I want you to be honest. This will never work if we're not honest."

The earnestness that, when it opposed her, seemed frustratingly insurmountable, now warmed her heart. "I agree, and I am being honest. I'm so ready to be back at the inn, back in the pub. I didn't realize how attached I'd become until I left."

"Oh." Cam's face relaxed and she looked relieved, if not entirely convinced. "I guess I didn't think of it that way."

"It's not a sacrifice, Cam. Netherfield is where I want to be. I have no doubt about that at all."

It was Cam's turn to take a deep breath. "I'm sorry it's hard for me to believe that. Seeing you here, so clearly in your element, makes me wonder if you're going to regret it in the end."

The conversation with Charlotte came to mind. "I'm not Amelia. I'm making this decision with my eyes wide open."

Cam paled. "Did Charlotte tell you about her?"

"She did." Lauren winced. "But not in a gossipy way, I promise. Just the broad strokes."

"It's fine. I'm not mad. I feel bad I didn't tell you about her. Or that we haven't really discussed past relationships at all."

Lauren smiled. "We'll get there."

Cam nodded. "Okay. Still, I'm not...I didn't mean to hint you were anything like her. Or that she's someone I'm still hung up on."

"I know. I don't think that." She really didn't. But she also knew some scars ran deep and triggers weren't always logical.

"The difference between Netherfield and New York is pretty dramatic, though."

The captain came over the intercom, announcing they were next in line for takeoff and telling the flight attendants to take their seats. Lauren turned her hand over in Cam's, lacing their fingers together. "I'll always love New York, but I'd be lying if I said it ever really felt like home. It was more like playing a part, if that makes sense."

"It does."

Only in articulating it did Lauren realize how true it rang. The thing was, she played the part so well, the lines had started to blur. Netherfield didn't feel that way. If anything, it felt like a piece of her she hadn't known was missing. "I'd be on this plane, or a plane at least, no matter what."

Cam chuckled. "Right."

"I'm really glad to be on this one, though, with you."

"Same."

The intermittent taxiing ended and the plane stopped moving altogether before hurtling down the runway. Cam closed her eyes and her grip on Lauren's hand tightened. "Are you afraid of flying?"

Cam shook her head slightly, but didn't open her eyes. "Not afraid. Just not my favorite thing."

The significance of Cam showing up at her apartment hit her. Not just a romantic gesture, but one that put her out of her comfort zone in every possible way. She waited until the plane leveled slightly, the ascent less pronounced. She brought Cam's fingers to her lips and kissed them. "Thank you for coming to New York."

Cam opened her eyes then. "I'm sorry I wasn't there for the deposition. You should have had someone by your side."

It felt, strangely, like a distant memory. And so insignificant in the grand scheme of things. "You came. That matters more than you could possibly know."

"It was the least I could do after being such an ass."

"I'm sorry I kept it from you. And I'm still sorry I handled the article the way I did, that I played along in the first place."

"No, I get why you did." Cam shrugged. "I reacted the way I did because I'm in love with you."

What a magical thing. Lauren let herself soak it in, imagine the future that was about to unfold. "The feeling is completely mutual."

CHAPTER THIRTY

Lauren hung up the phone and took a deep breath. She'd just turned down two million dollars. A small giggle escaped her lips. It was followed by another, then a guffaw. The next thing she knew, she was laughing almost hysterically. Two million fucking dollars.

She knew she wasn't going to take the offer. She'd not even gone forward with the listing. But when the VP from Atlas left her a message asking to talk about the property, she couldn't resist. She wanted to know what someone like him would pay for the Rose & Crown, for her own satisfaction, but also as a point of reference. Not that she was looking to buy another place to flip. No, if anything, she wanted to help others who'd made that leap. Having a sense of how the big fish valued properties like hers could come in handy.

She'd kept her composure when he tossed the number out there. It's not like it was more than she would have come up with herself if she'd had to put a price on it. It was that someone was willing to give her that much money—the reality of it more than some hypothetical list price. It was knowing what she could do with that kind of money. And perhaps most of all, it was knowing that money was no longer the most important thing in her life.

A knock on her office door pulled her back to reality. "Come in."

She thought it might be Mrs. Lucas coming in with tea, or Charlotte wanting to pick her brain about another idea she'd had.

But when she looked up, she found Cam smiling at her from the doorway.

"Should I ask about the maniacal laughter or do I not want to know?"

Lauren took a deep breath and stood. Part of her hesitated to tell Cam for fear it would make things weird, or that Cam wouldn't trust that she'd only taken the call out of curiosity. But keeping things to herself had gotten her into trouble. More, she didn't want her relationship with Cam to have secrets, even secrets of omission. "I just got an offer on the pub."

"You did?" To her credit, Cam didn't balk.

"I mean, I never went through with the listing, so not like a written offer or anything. I had a call from an executive at a hotel chain I worked with once and I wanted to see what he had to say."

"And?"

"And he offered me two million dollars." She looked up and did a quick mental calculation. "Like, one and a half million pounds. Maybe one and a quarter."

"Lauren, that's a lot of money."

"I know. I didn't accept, obviously, but I wanted to know what someone like him would value the place at." She closed the space between them and gave Cam a kiss. "Hi."

Cam frowned and her eyes got very serious. "Maybe you should."

"No, I shouldn't. I swear that wasn't my intention. Please believe me."

Cam shook her head, and Lauren's stomach twisted into a tight coil. Please don't let this turn into a fight. "I told you I was wrong to try to control what you did with this place. I meant it."

Lauren smiled, let relief loosen some of the knots. "I don't want to sell."

Cam continued to frown. "Don't want to or think I don't want you to? I don't want you passing up a golden opportunity for me."

Just like Cam's flying across the ocean to declare her love, the statement made Lauren's heart swell. "I'm not looking for a golden opportunity."

"But you don't want to be an innkeeper for the rest of your life, either. With that kind of money, you could start your agency. Here, obviously." Cam lifted her shoulder. "I'm not saying I want to let you out of my sight or anything."

Right. Because they'd worked that out. Lauren wasn't keeping secrets and Cam wasn't assuming the worst. "Do you know how much it means to hear you say that?"

"I wouldn't say it if I didn't mean it. We can't build a future on you doing things because you think it's what I want."

Lauren wound her arms around Cam's waist. "Do you know what I want?"

"To start your own agency."

"Yes." Lauren closed her eyes and tipped her head back and forth. "But that's not the only thing, or even the most important."

Cam tensed. "You're going to say me, and as much as I love hearing that, it worries me. You can't settle. If you settle you'll be miserable and, worse, you'll end up resenting me. I couldn't take that."

The worry in Cam's voice tore at her heart. She put a hand on either side of Cam's face. "I'm not settling. I like my life here and I don't want it to change. I'd rather take my time and start out a little smaller than sell out for the quick profit."

Finally, Cam smiled. "Watch it, Ms. Montgomery. You're starting to sound like me."

Lauren quirked a brow. "You say that like it's a bad thing."

"I've been told that I'm stubborn and resistant to change."

Much like the phone call earlier, the giggle manifested and escaped before she could stop it. Cam glowered, but there was no malice in it. Lauren bit her lip. "Sorry."

"I was trying to be nice, you know."

"I do. And I know what the Rose & Crown means to you."

Cam shook her head. "It doesn't mean anything if it costs me you."

"Well, like I said, I don't want to sell. So, it looks like you're stuck with it. And me."

"Good."

This time, Cam's arms went around her waist. Lauren couldn't think of a single place on earth she'd rather be. Cam leaned in and kissed her, long and slow. It felt like a thousand promises in that kiss. Lauren soaked them up and tucked them away in her heart. She'd never been big on promises, at least not the kind that weren't about meeting deadlines and satisfying customers. She was learning, though, and Cam was turning out to be a patient teacher.

Maybe that's why they clicked. They each had a lot to learn, after years of being convinced they had it all figured out. She'd managed to teach Cam a thing or two; Cam had taught her plenty as well. And some things they were figuring out together. That might be the best part of all. The realization made her smile.

"What are you grinning about?" Cam asked.

Lauren considered. "You. Us. The idea of happily ever after."

"That sounds like something I can get behind." Cam let out a sigh. "I wish I'd brought cocktails so we could raise a toast."

Happiness radiated out from her core, leaving her tingly and warm. "You know, I know this great little bar. The cocktails are on point."

"Really? Maybe we should check it out."

She took Cam's hand and led her back the way she'd come. In the pub, a couple dozen people chatted and laughed over drinks and food. Not bad for four in the afternoon. Charlotte stood behind the bar, chatting with a couple who'd checked into the inn the day before. She made some hand gestures and the couple left. She caught sight of Lauren and Cam and smiled. "Hello, love birds."

Cam said, "We need drinks, Charlotte. We're celebrating."

Her eyes lit up. "Ooh, what are we celebrating?"

Lauren grinned. "Not selling the pub."

"Is that news?" Anja, who'd arrived back in town the day before, gave her a questioning look. She and Charlotte remained resolute in keeping their relationship open, but they'd been spending more and more time together. Lauren imagined it was only a matter of time until Netherfield took the place of New York as Anja's home base.

Cam shook her head. "Apparently not, but she was just offered a boatload of money for it and turned it down, so it's official now."

"You did?" Anja asked.

"I did. I've grown quite fond of this place."

Charlotte nodded, as though getting confirmation of something she'd known all along. "Well, I'm glad to hear it."

Lauren considered how lucky she was to have Charlotte, who'd become not just an employee, but a trusted friend and colleague. "How would you feel about taking on more responsibility around here?"

"Really?"

"Yes. You're already running the bar. Mrs. Lucas has made it clear she's content with her role. There's going to be a lot more to do if reservations and pub patrons stay where they are. I don't want to sell the place, but I don't want to be a full-time manager, either."

"And you're offering me the job?" Charlotte's voice was incredulous.

"You know how things run better than anyone, wouldn't you say?"

Charlotte took a deep breath, stood up a little straighter. "I'd say so."

"You have great ideas, but a good head on your shoulders, too. Even more, I trust you completely."

She looked from Lauren to Cam. "Was this your idea?"

Cam shook her head. "This is the first I'm hearing of it. I think it's a bloody good idea, but it wasn't mine."

"We can talk about salary and such. You'll be wanting a raise with the extra work."

Charlotte nodded, although it seemed to Lauren that was the last thing on her mind. "Right."

Anja smiled. "I think this calls for drinks all around, then."

Cam said, "Agreed."

Charlotte gestured to the bottles behind her. "What'll it be?"

Could this day get any better? It was hard to imagine. "Gin Flips seem the most fitting, no?"

"Coming right up."

Lauren thought back to the day Cam had first made the cocktail for her, crafted specifically for her new drink menu. She'd been impressed with Cam's skill and more than a little attracted to her. At the time, the sentiments had seemed far from mutual. Those feelings hadn't gone away, of course, but now? She chuckled. Now, she had so much more.

"What are you snickering at?" Cam asked.

She looked at the woman she'd come to love more deeply than she thought possible. "I was just thinking about how far we've come."

"Should I be concerned you find it so funny?"

"Not funny, at least not funny ha-ha. It's more," Lauren searched for the right word, "magical."

Cam raised a brow. "Magical?"

"Think about it. The worst moment of my life set the stage for the best decision I ever made. And you hated me at first. Look at us now."

"I didn't hate you."

"Dislike, then, with a heaping side of distrust."

Cam frowned. "That's sort of true. I'm sorry for that."

Charlotte set a drink in front of each of them. "Cheers, lovelies."

Lauren leaned over and gave Cam a kiss. "I was marveling at the now, not complaining about the beginning."

Cam opened her mouth but seemed to reconsider. "Right. The now. I'll drink to that."

Lauren picked up her glass. Cam, Anja, and Charlotte followed suit. "Here's to the now."

Cam raised hers. "And to the future."

"And not selling the pub," Charlotte said.

Anja looked at them both, then at Charlotte. "And here's to love."

They clinked glasses to a chorus of "to love." Lauren sipped her drink, the notes of honey and lavender now familiar, but still exciting. Truly the perfect cocktail. Kind of like things with Cam. So much more than she'd bargained for, and utterly perfect.

EPILOGUE

One year later.

Lauren stepped back from the curb and put her hands on her hips. "A little to the left."

Cam adjusted the sign. "How's that?"

"Perfect."

A bit of banging and then Cam descended the ladder and joined her on the street. "That looks quite nice."

She'd slaved over the Wilspell logo for weeks, wanting something quirky but elegant. Something that was a far cry from the KesslerAldridge logo she'd come to see as stuffy and overbearing. Something that suited the name itself—Anglo-Saxon for welcome news. Cam had humored her, listening to her go back and forth and even offering some suggestions of her own. In the end, she was thrilled with the result. It suited her and the brand she hoped to build.

Technically, Wilspell had been open for a couple of months. She'd leveraged the press from the relaunch of the Rose & Crown to score three clients. Small, owner-operated inns, but still. It was a start.

She'd not expected to move from the cozy little office behind the bar for at least a year, but when the mess with Philip was finally settled, she found herself with a tidy nest egg. Half of it she set aside to start building a house with Cam and for them to take a trip to celebrate their engagement. The rest she poured into her new business, including its very own storefront right on Baker Street.

The space wasn't large, but it was right next door to Jane's office. And it wasn't like she had any employees. Well, local ones at least. She'd hired Anja to do all of her photography and a bit of graphic design. She knew better than to think Anja would settle in any one place for too long, but that didn't bother her in the least. Especially since she and Charlotte still seemed unable to get enough of one another.

Cam threaded an arm around her waist and gave her a gentle squeeze. "Are you ready to open your doors, madam CEO?"

"You're the CEO. I'm merely the mistress of my one-woman operation."

Cam smiled and got that aw-shucks look on her face. She'd been running the show at Barrister's since before Lauren met her, but only with the explosion of Carriage House had she taken on that title. The company had no plans to go public or anything, but funding an expansion of production had required someone to handle negotiations. And to be the public face of the company. What had started with Lauren's marketing campaign had morphed into a much larger, and much more consuming, endeavor.

It was all great for the company, but it took a toll. They'd recently started talking about ways Cam could delegate more and get back into the blending room. As far as Lauren was concerned, that would be good for both the company and Cam's state of mind.

"You're doing it again, aren't you?" Cam asked, her voice holding just a hint of accusation.

"I don't know what you're talking about." She did know, actually. Cam hated when she went into protective mode.

"Just because we're engaged, you've taken it upon yourself to worry about me."

Lauren angled her head. "It's my prerogative to worry about you. Besides, it's in my best interest that you and Barrister's are happy and successful."

"Your prerogative, huh?"

"Yes, it's a truth universally acknowledged that a woman will worry about the health and happiness of her betrothed. Have you not been fretting over Wilspell on my behalf?"

Cam gave her a bland look.

"I mean, I know I've fretted enough for both of us, so let me rephrase. Have you been worrying more about me, especially since you proposed?"

Cam seemed to think it through. "I suppose my worry about your professional happiness has increased, but now that you're wearing my grandmother's ring, I worry about other stuff less."

Lauren gave her a squeeze. "I guess I'll take that."

It had been a lovely proposal. Cam had conspired with Charlotte to close the pub a little early one night. She'd lit a fire and had candles all around, old time music piped in. They slow danced and had a light supper and Cam had gotten down on one knee. Lauren wouldn't have called herself a hopeless romantic, but in that moment, she'd turned into an absolute puddle.

Charlotte, Anja, and even Mrs. Lucas had been lurking in the library, waiting for the all clear to come in and help them celebrate. It had been so sweet, she'd cried even harder than when Cam flew across the Atlantic to tell her she loved her.

And now they were running two businesses and planning a wedding. It was so much more than she'd ever imagined and yet so much less stress than had defined her life before moving to England. Somehow, this tiny village and its people had been exactly what she needed, even when she didn't know what that was.

Like she did so often these days, she thought of Albert. The uncle she'd hardly known but whose decision had altered the course of her life, in the best possible way. Could he have possibly known how things would unfold? Surely not. Still, he'd seen something in her. She had to believe he had an inkling she'd do the right thing and love the inn as he had.

"He'd be proud of this, too, you know."

How did Cam always seem to know what she was thinking? What she needed to hear? "Thank you."

"I'm sure as hell proud."

For all that Cam puffed up about being a traditionalist, she was fully supportive of Lauren's ambitions. Even the conversations they'd started to have about kids hadn't swayed her insistence that

Lauren follow her dreams. It still left her a little bit in awe. "I love you."

"And I love you." Cam leaned in and kissed her. "I'll let you get to work, now. I know you're very busy, very important."

"Says the busiest and most important woman in town. I'll see you home for dinner?"

Cam raised a brow. "Are you cooking?"

"I am." She'd been getting lessons. Tonight, she was planning a roast chicken with potatoes and vegetables. It might not be as good as Cam's, but she was getting there.

"I can't wait."

Cam kissed her again and headed back to the distillery. Lauren watched her go, then took another minute to admire her sign. Then she headed inside to call a client and work on a new social media strategy for a line of boutique hotels in Ireland. She was, after all, open for business.

About the Author

Aurora Rey is a college dean by day and an award-winning lesbian romance author the rest of the time, except when she's cooking, baking, riding the tractor, or pining for goats. She grew up in a small town in south Louisiana, daydreaming about New England. She keeps a special place in her heart for the South, especially the food and the ways women are raised to be strong, even if they're taught not to show it. After a brief dalliance with biochemistry, she completed both a B.A. and an M.A. in English.

She is the author of the Cape End Romance series and several standalone contemporary lesbian romance novels and novellas. She has been a finalist for the Lambda Literary, RITA, and Golden Crown Literary Society awards, but loves reader feedback the most. She lives in Ithaca, New York, with her dogs and whatever wildlife has taken up residence in the pond.

Books Available from Bold Strokes Books

30 Dates in 30 Days by Elle Spencer. A busy lawyer tries to find love the fast way—thirty dates in thirty days. (978-1-63555-498-4)

Finding Sky by Cass Sellars. Skylar Addison's search for a career intersects with her new boss's search for butterflies, but Skylar can't forgive Jess's intrusion into her life. (978-1-63555-521-9)

Hammers, Strings, and Beautiful Things by Morgan Lee Miller. While on tour with the biggest pop star in the world, rising musician Blair Bennett falls in love for the first time while coping with loss and depression. (978-1-63555-538-7)

Heart of a Killer by Yolanda Wallace. Contract killer Santana Masters's only interest is her next assignment—until a chance meeting with a beautiful stranger tempts her to change her ways. (978-1-63555-547-9)

Leading the Witness by Carsen Taite. When defense attorney Catherine Landauer reluctantly becomes the key witness in prosecutor Starr Rio's latest criminal trial, their hearts, careers, and lives may be at risk. (978-1-63555-512-7)

No Experience Required by Kimberly Cooper Griffin. Izzy Treadway has resigned herself to a life without romance because of her bipolar illness but wonders what she's gotten herself into when she agrees to write a book about love. (978-1-63555-561-5)

One Walk in Winter by Georgia Beers. Olivia Santini and Hayley Boyd Markham might be rivals at work, but they discover that lonely hearts often find company in the most unexpected of places. (978-1-63555-541-7)

The Inn at Netherfield Green by Aurora Rey. Advertising executive Lauren Montgomery and gin distiller Camden Crawley don't agree on anything except saving the Rose & Crown, the old English pub that's brought them together. (978-1-63555-445-8)

Top of Her Game by M. Ullrich. When it comes to life on the field and matters of the heart, losing isn't an option for pro athletes Kenzie Shaw and Sutton Flores. (978-1-63555-500-4)

Vanished by Eden Darry. A storm is coming, and Ellery and Loveday must find the chosen one or humanity won't survive it. (978-1-63555-437-3)

All She Wants by Larkin Rose. Marci Jones and Tessa Dalton get more than they bargained for when their plans for a one-night stand turn into an opportunity for love. (978-1-63555-476-2)

Beautiful Accidents by Erin Zak. Stevie Adams and Bernadette Thompson discover that sometimes the best things in life happen purely by accident. (978-1-63555-497-7)

Before Now by Joy Argento. Can Delany and Jade overcome the betrayal that spans the centuries to reignite a love that can't be broken? (978-1-63555-525-7)

Breathe by Cari Hunter. Paramedic Jemima Pardon's chronic bad luck seems to be improving when she meets police officer Rosie Jones. But they face a battle to survive before they can find love. (978-1-63555-523-3)

Double-Crossed by Ali Vali. Hired thief and killer Reed Gable finds something in her scope that will change her life forever when she gets a contract to end casino accountant Brinley Myers's life. (978-1-63555-302-4)

False Horizons by CJ Birch. Jordan and Ash struggle with different views on the alien agenda and must find their way back to each other before they're swallowed up by a centuries-old war. (978-1-63555-519-6)

Legacy by Charlotte Greene. When five women hike to a remote cabin deep inside a national park, unsettling events suggest that they should have stayed home. (978-1-63555-490-8)

Royal Street Reveillon by Greg Herren. Someone is killing the stars of a reality show, and it's up to Scotty Bradley and the boys to find out who. (978-1-63555-545-5)

Somewhere Along the Way by Kathleen Knowles. When Maxine Cooper moves to San Francisco during the summer of 1981, she learns that wherever you run, you cannot escape yourself. (978-1-63555-383-3)

Blood of the Pack by Jenny Frame. When Alpha of the Scottish pack Kenrick Wulver visits the Wolfgangs, she falls for Zaria Lupa, a wolf on the run. (978-1-63555-431-1)

Cause of Death by Sheri Lewis Wohl. Medical student Vi Akiak and K9 Search and Rescue officer Kate Renard must work together to find a killer before they end up the next targets. In the race for survival, they discover that love may be the biggest risk of all. (978-1-63555-441-0)

Chasing Sunset by Missouri Vaun. Hijinks and mishaps ensue as Iris and Finn set off on a road trip adventure, chasing the sunset, and falling in love along the way. (978-1-63555-454-0)

Double Down by MB Austin. When an unlikely friendship with Spanish pop star Erlea turns deeper, Celeste, in-house physician for the hotel hosting Erlea's show, has a choice to make—run or double down on love. (978-1-63555-423-6)

Party of Three by Sandy Lowe. Three friends are in for a wild night at billionaire heiress Eleanor McGregor's twenty-fifth birthday party. Love, lust, and doing the right thing, even when it hurts, turn the evening into one that will change their lives forever. (978-1-63555-246-1)

Sit. Stay. Love. by Karis Walsh. City girl Alana Brendt and country vet Tegan Evans both know they don't belong together. Only problem is, they're falling in love. (978-1-63555-439-7)

Where the Lies Hide by Renee Roman. As P.I. Camdyn Stark gets closer to solving the case, will her dark secrets and the lies she's buried jeopardize her future with the quietly beautiful Sarah Peters? (978-1-63555-371-0)

Beautiful Dreamer by Melissa Brayden. With love on the line, can Devyn Winters find it in her heart to stay in the small town of Dreamer's Bay, the one place she swore she'd never remain? (978-1-63555-305-5)

Create a Life to Love by Erin Zak. When sixteen-year-old Beth shows up at her birth mother's door, three lives will change forever. (978-1-63555-425-0)

Deadeye by Meredith Doench. Stranded while hunting the serial predator Deadeye, Special Agent Luce Hansen fights for survival while her lover, forensic pathologist Harper Bennett, hunts for clues to Hansen's disappearance along the killer's trail. (978-1-63555-253-9)

Death Takes a Bow by David S. Pederson. Alan Keys takes part in a local stage production, but when the leading man is murdered, his partner Detective Heath Barrington is thrust into the limelight to find the killer. (978-1-63555-472-4)

Endangered by Michelle Larkin. Shapeshifters Officer Aspen Wolfe and Dr. Tora Madigan fight their growing attraction as they work together to destroy a secret government agency that exterminates their kind. (978-1-63555-377-2)

Incognito by VK Powell. The only thing Evan Spears is focused on is capturing a fleeing murder suspect until wild card Frankie Strong is added to her team and causes chaos on and off the job. (978-1-63555-389-5)

Insult to Injury by Gun Brooke. After losing everything, Gail Owen withdraws to her old farmhouse and finds a destitute young woman, Romi Shepherd, living in a secret room. (978-1-63555-323-9)

Just One Moment by Dena Blake. If you were given the chance to have the love of your life back, could you ignore everything that went wrong and start over again? (978-1-63555-387-1)

Scene of the Crime by MJ Williamz. Cullen Mathew finds herself caught between the woman she thinks she loves but can no longer trust and a beautiful detective she can't stop thinking about who will stop at nothing to find the truth. (978-1-63555-405-2)

Accidental Prophet by Bud Gundy. Days after his grandmother dies, Drew Morten learns his true identity and finds himself racing against time to save civilization from the apocalypse. (978-1-63555-452-6)

Daughter of No One by Sam Ledel. When their worlds are threatened, a princess and a village outcast must overcome their differences and embrace a budding attraction if they want to survive. (978-1-63555-427-4)

Fear of Falling by Georgia Beers. Singer Sophie James is ready to shake up her career, but her new manager, the gorgeous Dana Landon, has other ideas. (978-1-63555-443-4)

In Case You Forgot by Fredrick Smith and Chaz Lamar. Zaire and Kenny, two newly single, Black, queer, and socially aware men, start again—in love, career, and life—in the West Hollywood neighborhood of LA. (978-1-63555-493-9)

Playing with Fire by Lesley Davis. When Takira Lathan and Dante Groves meet at Takira's restaurant, love may find its way onto the menu. (978-1-63555-433-5)

Practice Makes Perfect by Carsen Taite. Meet law school friends Campbell, Abby, and Grace, law partners at Austin's premier boutique legal firm for young, hip entrepreneurs. Legal Affairs: one law firm, three best friends, three chances to fall in love. (978-1-63555-357-4)

The Last Seduction by Ronica Black. When you allow true love to elude you once and you desperately regret it, are you brave enough to grab it when it comes around again? (978-1-63555-211-9)

Wavering Convictions by Erin Dutton. After a traumatic event, Maggie has vowed to regain her strength and independence. So how can Ally be both the woman who makes her feel safe and a constant reminder of the person who took her security away? (978-1-63555-403-8)